Schmuel's Journey

Other novels by Steven P. Marini:

Connections
A Jack Contino Crime Story

This vigorous, well-plotted crime concoction takes a straight-on look at the tangles and snares involved in stepping outside the "social contract," and it's a kind of morality tale without the classroom lecture. It's pretty well done, too. The author has wisely limited his word count, so it feels just about right, and we're left with the sense of an inaugural job well done.

—The Barnstable Patriot

Aberration
A Jack Contino Crime Story

Author Marini again shows his mettle when it comes to creating a great storyline . . ."

—The Barnstable Patriot

Aberration takes off like a bullet with a cool hero: Jack Contino, a cop's cop, who knows a thing or two about criminals, breaking cases and chasing down a cold one. You'll find yourself rooting for him all the way. And if it's the late 1970s you're nostalgic for, you'll feel right at home with this nifty mystery.

—Jordan Rich
Chart Productions, Inc.
WBZ Radio

Calculation
A Jack Contino Crime Story

In Praise of *Schmuel's Journey*

Schmuel's Journey is an enjoyable thriller set in a small college town in New Hampshire in the seventies. Steven P. Marini immerses the reader in the culture of the time, doing a great job with all the little details. Throw in a couple of murders, fugitive Nazis, and Nazi hunters, and you have all the ingredients for a fun read. Fans of New Hampshire noir will find much to like in this story that keeps the reader guessing right up to the end.

—J.E. Seymour, author of the Kevin Markinson series from Barking Rain Press. *Lead Poisoning* and *Stress Fractures,* available now. *Frostbite*—coming in March of 2016.

Author Steve Marini has written a fast paced, intrigue-filled novel that not only reveals the internal machinations and interpersonal strife that intrude into the ivory towers of higher education, but secrets from the past that could result in scandal and termination, and just might wind up bringing another unwelcome presence to the hallowed halls . . . Death!

—Ric Wasley, author of *The Girl with the Faraway Eyes, Candle in the Wind* and *The McCarthy Mystery Series*

Schmuel's Journey

by

Steven P. Marini

❊❊❊❊

Gypsy Shadow Publishing

Marini

Schmuel's Journey
by
Steven P. Marini

Gypsy Shadow Publishing, LLC.
Lockhart, TX
www.gypsyshadow.com

Library of Congress Control Number: 2015957182

eBook ISBN: 978-1-61950-269-7
Print ISBN: 978-1-61950-274-1

Published in the United States of America

First eBook Edition: October 15, 2015
First Print Edition: November 15, 2015

Dedication

To all victims of the Holocaust and the atrocities of war.

Schmuel (Schmu—ELL)

From the Hebrew name *(Shemu'el)* which could mean either "name of God" or "God has heard." Samuel was the last of the ruling judges in the Old Testament. He anointed Saul to be the first king of Israel, and later anointed David.

~ http://www.behindthename.com/

Chapter One

APRIL 1944. AUSCHWITZ.

"I hate these men, and I hate being here. Why do we always have to do what they say? I wish they were all dead." Schmuel spoke harshly for a ten year-old boy. "Why can't I work outside, like my friend Eli? I'm always here in this hospital, working with you."

"Keep your voice down," his mother cautioned. "Eli is older than you and much stronger, so he can work at other things. We must do what they say and do it quickly, without error or they will do bad things to us, very bad things, just like they do to the others."

His mother worked in the kitchen during the day, in the building where the doctors did their work with the prisoners; their *patients,* as they were called. It was a drab building, with dull white paint and brown woodwork. There were no pictures on the walls or ornaments of any kind, except the one in the main entrance and another in the kitchen. They showed the face of a strange man with a funny little mustache, and the doctors spoke of him with great respect. Mother said not to talk about that man, so Schmuel never did, but he grew to hate the face just the same. If he was the reason why Schmuel and his family were forced to leave home and live here, Schmuel would always hate him.

The building was one story, very long, with two office rooms to the left, off the main entrance. There was another room past the offices that had a long table and several chairs. Sometimes the doctors and other men sat in there and talked for hours. There was a check-in desk, like the one at the hospital where he had his leg taken care of three years ago, and there were always women working there, other prisoners of the camp. Soldiers stood inside the entrance and always watched what the women were doing. The soldiers' guns were big and heavy-looking. They also had pistols at their sides. If he ever got to use a gun, he'd use a pistol.

His mother was making a small meal of sausage and sauerkraut. She put the food on two plates and sliced some bread as well. She was average height for a woman, a little thinner than she used to be. But she wasn't too skinny, like most of the women in the camp. Her dark brown hair was cut short and fell lifeless down her head, just below her ears. Unlike most women here, she got to wear a little bit of eye makeup and some lipstick. Some of the other women who worked here wore the same kind of makeup, but not all. Only the good-looking ones.

"Mother, will we ever get to leave this place? I don't like it. Everybody is sad and frightened and they don't seem to get much food. How come we get enough food?"

She never stopped working at her task as she tried to answer her son's questions. "Yes, we will get out of here one day, I'm sure of that. God will provide for us, but we have to help ourselves, too, by doing our work without complaining. You understand that, don't you Schmuel? It is very important that we do our work."

"Yes, Mother, I guess I do." Schmuel stood beside his mother as she finished preparing the meal.

She put the plates on a tray and filled two steins with beer, placing them gently on the tray, too. "Now, take these to the doctors, Schmuel, and don't drop anything." Sadie was being very cautious, for she knew a slipup could be very costly to her son. But her orders were to make the meals while he was the servant.

Schmuel worked his way along the route from the kitchen, out through a long hallway and into the entrance area of the building. A woman at the main desk called out to him. "Good afternoon, Schmuel." He tried to smile at her and answer, but he felt the movement of a beer stein as it slipped slightly on his tray.

His smile vanished and his eyes went directly to the tray and his hands. It moved only a fraction of an inch, but he thought the stein was going to tumble to the floor with a deafening crash. His feet became motionless, and he recovered his balance like a tightrope walker regaining control after giving the audience a sudden scare. He turned his entire body, tray and all, toward the voice. "Good afternoon, Madame." He waited for his voice to be silent, as if it was not in his control, before he turned his body back to its original position and resumed traveling.

When he reached the intended room, his mouth filled with saliva when he saw that the door was closed. What would he do? Did he dare put the tray down on the floor to open it? Before he could decide upon his action, the door swung open with a slight creak in the hinges and he saw a tall doctor in a long, white smock holding the knob. The doctor didn't say anything, but he smiled at Schmuel as he brought in the meal like an obedient servant. His body continued on its trek to the table even as his eyes held fast on the tall man in the white coat.

"Watch what you are doing, boy," said the other man seated at the end of the table. The man's voice startled Schmuel, forcing him to make a sudden stop. Again, he felt the contents of the tray shift position. His eyes opened wide as he focused on his burden, struggling with both hands to regain control. His left hand was lower than his right, and he watched everything slide. He swiftly lowered his right hand and succeeded in stopping the slide before it could bring his whole world toppling to the floor. He eased it to the table and stepped back, taking a deep breath.

"You little idiot," said the man in his seat. "You almost spoiled my lunch. You know what I would do to you if you dropped my food on the floor?"

The boy shivered, but kept silent.

"Answer me, you dumb one."

"No sir," said Schmuel. "I don't know."

The man blurted out a laugh. "*Nothing*. That's what I would do to you, absolutely nothing. But I would cut off one of your mother's hands. That's what I would do."

"Really, Dr. Rauf," said the man in the coat.

"Oh well, all right," said the other. "Maybe just a finger, eh?"

Both doctors laughed, although the one in the white coat tried to stifle it with his hand, as if sneezing. He took a seat across from his colleague and dismissed Schmuel. The boy started to exit, but the doctor stopped him. Reaching into his coat pocket, he produced a piece of hard candy and offered it to Schmuel. The young boy hesitated momentarily.

"Go ahead, Schmuel, you can take it. Go ahead." The doctor's voice was soft and comforting. Schmuel took the candy and backed out of the room after giving a soft thank you to the man. "And Schmuel, send your mother in here," said the doctor. "I just need to talk to her for a moment, so please, send her in."

✶✶✶✶

"Why do we bother with that one, Josef?" said Dr. Rauf. "He's lame and pathetic."

"Then why waste good gas on him, Doctor?" Both men laughed. "Besides, he makes his mother happy and she makes me happy when I want it. That is a workable arrangement for me."

"Personally, I don't know how you can touch these Jews, Josef. They are repugnant to me."

"War time is tough time, Doctor. We must all make sacrifices. Forget that she is Jewish for a moment and you must admit that she has all the right parts in a most appealing way. You'll come around someday. Wait and see."

✶✶✶✶

When Schmuel returned to the kitchen, he unwrapped the candy and looked at it as it rested in his palm. He studied it, as if it were a rare jewel he had discovered.

"What is that, Schmuel?" asked his mother, who was wiping off the table where she had been working.

"Just a piece of candy," he replied before popping it into his mouth. He was puzzled how anything in this sad, bitter place could produce such a sweetness.

"Mother, the tall doctor said he wants you to go see him right away."

She stopped wiping the table and straightened up. "What does he want, Schmuel?"

"I don't know, Mother. He said he wants to talk to you, that's all."

Sadie dropped her towel onto the table top and looked at Schmuel. "Finish cleaning the sink for me, Schmuel. Be sure to do a good job. Then take the trash out, too." She walked past her son without looking at him, resigned to her task.

4

When Sadie walked into the conference room, she stood at the end of the table, away from the two men who enjoyed the meal she prepared for them. Neither of them rose when she entered. "Ah, Sadie, you look wonderful today," said the tall doctor in the white coat. "There is something we want you to do for us. We know there are several pairs of identical twins in the camp, but we also know there are a few fraternal twins as well."

Sadie's face became drawn and her lips taut, as if she could not speak.

"Yes, we are very thorough in our work, Sadie. We know you are a twin, although your sister is not here in this camp. But there is a new woman here, she came in yesterday. She is also a fraternal twin, separated from her sister."

"We think you should meet her, now," said the other man. "Go tell your son to fetch her from the barracks. She was told to expect a boy to come for her, that he will lead her to you because you have something in common. Do this, now, woman."

The man in the white coat stood and approached the puzzled woman. "This is not your sister, Sadie. We know that, so don't look so nervous." He placed his hand on her back and caressed her shoulder, then ran his hand down her spine and slowly back up. "So, go tell your son to go to building number seven and bring her here to the front desk."

Sadie's head turned toward the tall doctor, glimpsing his deceptively warm smile. She knew this woman was in trouble. Her crime was to be a Jew and a twin. She heard the doctor was doing research about twins. Many of those who came into this building were never the same when they left, if they left at all.

"You don't have a problem with this simple assignment, Sadie, do you?"

"No, no, of course not," she answered. "I'll tell him to do it right now, just as you want . . . Dr. Mengele."

Chapter Two

FRIDAY, SEPTEMBER 13, 1974. HENNIKER, N.H.

There were worse ways to start employment at a college. Sam had been on the job since June, but this September afternoon was the kickoff for the academic calendar. A cocktail party put the entire faculty and staff in a good mood.

Sam poured himself a glass of red wine at the makeshift bar set up in the lobby of the administration building, also called The Inn. The old wooden structure, like something out of a Rockwell painting, was set on the north side of Main Street in the center of town. It had once been a New Hampshire country inn before it was rescued from demolition by the New Sussex College in 1946, its inaugural year. The vast lobby and its colonial décor was a perfect setting for college president Seth Walpole to use for a welcoming cocktail reception for faculty and staff at the end of the first Monday of the semester. The white wainscoting adorned every wall and provided nice contrast to the blue wallpaper above it. White crown molding ran along each wall at the ceiling.

There were worse ways, indeed.

It didn't take long for the room to fill with college employees, many of whom worked in this fine building. Sam knew many colleges had reputations for partying, rather than academics, but that reputation usually focused on student behavior. Employees didn't waste time getting to a party at this institution.

"Sam, let me introduce you to Arthur Vasile and his wife, Carol. Arthur is a Biology professor, and Carol works in the business office," said Bob Hill, the Director of the Danton Library, and Sam's new boss.

Sam extended his hand toward the man, who sported a salt and pepper goatee and was a husky six-footer with a full head of graying hair. "Nice to meet you, Professor Vasile, and you, too, Carol," said Sam. The woman looked much younger than her husband.

"Oh please, call me Arthur. We're usually very informal here and don't bother with academic titles. I think they're a bit stuffy, don't you agree, Carol?" The man's accent was European, but Sam couldn't place it.

"Absolutely," his wife replied. She reached out to Sam, who took her hand gently, giving it a slight squeeze without shaking it. Something about her face anchored his eyes on her, as if a flash of light had gone off. He scanned her figure as rapidly as possible, trying not to be noticed. He didn't know much about perfume, but whatever it was she was wearing, he liked it. Her light brown hair was long and straight, reaching well below her shoulders. He liked that, too.

"Sam runs our Educational Technology Department on the second floor of the library. He has a wonderful collection of films and other teaching aids," said Hill. "What we don't have, he can rent for you, but you know that, Arthur."

"Yes, I do. Thank goodness, Sam, for *Time Life Films,*" said Arthur. "I make my selection of films to rent. You type up the requisition and bring it to Carol and she processes the order. Very neat and tidy. It's a process that will enable the three of us to get to know each other, one of the benefits of working at a small college. It's a rather intimate setting, not like those diploma factories in Boston."

Sam listened to Arthur, but his eyes fixed on Carol. He figured her to be in her mid-thirties. Her light blue dress was simple, but fit her well in the right places, stopping a few inches above the knee, flattering her beautiful legs. She looked at Arthur as he spoke, but her expression was empty.

"Aren't you going to introduce me to your friend, Carol?" The voice came from behind Sam at the same time he felt an arm encircle his. She stood between Carol and Sam, smiling as if she'd won a prize. "Hi, I'm Martha Sanborn. I'm also on the library staff and I've seen you around, but the boss didn't bother to introduce us." She shot a scowl at Bob.

"Hi, Martha," said Sam, unpleasantly surprised by the grab on his arm, despite the obvious pressure of her full breast against him. He noticed Arthur and Carol making disapproving expressions simultaneously. Bob Hill simply walked away. "I'm Sam Miller. It's a pleasure to meet you," he said, as she inched closer to him.

"The pleasure is mine," she replied. "Where's your wife, Sam?" asked Martha.

The real intent of her question was obvious to Sam and the others. The Vasiles shrugged and Sam looked at his feet, avoiding eye contact with Martha. "She's where she likes to be," said Sam, "in the arms of another man. I'm divorced."

"I'm sorry to hear that, but I understand," she said. "I'm divorced myself, twice, in fact. Oh, it was a long time ago. I married young, too young. But that's a boring story. I'd rather talk about you, Sam. I couldn't help notice that you have a slight limp. What's that, an old football injury?" she laughed.

"Actually, I was about to ask Prof . . . Arthur, about his homeland." Sam shifted his head to meet the professor's gaze. "I can't place the accent."

"I'm originally from Romania, Sam, but I've been in the United States for nearly thirty years. The war caused many of us to flee Europe, you know. I had started medical school, but wasn't able to finish my studies. When I arrived here I had no money, but I worked my way through a Ph. D. program at Boston University and began my academic career. It's been most rewarding." Arthur glanced at Carol as he said *rewarding,* a move not lost on Sam.

Sam knew all too well about fleeing Europe because of the war. He hoped to avoid lengthy conversations about it.

"Oh, Sam, look at this," said Martha. "My wine glass is empty. Would you get me a refill, white, please?"

"Ah, sure, Martha." Sam took the empty plastic party glass and wove his way through the crowd to the bar. A tall, heavyset man stood there, plopping ice cubes into a glass while eyeballing the bourbon bottle on the table. "Going for the strong stuff, eh, Ian?"

Ian Barnstead was a History professor whom Sam had met several days earlier. He was a pleasant, jovial man with a strong voice and a broad smile, the kind of guy who you felt you'd known for years. "Oh hi, Sam. Yeah, time for the heavy artillery. I get to sneak one or two of these when the wife's not around. Fortunately for me, she's at home." He followed his comments with a hearty laugh. "I see you've met the Vasiles," said Ian. "Something about Arthur, though. Maybe it's the cultural difference, I don't know, but whenever I've tried to talk to him about the war in Europe, strictly from a historic perspective, mind you, he usually talks about Germany's positive contributions, technologically. He's from Romania, so why such cheerleading for Germany? I don't know."

"Well, he's a science-oriented guy, maybe that's why," said Sam. "Maybe that's what he thinks of instinctively."

"Well yeah, Sam, but I don't know. If you talk about the air attacks on London, you know, with V2 rockets, he starts telling you how important those rockets were in contributing to our space program. Oh, and he can't say enough about the Autobahn and how it's the model for our interstate highways. I don't know." Ian shook his head and eased some bourbon into his mouth. "I guess he's got a point. The Germans were technological innovators, for sure. I once read somewhere that the American and Russian space race was all about which country had the best German scientists. I don't know."

"That's one way to look at it, Ian. What about his wife, Carol? What's she like?"

"She's a top shelf gal. I guess he met her at Boston University about ten years ago. They got married and moved up here a few years later. They both like the things most of us like about this place: small, quiet, out of the way, no hustle and bustle. She's very bright and likeable. But he's a bit stiff. They seem like an odd fit to me. I don't know." Ian swigged his drink again.

Sam peered in her direction, but his gaze was interrupted by Martha looking back at him, raising her hand to her mouth as if drinking. He came back to Earth, recalling his mission, and reached for the white wine.

"I see you've met Martha," said Ian. "She's a trip."

"How so?" asked Sam.

"She gets along with everyone, especially the guys. The life-of-the-party kind of gal, she is. She flirts with anything with a dick and has been known to get pretty schnockered at social engagements. But I guess she's harmless. I don't know."

9

Sam delivered a freshly poured glass of wine to Martha, who eased both hands around it as if cradling a baby bird. "Thanks, Sam. I was afraid you were going to let me die of thirst."

"I'm sure that would never happen, Martha," said Arthur. His remark struck her sharply and her smile vanished. "If you will please excuse me, I've made my obligatory appearance and now must go home to assume my role as kitchen slave."

"Oh, yes," interjected Carol. "Soon I hope to have him doing the laundry and scrubbing the floors. Cooking has become one of Arthur's hobbies, and I'm happy to yield the kitchen when he offers to cook dinner, such as tonight."

Arthur smiled. "Actually, tonight looks like a good night for using the outdoor grill. I just love to build a fire." He laughed and nodded to the group, a light clicking sound emanating from his shoes as his heels touched quickly.

"I think I need a refill, myself," said Sam, and he scurried over to the bar. As he finished refreshing his drink, he looked back to see an unknown man trying to start a conversation with Martha. It seemed like a great opportunity to make his way to the front door and step out onto the vast porch that ran the entire length of the building. He found an inviting bench to his left and settled onto it. He sipped from his glass after exhaling a sigh of relief. He wasn't in the mood for Martha.

"Nice move, Houdini." A woman's voice surprised him. It was Carol Vasile, emerging through the door. "That's the slickest escape I've seen in a long time."

"Oh, please, I didn't mean to be rude to you," said Sam.

"Don't apologize. I saw the predicament you were in. She comes on pretty strong sometimes, not very subtle. Of course, I could be insulted. First my husband abandons me and then you do a disappearing act. Swoosh, the men are gone."

Sam peeked at Carol with guilty eyes.

"Maybe I should go inside," she said.

"No, no, don't do that. Please, have a seat," he said, motioning to one half of the bench.

"Okay, Mr. Houdini, but no vanishing act this time." Carol slid onto the bench, folded her bare arms across her chest and crossed her legs, causing her skirt to rise up a bit further on her thighs. She looked straight ahead onto Main Street, nearly the entire commercial center within view. "This is really a pretty little town, Sam. I believe you'll like it. We're all country mice up here, each and every one of us turning away from city life, except an occasional trip to Boston or New York for the Pops or a Broadway play. We're not altogether without culture, after all."

Sam focused on her as she continued to gaze upon the small town's Main Street. She was a class act, alright, with subtle beauty, bright blue eyes; she was intelligent and well spoken. He felt at ease in her presence, a sharp contrast to Martha.

Chapter Three

On Monday afternoon, the conference room located beside President Seth Walpole's office on the first floor of the administration building came to life with Seth, the deans of the college, department heads and several staff members. The room sat adjacent to Seth's office and that of his personal secretary, Irene Preston. It boasted a large, round table in the center, with eight upholstered chairs around it. Several similar chairs hugged the walls. The room was on the southeast corner of the building, so at three in the afternoon, the sun posed no problem, and the drapes were left open on the large windows on the two outside walls. There was a white chair rail along each wall, its line broken by the doorway and the windows. The blue walls matched the color of the lobby.

As people took their seats around the table, Seth called the meeting to order. His secretary had set up an easel behind Seth, just to his right, and Seth placed a large mounted drawing on it. Irene sat against a wall, her notebook at the ready for taking the meeting minutes. The drawing showed a new, white clapboard building being proposed as an addition to the campus.

Sam squirmed into a seat at the table as Seth started the meeting. "Welcome, gentlemen. I've been working on making this announcement for some time. Some of you have heard rumors, I'm sure, but it now seems close enough to reality to officially let the cat out of the bag. Since he's done most of the heavy lifting, so to speak, in bringing this project along, I'm going to let Bill Woodruff tell you about it."

Bill Woodruff, the Dean of College Development, was in charge of an office that did the fundraising for New Sussex College. Sam admired Bill and his staff for doing a necessary job, even if it did mean harassing alumni and doing sophisticated begging from merchants, bank presidents, and searching for every possible source of funding in the state and federal governments. He could never imagine doing such work. But he knew from experience that sometimes one has to perform distasteful labor.

Bill had taken off his sport coat and remained in his seat as he spoke. His white, long-sleeved shirt with dark red tie gave him about as close to a businesslike look as anyone at the table. Most of the men were without ties, and many had sleeves rolled up to the elbow. Seth wore a gray tweed sport coat with brown elbow patches, preferring the traditional academic look.

"This is an uncommon college, geographically speaking. We've had to make use of old buildings spread all over town, surrounding the commercial center of little Henniker. Fifteen years ago, the college drafted a plan that called for relocating most of its new building construction south of the river that bisects the town," said Bill. "We've been following that plan effectively, with the new dorms, the gymnasium, cafeteria, library and science building, all contributing to the evolving campus. The large lot between the library and women's dorm has long been considered for an open, landscaped section of the campus or for a new building. We are happy to say that a generous alumnus has worked with us not only to provide major funding, but also to help design the building that we believe will serve as the new focal point of the campus."

Although each man at the table had an 8x10, full color rendition of the drawing placed in front of him, everyone glanced at the large poster; those seated in front of it even turned in their seats, before choosing to focus on their own copy. Within a few seconds, spontaneous applause filled the room.

Bill continued. "We can thank Mr. James Kirkson for his most generous donation, stipulating that this building be constructed in his family name. Not only did he attend New Sussex College, but he has put three children through here as well. The building will bear his name as the Kirkson Center. There will be classrooms of various sizes, the campus bookstore, a food court, the college radio station and a large patio behind the building. The exact layout has not been determined, so we will seek further input from all of you before the architect comes up with final plans. This truly will be the center of the campus and will provide a location for many college functions and activities."

Sam held up his hand and Seth pointed to him in acknowledgement. "This is the first time I've heard mention of the college radio station being located here. I just want to say that I think that's a great idea. As the faculty advisor to the radio station, I know that we could use more space and I'll be happy to give input about its design."

"Yes, Sam, I thought you might. Thank you."

Further discussion took place among the group, with questions about the construction schedule, publicity, additional funding needs and possible input from the Alumni Council. Sam didn't care much about these specific details. He was glad to hear that the rumors about construction plans were true and wanted to see the building take place. He knew it would help transform the campus, and he was in no hurry.

Seth went on to discuss the overall fiscal health of the college, which was very good, and that an Arts program was being considered as a possible replacement for the failing Engineering program, which was drawing fewer and fewer students each year. The Arts could draw more interest and perhaps enable the college to broaden its enrollment and enjoy a boost in cash flow.

Seth adjourned the meeting and he rose from his seat, ready to exit. Meetings weren't Sam's favorite thing, but this one was short and sweet, much to his pleasure. Several of the men at the table remained seated, buzzing to each other about the Kirkson Center.

Sam noticed Seth motion to Al Turner, the Dean of Academic Affairs. He saw a strong scowl on Seth's face. *What is that all about? Isn't this a feel-good session?* Al Turner had a strange expression, too. He looked like the cat that swallowed the canary and had feathers on his face. The two men moved out of the conference room together, one behind the other, like they were headed for the woodshed.

Sam recalled that Carol Vasile worked in a room on the second floor, so he decided this would be a good time to make a friendly visit. He could honestly claim to be in the neighborhood, so why not?

He made his way out to the lobby, climbed the large, straight stairway to the second floor, passed through a short hallway and turned to his left, finding his intended room at the end of a connecting corridor. Years of additions and modifications to the building were obvious to Sam. The door was open and Sam went in, slowing his pace. His eyes went to Carol, at his right as he entered, her desk against the wall. He didn't notice anyone to his left, since he looked straight in Carol's direction. But Doris Brewer noticed him and announced his presence.

"Hello, Sam, how nice to see you. To what do we owe this surprise visit on a Monday afternoon?" Sam was still looking in Carol's direction when Doris spoke. He finally caught her gaze as she tilted her head, as if to say she had her answer.

"Hi, Sam," said Carol. Even though she was seated, he could see her faded jeans fit tightly around her athletic figure. A yellow, long-sleeved blouse had lace down the front, offering a feminine contrast to the old jeans. The top three buttons were open, teasing Sam. Her smooth complexion pleased him almost as much as her blue eyes. They demanded his attention.

"I have to run a quick errand, kiddies," said Doris, who grabbed her purse from a coat rack near her desk. "Be back soon, so stay out of trouble, now."

"What's up, Sam?" Carol swiveled her chair to face Sam, a high, creaky sound coming from that old piece of furniture. This historic, aging building and many of the items in it offered a glimpse back in time to the early 1900s. Sam thought about how it must have been when it was new, a grand tribute to the progress of the emerging new century. Its location kept it sheltered from the damages of war-torn Europe, where many great buildings were destroyed.

"I just came from an interesting meeting with Dr. Walpole and the Deans," said Sam. He brought her up to speed on the new building. Her smile was without the enthusiasm he expected. "That's great news for the students. I'm glad the rumors were true, but I hope the administration stays right here at The Inn. I love working in this old place."

"Funny thing, though," said Sam. "Seth called to Al Turner and they left the room together, not exactly singing

Happy Days Are Here Again, if you get my drift. Turner's in his doghouse about something."

"You know, Sam, they're the top administrators at this college, so they work closely together on many things. Maybe they disagree about some issues. It could be anything, really."

"In the short time I've been here, I've already heard that they aren't exactly bosom buddies," said Sam. It probably didn't have anything to do with the new building. I just thought it strange, to be showing teeth right after such an upbeat get-together."

They fell quiet for a moment, their eyes locked together. Sam broke the awkward pause. "How about taking a break and grabbing a cup of coffee?"

"That would be great, but maybe another time. I'm really swamped with work and have to catch up. Give me a few days, and well, maybe my head will get above water."

"Okay, that's a deal," said Sam. He tried not to look disappointed. "I admire your dedication. Say hi to Arthur for me." He didn't know why he said that. It just rolled out.

Sam wound his way back through the passageways of the building and down the front stair to the lobby. He was about to exit through the front door, but he remembered the large bulletin board outside the business office and decided to go check it out. It was like checking a rural mailbox, regardless of the time of day. There just might be something of interest.

As Sam approached the board, he could hear loud voices, Seth Walpole and Al Turner, coming from the president's office a few feet away. There was nobody else around, so he inched closer to the sound, still looking at the bulletin board.

"I don't care what you've heard. I'm not involved with any such wife-swapping thing, or adult club as you call it. Really, Seth, I'm surprised and hurt you'd even suggest such a thing." It was Al Turner.

"Well, I hope not, Turner, for your sake and that of the entire college. We're on the verge of this major alumni contribution that could help put New Sussex College on the map. If this club exists and it gets to the news media, it would be a most damaging scandal. What's more, it would

16

certainly destroy your career in academia." Seth's voice got louder, like a pianist pounding the keys harder and harder.

"Are you threatening me, sir?" barked Turner. "You have no right to accuse me of anything. I don't have to take this from the likes of you. You're just a UNH castoff. Don't play high and mighty with me."

"How dare you, Turner. I had an exemplary career at the university. My record stands for itself. I'm not threatening you. I am warning you. You'd better wash your hands of this club, and thoroughly."

The voices stopped and Sam heard the sound of footsteps a few feet away, coming from Seth's office. He looked up and saw Al Turner stomping along the corridor. Their eyes met briefly, and Sam froze in place. Turner looked startled, pausing before taking a turn toward the lobby. Sam waited a minute before going in the same direction. He left the building, heart racing, and rushed to his car. He wanted to tell someone about what he'd seen and heard, but learned long ago that sometimes silence is the best choice.

Chapter Four

THURSDAY, OCTOBER 3.

Sam still carried the image of Al Turner's eyes peering at him when Turner made his fast exit from Seth Walpole's office on that September day. Everyone else left that meeting with a sense of euphoria at the news of the imminent construction of the Kirkson Center. But Seth and Al had a knockdown, drag-out fight over something Seth said could be very damaging to the college. It sounded like an adult club of some sort that involved wife swapping. How could that be true? In such a small town, it seemed like everybody knew everybody else, except newcomers.

Sam often liked to go off by himself at work, so he left his second floor office and took the day's mail arrival of packages down to a workroom on the basement level. He spread the packages out on a table and opened them, sorting the contents: projection lamps of various sizes, a film storage rack in need of assembly and four rental films from Janus Film Distributors. A woman's voice from behind startled him.

"I'm glad you like to wear casual clothes to work, Sam. Those Levis fit you perfectly."

He turned to find Martha Sanborn. Her knee-length skirt fit loosely and revealed shapely legs. Her white blouse, buttoned to the neck, clung to her full bosom. Sam's eyes surveyed the length of her before replying.

"Oh hi, Martha. Are you lost? I wouldn't expect to see you down here."

Martha moved from the doorway into the large work room. Her walk was slow and rhythmic, like she was about to start a dance.

"I know my way around, Sam. I'm never lost. You've been very busy and I haven't had a chance to chat with you much. So, I thought I'd come see what keeps you so busy."

"There's always a lot to do at the beginning of a se-mester, especially this year, since we began occupying this downstairs space. I'm about to build some shelving here and install soundproofing in the two listening rooms in the back. How about you? Keeping busy?" He watched Martha turn around slowly, gazing at the workroom as if it mat-tered to her. She was putting herself on display for Sam, a move he enjoyed more than expected.

"Yeah, sure, always busy. I need an occasional break, though. Don't you?" She moved a little closer to Sam, even-tually standing beside him at the table and letting her arm bump softly against his a couple of times. "Aha, you got some films in, I see," she said, reaching across Sam and touching the large box with the Janus label. "Got any good anatomy films for the Biology professor?" A girlish smile spread across her face.

Sam caught her impish look. "Probably just an instruc-tional piece on how to dissect a frog. Of course, if that's your thing, it'll keep you happy for thirty minutes."

"Oh yuk. No, that's not my thing."

"Well then, what is your thing?"

"I'll tell you what. Why don't you let me take you out to dinner tonight and you can learn about my thing. Just a casual dinner after work. We can ride out to Hillsboro, to Govoni's. I'm in the mood for Italian food. What do you say?"

Sam hesitated.

"Oh come on, Sam," she said, breaking the silence. "We're grownups here. Co-workers often socialize at this college. Besides, I'm buying. Unless, of course, you've got a date with Carol Vasile. You two seem to spend a lot of time together, so I wouldn't be surprised."

"Oh, please, that's ridiculous. Like you just said, co-workers socialize often at this college. Carol and I have be-come friends. That's all."

"Well, I'm not the only person around Henniker that notices you and her together a lot."

"Then I guess there are a few more busybodies in town than I counted." Sam felt boxed in, with no retreat other than to accept Martha's offer. "Okay, it's a deal." Sam won-dered if he was making a wise decision.

"Okay, Sammy boy. That's the ticket. Meet me in the parking lot after work. We can take my car."

Sam nodded and watched Martha turn and ease her way out of the room, disappearing in the hallway. He liked the way she moved and felt a manly urge rush through him. Sometimes Martha could look pretty damned good.

Sam met Martha as planned but insisted on driving, taking his car. He still had old world values, despite the so-called *New Age* and the emerging women's movement.

"Okay, Sam, if you insist. Besides, that way it will keep my hands free," she laughed.

Govoni's was a quiet Italian restaurant one town over, about a ten minute ride to the west. Soft music was playing as they entered. Sam never cared for the sounds of Frank Sinatra, Tony Bennett, or Perry Como, but he could take it in small doses. The food, however, was outstanding, so he didn't mind coming here. They settled at a table for two, complete with checkered tablecloth and wine glasses ready for filling. The service was quick and they enjoyed some red wine while waiting for their meals.

"How'd you get that leg injury, Sam? You limp just a bit, but it doesn't seem to slow you down any," said Martha. She had no problem getting personal, it seemed.

"It was a long time ago, when I was a little boy. I had a broken leg that wasn't set very well, but I get around."

Their first sip of wine was almost in unison, like trained performers. After finishing his first glass quickly, Sam felt relaxed and ordered another. Martha was still good with hers.

"Another thing, Sam, I detect a faint trace of an accent of some kind. My guess is European. Am I right?"

He stared into his glass as if searching for words, cupping it with both hands. When he reached the decision about his answer, he raised his head and peered into Martha's eyes. "Yes, I'm originally from Poland. My family tried to escape Europe during the war, but we didn't make it out."

"Sam, I'm so sorry to hear that," said Martha. "Were you and your family in one of those camps?"

Sam nodded and diverted his gaze away from Martha. For a moment he was transported back to that time when he was by his mother's side, working with her in that kitchen. "Yes, my mother and I. We were separated before the liberation and I never saw her again. I traveled with a teenage friend, and we eventually made it to this country. It was a long time ago. It doesn't make for good conversation. I want to learn about you."

"I'm just a simple country girl who's learned how to make her own way and enjoy good times when they happen. Of course, sometimes you have to nudge those good times along."

Sam felt a shoeless foot caress his lower leg, a movement that added clarity to Martha's statement. He made no effort to break the contact.

When dinner was over, Sam drove back to Henniker, with Martha sliding as close as she could, despite the bucket seats. The console became her enemy.

"Sam, are you up to meeting some people? I know some folks who are getting together tonight in West Henniker. Let's stop by for a short visit. What do you say?"

Sam fell into the childhood mode of gauging all nights as school nights or weekends. It was early, so why not go? "Sure, but just for a short time, if you don't mind."

Martha smiled, folding her arms across her chest in victory. She directed him to a colonial house in the neighborhood north of Route 202, filled with beautiful old farmhouses mixed in with newer colonials.

"I like this area," said Sam. "It's an interesting mix of old, well-kept houses and new."

"Farming has given way to new occupations for people, so original owners are subdividing their acreage and selling it off to folks moving in, like college faculty and staff. Think you'll want to buy and build here someday?"

Sam didn't answer. He focused on a two story, white clapboard house up ahead with several cars parked in the long driveway and on the shoulder of the road.

"That's our place, Sam," said Martha. "Pull over and let's go inside."

The house had a covered front porch which Sam admired as they stepped up onto it. Martha rang the bell, which was answered by a petite woman about Martha's age. She wore tight, red ski pants, a white turtleneck sweater and small, soft-looking gray boots with pointed toes, typical après ski. "Hello, Martha. Who's your friend? Come in and be sure not to leave him outside." Her voice was tiny and she spoke slowly, watching Sam make his entrance behind Martha.

Sam recognized the sound of music from the 1940s, the upbeat *In the Mood* playing as they entered a large living room filled with people. Some gathered at a table where liquor and finger foods were served and others scattered about in chairs or leaning against a wall, in conversation. The chairs were pushed to the room's perimeter, providing a hardwood surface in the center suitable for dancing. Apparently, nobody was in a dancing mood yet. It seemed to be an even split of men and women, a nice collection of couples, all unfamiliar to Sam.

Martha led Sam to the drinks table and poured red wine from an open bottle for both of them. The woman who answered the door reappeared at Sam's side and introduced herself as Bonnie West. "Nice to meet you, Bonnie," said Sam, his eyes glancing about the room. "Welcome to my home, Sam," she said. "That's my husband, Tom, across the room." A tall, husky man in a red ski sweater and brown slacks waved to them, acknowledging the introduction.

He broke off his conversation with a tall woman and came over to join them, grinning like a department store appliance salesman working on commission. "Hello," he said, extending a hand to Sam. "My name's Tom, but I guess you know that by now. You and Martha getting along, are you?"

Sam sensed that he meant something deeper than that. "We work in the college library and just grabbed a casual dinner, that's all. Nice to meet you."

"Ah," replied Tom, nodding and shifting his gaze toward Martha.

"He sure is a cute one," said Bonnie. "Glad you brought him along. Your timing is excellent."

Bonnie and Tom joined hands and walked to the center of the hardwood floor. Sam looked at Martha. He thought there was some unspoken meaning he was missing. Martha raised an eyebrow and motioned for Sam to look toward the dance area as she drank from her glass. Tom and Bonnie came together as the music changed to the romantic tune, *Moonlight Serenade*.

Tom swept Bonnie up into a slow dance position, bending down to guide his small partner, his left hand holding her right at his shoulder height. They swayed in a gentle foxtrot, somehow working their contrasting sized bodies as one, in a smooth, rhythmic dance. After spinning Bonnie with one hand as a guide, Tom turned away from her and peered at Martha. Bonnie wasted no time in ambling up to Sam, taking his hand and leading him to the dance floor, which soon had two couples. Martha and Tom snuggled close as they danced, while Sam held Bonnie at a distance, doing a less than spectacular version of the dance.

Bonnie looked at Sam, easing herself in closer, pressing against him. "This is the snowball dance, Sam. Ever heard of it?"

"No, not really. I don't dance much."

"Well, it's fun. Soon, we split up and find new partners. The pack on the floor gets bigger and bigger, like a snowball rolling down a white covered hill. Time for a change." She slid away from Sam and walked around the perimeter of the dance area, inspecting the other men, who had put food and drink aside in anticipation of using their hands for more pleasurable pursuits. Bonnie found her prey and began dancing anew. Martha and Tom had also taken new partners, but Sam stood alone.

"Get with it, Sam," called Tom. "Don't be shy with these women. Grab a dame and take to the floor."

Before Sam could respond, a woman his own height, with long brown hair and wearing a green mini dress, grabbed his hand and led him to the center of the dance floor. "Oh, look, he chose me," she laughed. She moved in close and Sam felt her warmth.

The snowball effect continued until everybody had a partner. Somehow, Martha wound up back with Sam, a move that didn't surprise him. "Isn't this a coincidence," laughed Martha. She nudged Sam with her full body. He relaxed, finally reunited with the only dance partner he knew.

"This has been . . . nice, Martha, but I think we should go now."

"That works for me, too, Sam," she said with a smile. She looked around for Tom and waved to him when their eyes met. Sam felt her hand grab his and they moved away from the dancers. As they neared the door, Sam looked back and noticed Al Turner embracing a woman, his hands moving along her side, his arms wrapped around her, as if he was protecting his catch. Sam didn't recognize anybody else.

The air was warm for an October evening. He could sense Martha looking at him, but kept his eyes fixed on the road. "Sam, there's no need to go to the library parking lot. Let's go to my place for a nightcap. We'll fetch my car in the morning."

He felt her hand clutch his thigh, giving clarity to her message. He said nothing for a moment as he slowed the car, approaching the blinking overhead light at the main intersection in Henniker. He came to a full stop and looked to Martha, who pointed left. A right turn would lead to the library. Her hand caressed him as he put on the left turn signal.

Chapter Five

As Sam entered Seth Walpole's ground floor office for a Friday morning meeting with the college president, he admired the fireplace on an inside wall and built-in book-shelves on either side of it. The fireplace was no longer in use, but there were iron utensils with shiny brass handles on the hearth. Seth's desk was a few feet in front of the fireplace, sitting on a large plush carpet that seemed out of place. This room screamed for uncovered hardwood, but that would have added significant noise from passing feet. A round table sat across the room, close to the corner, getting light from windows on two walls. A floor plan of the Kirkson Center lay spread out across the table.

After quick greetings, Sam made a beeline to the floor plan and studied it carefully before speaking. He had his own 8x10 copy in a folder, which he'd used to prepare for the meeting. He'd learned as a boy that preparation was vital to good performance. Sometimes it was a life saver.

"I think the radio station should be located near the rear, southwest corner door," said Sam. "There'll be a lot of student traffic at the studio, so let's keep it away from any classrooms. We could also place the transmission antenna on the roof in the same corner of the building, so as not to stand out against the façade."

"I agree, Sam," said Seth, bending over the table like a new father admiring a baby. "Any thoughts on the class-rooms?"

"Just that they'll need some closet space for audio vi-sual equipment. They should each be equipped with their own collection of film, overhead and slide projectors. Wheel-ing them around on carts, from room to room, will just add disruption. The walls and ceiling should have sound ab-sorption materials."

"Yes, Sam. That's good. We'll house the radio station, student union and bookstore on the ground floor. The classrooms will be upstairs."

Seth stood tall and backed a few feet from the table, turning as if he was about to walk away. He scratched his chin in deep thought, before turning toward Sam.

"I'd like to ask you something, Sam, and I need a totally honest answer. Is that okay?"

The change of tone puzzled Sam. His impression of Seth Walpole was that of a straight shooter, a man who got to the point. "Of course, Seth, what is it?"

"You've been here long enough to have met everybody on the faculty and administration of this tiny college. But I hope your mind still holds an unbiased view of those people. Sam, is there anyone here who strikes you as very secretive, who might have something to hide and is putting up a false front?"

Sam felt his jaw tighten. He pressed his hands together and looked to the floor, carefully waiting for his words to arrive. "I'm not sure I know what you mean, Dr. Walpole."

"It's hard to explain, Sam. I have to be careful not to say the wrong thing. I don't want to put you in an awkward position. Can you just tell me about your general impressions of the people you've met?"

Sam began to feel as if the walls of the room were moving in around him. He struggled to answer. "I guess a lot of people have secrets. Some people seem to be very friendly, some seem like real . . . Well, I guess I haven't noticed anyone who seems very unusual. The only one from a different culture is Arthur Vasile, but he keeps to himself most of the time." Sam swallowed hard, realizing that there were two people from foreign cultures.

"As I said, Sam, this is hard, but I have reason to believe that there is someone working here who can't be trusted, someone whose sense of morality could be brought into serious question, particularly regarding that person's past."

Sam shook his head, eyes down, his face beginning to feel flushed. Was Seth trying to put him in a corner? Was he talking about Al Turner or himself? "Dr. Walpole, I . . ."

Seth cut him off. "No, Sam, let's stop now. I'm sorry I brought this up. I can see this is not the time or the place for these questions. I'll note your suggestions about the building. As for this other train of thought I had, I'll have to think that out on my own. I'm sorry to have bothered you with the subject."

Sam was at a loss for words, his thoughts muddled. He rubbed his palms together and made his way out of the office. "See you later, Dr. Walpole."

Sam's breath was rapid as he entered the lobby. He wanted to visit with Carol after the scheduled meeting with Seth Walpole, but now he thought the better of it. What was Walpole really getting at? He thought about his time at the camp with his mother. *I never did anything wrong or distrustful there. I always did what I was told to do.*

He struggled with the meaning of Seth Walpole's questioning as he drove back to the library and scrambled up the stairs to his office. The two young men who made up the rest of his department were working at their desks across the room. He crossed to his desk in silence, as if they weren't there.

"Hey, Gene, either the boss had a bad night or a bad meeting this morning. What's your guess?" Fred Reilly was a technician Sam relied on to do a great deal of the hands-on work with the media equipment and the college radio station.

Gene Allen was the other staff member, handling most of the clerical tasks like ordering media materials and scheduling their use among the faculty. Both were in their mid-twenties.

Sam peeled off his light jacket and draped it over the back of his chair. "Sorry, guys, I didn't mean to be rude. You're right, Fred, I had a meeting this morning with Seth Walpole. It was fine, though, nothing to worry about. I just zoned out, I guess. How are you guys this morning?"

Sam and Fred's desks were each located in opposite corners of the large room, and Gene's was halfway down a wall common to him and Fred. The three desks formed a right triangle. The young workers exchanged looks before they responded in unison, "Good morning, Mr. Miller."

Sam smirked. "Very funny, you two. Very funny." They had used this greeting several times before, acting like schoolboys greeting their teacher.

"Sorry, boss," said Fred. "We couldn't help it. Sometimes you come in here looking like you're someplace else. Don't know if it's where you just left or are going to next."

"I've got a lot on my plate, so to speak, which is why I get paid the big bucks," said Sam. "It's lonely here at the top."

The three men chuckled and resumed their work. Gene was immersed in paper work, with invoices spread out on his desk, all tucked inside manila folders. Fred stood up, grabbed a box full of projection lamps and other electronic odds and ends. "Off to resupply the projection booths in the Science Building and the Little Theater. I'll be back before the snow flies."

Sam watched Fred shuffle out of the room, then glanced at Gene, who had resumed spreading folders and papers across his desk like he was in a giant game of solitaire. He wondered if these young men harbored any secrets. Not likely, but you never know. Henniker was a very small town where everybody gets to know everybody else. In time, he'd fall into that category, too, if he settled in here. But apparently they didn't know each other as well as they thought. Even a small New Hampshire town had secrets.

Chapter Six

FRIDAY AFTERNOON, OCTOBER 4.

The hours flew and Sam's staff had long ago left the building. He was about to do the same when a female voice surprised him. Carol Vasile glided through the door, smiling as she made her way into the large room. He didn't greet her with the traditional phrases, but simply returned her smile. A pleasant feeling warmed him, transforming his entire day. The uneasiness he experienced earlier vanished, as if Carol had worked some magic on him.

He stood at his desk stuffing papers into a folder. "Hey, lady, didn't you get the memo? This place closes at five."

"I know," she said. "I probably should've called, but I haven't been over here in a long time. I thought I'd chance a visit." His chair was behind him as she spoke, sliding in behind him and easing her way onto the chair.

"Make yourself at home, Mrs. Vasile. We have a wealth of comforts in this library, especially as you can see, in the Educational Technology arena."

"That's no lie," she said. "Your chair is much more comfortable than mine. How do you rate this?"

"I guess they wanted to make a good impression on a first year employee."

"Yes, that's the spirit of the place. We always want to make a good impression, so that's why I'm here. In that spirit of good impression-making, I have a proposition for you."

Sam turned to look at Carol with eyes wide open. "Hmmmm. That sounds interesting, but what would Arthur say?"

"He says go for it. Yeah, I already talked to him about the idea."

"What? You're losing me, Carol."

"Oh, Sam. It's not like that. Here's the deal. Arthur called me a half hour ago and said he had to go out of town, probably for the weekend. He was at home packing a few things and was about to take off for Massachusetts. He has a big project of some sort that he's consulting on with an old buddy in Norwood. The guy just called him and said he needed to see Arthur right away, that they had something happen that looked good for the project and might take them the whole weekend to work on it. I said that's just ducky."

Sam laughed. "Ducky?"

"Yeah, well, there goes my weekend. My old man is leaving town on short notice and I'm left with a pork roast to cook. Oh, and don't ever let on that I called him that. It's just an expression, but he gets a little touchy about our age difference sometimes. Anyway, he said that I should call up some friends and get something going. Then he said that I should try that new fellow, Sam. Why don't I ask him to a friendly dinner at our house? So, that's what I'm doing."

Sam lifted the folder off his desk, took it to a nearby file cabinet and deposited it in the top drawer. There was barely a sound to the action of the drawer in the shiny, metal cabinet. "A pork roast?" He had long lost his Jewish faith, so the idea was growing on him.

"Yes, with baked potatoes, fresh carrots and a salad. Red wine, too, of course. You look like you're searching for an answer to a classroom quiz. Well, if you don't think you'll like my home cooking, I'll just have to . . ."

"Stop right there, lady," he said. "You've sold me. What time? And I need your address."

"Seven should do," said Carol as she searched Sam's desk for pen and paper. In a moment, she scratched her address down on the paper and slid it into Sam's hand. "This is VERY casual, Sam, so stay in something comfortable."

"Comfortable is my middle name," said Sam. "I'm with you on that."

"Then why are you starting to blush if you're Mr. Sam Comfortable Miller?"

Sam's mouth opened, but no words escaped.

"Oh, Sam, I'm just kidding. Actually, you're looking a bit pale. Look, this kind of friendliness is quite common in our tiny town."

"I've heard that," said Sam.

"Hell, people don't even lock their doors around here."

"Yes, I've heard that, too." Sam's thoughts raced back to the camp at Auschwitz, where strong doors, locks and Nazi guards were everywhere.

"Okay, Mr. Comfortable, see you at seven thirty. The roast awaits you."

"That's fine. See you then." Sam watched as Carol turned and eased her way along the floor, making her exit. Her gait was smooth and natural, without a hint of pretense. *How fortunate is Arthur.*

Sam spent a few minutes filing some papers, straightening up his desk before closing his office and scrambling down the stairs. On the first floor, he passed the circulation desk just as Bob Hill emerged from his office, a set of keys jangling in his hands. "Got big plans tonight, Sam, or in a hurry to get to the Pub?"

"Oh, nothing special. I'm just having dinner at the Vasiles' tonight. That's all."

"I promise not to tell them that dinner at their house is nothing special."

Bob's remark startled Sam. "I just meant that it's casual, not a big deal."

"Hey, that's the way we do things around here, Sam. There are very few big deals in Henniker. Maybe the wife and I should join you."

Sam jumped at the suggestion. "Yes, that would be great. I mean, I'm sure it would be okay with Carol. She's cooking a roast. I can call her and tell her so she can prepare enough for four."

"Four? What about Arthur?"

"Arthur is out of town, working on a project in Massachusetts."

"Oh, I see," said Bob.

"Hey, it's not like that. Carol was just here and asked me over after explaining about Arthur."

"Relax. Like you said, it's no big deal. Actually, Sam, I was just busting you. I can't make it, since we already have plans to go out with friends. Maybe another time. Go home and enjoy your evening. I believe you're getting into the swing of things in your new town."

"Yeah, sure, Bob, you, too." *The swing of things.*

Chapter Seven

FRIDAY EVENING, OCTOBER 4.

Early October nights can be cool in New Hampshire, so Sam wasn't surprised by the distinct smell of a fireplace, fully stoked. Sam stepped out of his car onto the paved driveway in front of a barn serving as a two car garage, with an overhead door where conventional barn doors once swung open and shut. He assumed Carol's car was inside.

To the right stood a two-story farmhouse, with a covered porch running the length of the front, a common look in a rural town. Flood lights above the garage door illuminated the way to the porch and an outside light beside the front door aided his way up the two steps. Carol answered his doorbell ring, wearing a red apron over her matching red sweater and snug fitting blue jeans.

"Welcome, Mr. Comfortable, come on in," she said, holding a cocktail in one hand. As he entered, she turned and spoke while sauntering back to the kitchen. "This is a bourbon rocks." She held her drink up high, with her back still turned. "Want one of these or something else?"

"That sounds good." He loved her attitude, after all, this was supposed to be a casual evening. He loved her gently swaying figure, too.

He wasn't aware of music playing until she turned her head toward him while walking away, singing along with the stereo, "Rocky Mountain high, da da, da da da. Hope you like John Denver, 'cause I'm in a Rocky Mountain mood. Ha. Nothing like a Friday night and good company."

Sam didn't reply, afraid he might say something stupid.

They got to the kitchen, a rustic looking room with pine board cabinets, lightly stained, with a red brick fireplace at the far end. It had a low hearth and a compartment to the left for firewood, full to capacity with small cuts of oak. In contrast, the appliances were modern. Sam eyed the tall, double-door fridge with a light yellow coating. The dishwasher matched. A stainless steel sink rested in an *L*-shaped, granite-covered counter that separated the working half of the kitchen from the eating side, with a table for four. It was warmed by the fireplace.

"Just drape your coat over one of the kitchen chairs," said Carol, as she fetched a highball glass from a cabinet and placed it on the short end of the *L* counter, along the wall where a collection of liquor and wine bottles stood. "Mix your own, mister. The ice comes out of the door. Just press the button for cubed first, or you'll be drinking bourbon and water."

Sam examined the slot in the door for glasses, found the buttons and did as instructed. After a couple of cubes tumbled into his glass, he stepped to the bourbon bottle and poured his beverage. "I really like your place, Carol. This is the most interesting kitchen I've ever seen."

"Glad you like it. I'll give a limited tour in a minute after I've checked the roast." Carol did as stated and then motioned for Sam to follow. The living room, with flower-patterned pale green and white wallpaper, had a fireplace at one end with a wood-burning stove mounted in the opening. A recent model TV filled a corner, while colonial style furniture sat atop a carpeted floor. Numerous pictures on the walls completed the décor.

Sam stopped in front of one particular photograph, eyeing it carefully. It featured two women, perhaps teenagers, who were identical. It evoked a quick memory of his mother and her lost twin sister.

"Two of Arthur's cousins," said Carol. "He said they didn't make it out of Europe during the war. He didn't know them very well, but he likes the picture because it reminds him of family members lost. He says we shouldn't forget them."

The tour continued into the dining room, which was also colonial style, and large enough for a tall corner hutch and a table with seating for eight. More photos were scattered over one wall and Sam found another one featuring twin girls, this time mature women, about in their thirties. "The same twins, no doubt," said Sam.

"I guess so," said Carol. "I asked Arthur about that once and he just kind of nodded his head. Who else could they be?" Carol blurted out a short laugh. "It's pretty unusual to have more than one set of twins in a family."

Sam crept closer to the picture, which hung at eye height, raising an index finger near the glass cover, almost touching it. The subjects were twice as old as the ones in the other photograph, but they were different looking somehow. One woman seemed to have a pronounced slouch to her frame. Of course, the growth into adulthood can bring about facial and body changes. Perhaps she was injured. The war brought much suffering to many. *Poor girl.*

They returned to the kitchen and Carol extracted the roast from the oven. "How can I help?" asked Sam.

"By being patient and enjoying your drink," said Carol. "We're going to let this piggy sit for about five minutes."

"You're going to starve me, woman."

"You'll find it worth the wait. Haven't you ever cooked a roast before? You've got to let the juices settle back down. It fills our little meaty guy with flavor. The table is set, the veggies are in the roasting pan with piglet, the wine bottle is opened and the vintage is breathing life. Sit back, Jack, and relax to the sound of Johnny D."

"You're starting to sound like a DJ. Maybe you should be on WNSB-FM," said Sam. "You've got a rich voice, a little deep for a girl. You'd be great."

"Maybe I should," laughed Carol. "When can I audition?"

"I'll set it up with the station manager."

"Hey, I'm just kidding. Let's pass on it."

"Okay, Carol, but you really should consider it. You'd have fun."

Carol ignored the last comment and dug into a kitchen drawer, removing a fine looking chef's knife. "In a minute or two, you can help by slicing the roast. You're going to be the Hog Cutter of Henniker, my man. Just take it from the pan, put it on the tray over there and do your stuff. I'll get the juice ready for pouring and fill the tray with the vegetables when you're done. You can pour the wine."

The meal was excellent and so was the conversation. Sam finished eating and pulled his wine glass closer. He looked up at Carol, hoping to steal a private glance at her lovely face, but found her staring directly at him. Their eyes locked in an awkward moment. He turned his eyes back to his wine glass. She never blinked.

"The roast was delicious. I've never . . ."

Carol's soft, deep voice stopped him. "I'm glad you came to work here, Sam. Arthur feels the same way. He said you're an interesting young man and he feels comfortable around you. That's not true with most of the people here. Oh, he likes them all right, but he knows he's a foreigner to them and isn't truly at home. He said he senses something different about you, different from the locals. He'd like to know more about you. Me, too."

"There's not much to know. I'm divorced. I work in Education. I prefer a quiet place to live versus a big city."

"I figured that much, Sam," said Carol. "But what's down deep? Just when we start to talk, you give me a little and then stop. You seem to back away. Why? Do you have a deep, dark secret? Or are you just a shy guy, you know, horny but shy? They stared into each other's eyes and broke into laughter.

"I'm not the only rooster in the hen house."

"Oh, Sam, I'm sorry. You're divorced, not just some single young guy on the make. I shouldn't have said that." Carol held her smile, but turned away. When she turned back, she cradled her wine glass, staring into the redness. "I just want to know more about you. I want us to be friends. I feel that kind of closeness to you, Sam. There aren't many men around here that I can say that about. In the city it was different. There were lots of male peers, lots of grad students, lots of professors . . ."

"And there was Arthur," said Sam.

"Yes, there was Arthur. And I loved him right away. But I still needed the friendship of people my age and that included men as well as women. It's funny how you can love someone with everything you've got, and yet, there still can be something missing. For me, it's that social interaction with my own generation. I guess I never realized that loving an older man might leave such a social void. It hasn't taken long for us, Sam, but I feel that closeness with you. I hope you can understand. It's a bit strange, but wonderful that in this little town, friendships can develop easily between

men and women and it doesn't have to mean anything il-
licit."

It was Sam's turn to stare into his glass. If what Carol
said was true, then what had Seth Walpole and Al Turner
been arguing about? What was going on at the party Martha took him to? Was Carol unaware of the alleged swap
club?

"Arthur seems like a nice guy. He gets along well with
everybody, from what I've seen."

"Yes, most everyone," said Carol, "but there's something between him and Seth Walpole. Seth shows a cold
shoulder to Arthur most of the time. I don't know why. Of
course, Arthur hits back. We've had dinner parties here
with faculty and staff people, but Arthur refuses to invite
Seth. I can't blame him, though."

"Sometimes, people just don't see eye-to-eye about
things," said Sam.

"Oh, it's not that they disagree about issues. They just
seem to repel each other, like magnets working in reverse.
Instead of pulling together, they push apart. I get along
with him, considering what little interaction I have with
Seth, you know, always cordial when passing each other in
the hallway, stuff like that. But if I'm with Arthur, it's like
we don't exist. I don't know what it could be, but it's been
like that all along."

Sam sipped his drink while his mind wandered back
to the meeting with Seth and his strange question about
somebody at the college who was not trustworthy. At first,
he wasn't sure if Seth was talking about Al Turner or himself. Now he added Arthur Vasile to the list.

*"Someone working here who can't be trusted, someone
whose sense of morality could be brought into serious question, particularly regarding that person's past."*

"That certainly does seem strange, Carol. Is there anybody else who doesn't get along with Arthur?"

"Well, like I said, he feels a little uncomfortable at
times, but basically he likes it here. He keeps to himself a
great deal and often has to go out of town on business trips,
like tonight. I guess you could say he keeps a low profile,
but he goes into introvert mode often and even shuts me
out at times. I've learned to accept it over the years. It's just
who he is, that's all."

"He must be very dedicated to his outside work," said Sam. "The extra money from consulting fees can be very attractive."

"Oh, there's no extra money. Arthur works pro bono with these people."

Sam turned his head slightly to one side, as if listening for a faint sound. "Wow, I guess he's *very* dedicated. He runs up travel costs, at least mileage, doesn't he?"

"Yes, but he doesn't mind."

"What about taking a tax deduction?"

"Nope. He doesn't do that, either. He says he prefers to pay his taxes and not make a big fuss about it, like so many Americans do. He says we don't need to act like poor people."

"He really is different," said Sam. "What about the license plate in New Hampshire? What does he think about that?"

"You mean the motto, LIVE FREE OR DIE? You know, he never says anything about it. I've seen him just walk away from a person if that subject came up. He'd rather talk about scientific achievements than politics. He was riveted to the TV when Armstrong walked on the moon. He says Von Braun is a genius who will never get his just due as a space pioneer. The United States would never have gotten to the moon without him, that's what he says."

"He doesn't comment, even to you, about Nixon and Watergate?"

"Only once, when I was watching something about it on the TV news. He said he couldn't believe that such a smart man could be so dumb. When I tried to ask him about it, he held up his hand and walked away, like the whole mess disgusted him." Carol made a hand movement, mimicking Arthur's gesture.

What a woman. She's bright, strong and competent, yet totally subordinate to Arthur. She must love him very much.

"Care for some dessert or coffee, Sam?"

"No thanks, I think I'll just squeeze down another bourbon before I hit the road."

"Don't be in a big rush. Relax, Sam, and enjoy the music on a Friday night."

"Yeah, but about the music, do you think we could make a change?"

"What, you don't like John Denver?"

"I do, but he gets to be a bit much after a while, a little too sugary. How about some jazz?"

"Got it," said Carol. "How about some Herbie Mann? I've got his *Push, Push* album."

"That's the ticket. I guess you're a fan, like me."

"Of course I am. Hey, a well-built shirtless guy on the album cover, what's not to like?"

"Maybe I should take up the flute." Sam watched Carol ease her way out of her chair and leave the room to change the stereo. *And lose my shirt.*

They resumed their conversation at the kitchen table, drinks in hand. "Do you ski, Sam? We're lucky to have our own little ski area just down the road, Pat's Peak. The runs are short, but fun."

"No, I've never taken to the sport. I broke my leg when I was a kid and I have no desire to repeat the injury."

"Oh, is that why you have the hitch in your walk?"

Sam was surprised at the reference to his limp. She had never mentioned it before. "Yes," he said. "It didn't heal properly, so it's a gift that keeps on giving."

"But you seem to get around very nicely. I'll bet I could teach you to ski in no time."

"Don't hold your breath waiting for me, Carol. Fortunately, the ski season is a couple of months away, so I'm safe."

"Watch out. Three years ago we had a couple of early storms and a cold snap. The Peak opened Thanksgiving weekend that year."

Sam shook his head and finished his drink, feeling that this was a good time to make his exit. After the usual thank yous, Sam slid his arms into his coat, zipped it up and began making his way to the front door. Carol's hand on his shoulder startled him.

"Great dinner, Carol. Thanks again."

"Don't mention it. I'm glad you came over." She stood directly in front of Sam and planted a kiss on his cheek.

Sam smiled and nodded, resisting the temptation that raced through him. *Definitely time to leave.*

Chapter Eight

MONDAY, OCTOBER 7.

THE LIBRARY AND THE ENTIRE NEW SUSSEX COL-
LEGE CAMPUS IS CLOSED UNTIL FURTHER NOTICE.
LIBRARY EMPLOYEES ARE TO REPORT AS USUAL THIS
MORNING FOR A SPECIAL MEETING IN THE SUSSEX
ROOM.

The sign was posted on the library's main entrance as
Sam approached for work on Monday morning. Swinging
the door open he did a double take, almost ignoring the
stunning message. *What could this be?*

The Sussex Room was a large sitting room, with sofas
and padded chairs scattered about, easily accommodating
twenty people. A door on the left side wall concealed a galley
kitchen used for food service at special events. A pristine
brick fireplace sat at the south end of the room. The U.S
and New Hampshire flags, draped from wooden flagpoles on
each side of the hearth, gave a pleasant yet distinguished
air to the room. Wall-to-wall carpeting softened footsteps.

Sam entered the handsome room, finding himself alone
with Bob Hill.

"What gives, Bob?"

"Hold on a minute. Let's let the others get here. I don't
want to have to repeat this." Bob lifted his eyes to look past
Sam. "Here they come now."

Sam turned to see Fred, Gene, Martha and the rest
of the day staff entering. Bob held up his hand, asking for
silence before anyone spoke. "Please come in and take a
seat." The group fit into a sofa and a couple of chairs that
were not far apart. Sam stood behind the sofa.

"I'm afraid I've got some terrible news," said Bob. The
staff members groaned in unison, echoing Sam's fears of
another fiscal crisis. "No, no, it's not what you think. I'm

afraid it's actually something worse than whatever you can imagine."

"What could be worse than bouncing paychecks again?" asked Martha.

For a moment, Bob seemed to be searching for the right words. Unable to find sugar coating, he spoke. "Seth Walpole is dead. He was apparently murdered last night in his office."

The staff members' groans turned into muffled screams.

"Murdered?"

"Last night? I saw him yesterday afternoon!"

"What happened? How?"

Sam stared at Bob Hill for a few seconds before looking away in disbelief. It had been decades since he faced shocking death. They were all too frequent at Auschwitz. One day, he was playing outdoors with another child and the next day the child was gone. Sometimes days would go by before Sam's mother would tell him what happened. She would usually say that the friend had a bad accident, or he was very sick, or whatever she could think of to spare Schmuel the awful truth. But nobody could hide the truth forever. Not that truth.

"Our local police chief, Cal Powers, is working with the State Police. They're at Seth's office right now. Department heads were told to close the campus until further notice and to post signs on entrance and exit doors to all buildings. Campus Security has issued a request that everybody, students and staff, stay in Henniker. The Student Union is the only college building open. Security personnel will go from dorm to dorm to explain things as best they can. Faculty and staff are instructed to report to the Science Building auditorium at 10 o'clock for an announcement from Dean Al Turner."

Sam glanced at his watch which read 8:10 a.m. "What about the radio station? Shouldn't we keep it on air?"

"Yes, that's a good idea, Sam. It will help provide a distraction for the students and a vehicle for any news we can give. Why don't you power up the transmitter, and see if you can get the student operators to come in."

"Will do, Bob. Before I go, is there anything else you can tell us about it? How do we know it was murder?"

"I'll tell you what I know, but I want you to get Chief Powers to make a statement for broadcast. The commercial stations from Manchester and Concord will be here soon, so he'll have to make a statement. What I've been told is Seth was attacked while apparently working late last night in his office. He was struck in the head by a lethal object, possibly a fireplace poker."

Groans filled the room. Martha and others began to weep. The people seated seemed to be stuck in position, unable to rise. They turned to one another, as if someone could supply answers to ease their shock.

"I'll go contact the students scheduled for Monday broadcasting, Sam," said Fred.

"Okay, Fred. Gene, why don't you stay near the back entrance, in case any radio personnel show up there? You can let them in, but just them. I'll get a tape recorder and broadcast mike and go up to Seth's office to get that statement from Chief Powers." Sam broke away from the group, heading for the radio station in the library's basement. Fred and Gene followed him like obedient soldiers.

"Jesus Christ, a murder," said Gene. "This is unbelievable. Who would want to kill Seth Walpole? He was as nice a guy as you could want to meet, at least as far as I knew him, which I admit wasn't very much. Hey, Sam, did you ever know someone who was murdered? I certainly never have."

Sam looked back toward Fred without answering, as they descended the back stairway leading to the lowest level of the building. The library was built into a small hill, so the back section, which faced the road, was at ground level in the rear, with a sidewalk leading up to an entrance. There was a wide hallway inside, with a small classroom to the left and Sam's work areas to the right. Straight through the entrance across the wide hall was a solid door that led into the radio station, with two studios, a control room and a sitting area.

Sam hustled into the control room, turning on room lights as he went. That done, he flipped the switches needed to power on the transmitter and made the proper entry into the station log.

"Gene, go queue up the tape with the on-air announcement and the national anthem. Wait for me before starting anything."

"Got it, Sam."

In the sitting area, a typewriter sat on a table. Sam made his way to it, curled in a piece of paper and sucked in a deep breath before typing. The words came quickly. Once ready, he extracted the paper and handed it to Gene.

"Go start the broadcast, Gene, and after the tape is finished, read this announcement. It tells the listeners why the campus is closed and that there will be a police statement very soon. Play some music and repeat this message after every three songs. Stay with it until the student DJ shows up and give those instructions to him. Check for the students at the back door while music is playing." Gene nodded and rushed to the studio controls to follow Sam's orders.

Sam hurried back into the control room, which was also the backup studio, and housed a small storage cabinet with a couple of portable cassette recorders, blank tapes, patch cords and three boxes holding microphones. He took a recorder with the station call letters, WNSC-FM printed on the side, popped a tape into it, and grabbed a mike box. After checking to see that the box wasn't empty, he jogged back upstairs and out to his car.

In a couple of minutes, Sam was uptown. He found a parking space in the lot behind the administration building, and equipment in hand, hustled to the rear door. It was guarded by a campus security officer, a man about Sam's age. He recognized Sam.

"Gotta get a statement from the police chief," said Sam. "Gonna put it out over the campus radio, the best way to inform the student body in a hurry."

The officer nodded and opened the door, letting Sam pass. The guards he encountered much earlier in his life were never this accommodating.

As he moved into the hall that led to Seth's office and the conference room, Sam saw several uniformed State Police officers and a couple of plainclothesmen moving in and out of the office. A tall uniformed officer was in the hall next to the Henniker chief, Cal Powers. They disappeared into Seth's office.

One officer stopped Sam as he approached and simply pointed toward the building lobby, indicating that he was to go there. The tape recorder and microphone in Sam's hands must have given the officer all he wanted to know about Sam.

Al Turner was standing in the lobby, along with other department heads. They all paced slowly, like windup toys in need of a twist. Turner had a Styrofoam cup in one hand, sipping from it when he saw Sam.

"You must be using that for the radio station," said the Dean. "You'll have to wait awhile. Chief Powers is giving the other stations a chance to arrive. There'll be radio and television."

"I hope that the Boston stations can get their feed from Manchester, so we don't have to wait for them," said Sam.

"Is that how it works? I guess so. I doubt that Powers wants to wait half the day, either."

Their conversation ended and their eyes locked on one another. In an instant, Sam recalled the argument Turner had had with Seth Walpole. Turner's face suggested that he knew what Sam was thinking about.

There was a sound on the front porch and both Sam and Dean Turner swung their heads in the direction of the door. Guys in jeans and parkas were coming in with equipment boxes in hand. A clean shaven, neatly dressed man followed, wearing a tan trench coat over a gray sport coat. His white shirt, red necktie and combed hair set him apart from his colleagues.

One of the technicians spoke to the clean-cut reporter, pointing to a spot along the back wall of the lobby. Dean Turner approached the reporter and determined his was the Manchester television crew. They needed a place to set up a microphone and stand. Turner nodded his head, approving the spot they'd chosen, and the crew went about their business. One of the crewmen pulled a spotlight from a box and a 16mm camera, while another handled the sound equipment. Sam, with his tiny cassette recorder, felt humbled.

In a few minutes, other radio station people had arrived and set up mikes next to the one from the TV station. The well-groomed reporter spoke to Dean Turner again, who listened for a few seconds then exited the lobby toward the busy crime scene. He emerged shortly and stood near the mikes to address the people.

"If you will all be patient, Chief Powers of the Henniker Police Department will be ready to make a statement for you in just a few minutes. Thank you."

The technician with the camera turned on his spotlight and aimed his camera at Turner. The slick-looking TV reporter started to ask him a question, but he waved it off and walked away from the microphones. The reporters congregated in a spot a few feet from the mikes, and Sam decided to work his way in among them, his recorder hanging from his shoulder and his microphone in his right hand. Sam felt a strange exhilaration, in stark contrast to the horror of the murder. But he kept to himself, avoiding any chit-chat opportunity with the media people.

When Chief Powers entered the lobby, he was accompanied by the tall State Police officer, both walking in a rigid manner, not gazing about. The Chief stood at the microphones and made his statement. Sam went down on one knee and extended his arm with the mike, trying to get a clear recording. The statement included the information that Sam already had and also explained that the Henniker PD was cooperating with the State Police in the investigation. He offered his condolences to Mrs. Walpole and her family and promised to bring the killer to justice. He urged people to lock their doors because they had no idea about the killer, so it could be a stranger in town. Sam thought how odd that would be to these citizens, the free-spirited people of Henniker locking their doors. And every college employee was going to be subjected to fingerprinting.

"Chief, can you tell us anything about the cause of death?" It was the TV reporter.

Chief Powers stood with his hands clasped behind him, his face as straight as a guard at Buckingham Palace. "It appears to be an attack to the head with a heavy instrument, specifically a fireplace poker, which was found lying near Dr. Walpole. The medical examiner will have to make a final determination about that."

All of the reporters tried to squeeze in the next question, but the TV guy won out. "Any idea, Chief, about the time of death?"

"Again, the medical examiner will have to tell us more specifically, but it apparently occurred last evening, while Dr. Walpole was working in his office. A campus Security officer said he noted Dr. Walpole in his office at nine-fifteen, while making his rounds. He was alone at the time. His body was discovered this morning by Mrs. Irene Preston, Dr. Walpole's secretary."

"Can we talk to her, Chief?" asked one of the radio reporters.

Chief Powers turned his head in the direction of the question. "No, she's not available. The woman is terribly upset. We took her statement, and an officer helped her get home."

Sam was impressed with Cal Powers, whom he had met a couple of times around town. At first, Sam saw him as a country bumpkin type, but his immediate control of this situation proved that first impression to be false. He also noted that Cal ran this news conference, not the State Police. Maybe they wanted it that way. Either way, there was more to Cal Powers than Sam expected.

Chief Powers concluded his remarks and returned to the crime scene room with the State Policeman. The radio reporters began to converse off-mike, apparently knowing each other from covering news events together. Their technicians busied themselves collecting their equipment.

Sam fixed his gaze on the TV reporter, who stood his ground, still facing the area where Chief Powers had stood. His cameraman swung around to face the reporter, his light and camera aimed at the reporter. The man repeated his earlier questions and those of the radiomen, too. Sam understood that these questions would be edited into his TV report, so that the final piece would look as if this reporter was asking the questions and Chief Powers was answering just for him. Broadcasting was an exciting field. Sam wondered if he had made the right career choice.

As the hustle of the news conference died down, Sam made his way to the back door of the building and out into the parking lot. The march to his car was stopped by the sight of Carol Vasile, who was getting into her own vehicle, just three spaces away from his own.

"Carol," he called.

She stopped, looking toward the voice. Relieved to see Sam, she ran to him, throwing her arms around his neck. "Oh, Sam, this is awful. How could such a terrible thing happen here?" Sam held her tightly, his recorder hanging loosely off one shoulder.

"I know. It's unbelievable."

"Sam, I was just coming to work and found out. They wouldn't let me in. I didn't know what to do. I wasn't sure where to go. I . . . I . . ."

Sam embraced her again, trying to calm her. "What about Arthur? Doesn't he know yet?"

"He's not back yet from Massachusetts. He may not be back until later. Sam, please stay with me for a while."

Sam saw fear in Carol's eyes, a look he remembered from women at Auschwitz. They didn't know what lay ahead for them, in the next hour, in the next moment. They were in a constant limbo. Carol was there now.

"Look, I have to get this tape to the radio station," said Sam. "Come with me. After I drop it off, we can go to the Science Building together for the meeting. Al is going to address the faculty and staff."

They both got into Sam's car. He eased it out of the parking lot and motored his way through town, heading south to the library. Carol looked about as they went, eying the multiple police and media vehicles. "I don't know what to make of all this, Sam. It's like we've been transported into another place." She saw him turn toward her, giving a quick glance. Yes, he was in another place.

Once at the library, Sam told Carol to wait in his car while he ran the tape into the radio studio. Fred and Gene were both there, along with several student broadcasters. He instructed them to play the tape immediately and then repeat it at the scheduled newscast. He added for them to check in with campus security every half hour for updates.

When he first saw how the students ran their radio station and performed on-air, Sam was impressed with their level of talent and professionalism, despite the fact that there was no Broadcast Communications major offered at New Sussex College. He was doubly impressed now that they were working in crisis mode.

On his way out, he stopped by his boss's office and found Bob Hill at his desk. Sam gave him a rundown of the news conference and told him that the college radio station was on the air, running his tape.

"Good work, Sam. I'm going to walk down to the Science Building. Want to come along?"

"I'll meet you there, Bob. I ran into Carol Vasile at the Administration Building. She's in my car waiting for me. Arthur isn't back from his weekend trip, so I'll go with her to the meeting."

Bob didn't answer, simply nodding, but Sam perceived a look of disapproval. He shook it off without comment and returned to his car. Carol needed him.

When he saw Bob leave the building, Sam persuaded Carol they should walk to the meeting, not enough parking at the Science Building and all that. As Bob walked near them through the parking lot, they caught up with him. Sam felt this was better than being seen alone with Carol.

Sam watched the people file into the auditorium with surprisingly little talk. He, Carol and Bob saw other library staff, including Martha, sitting a few rows down from the back and joined them. Soon the room was full, but the group remained silent, as if a memorial service was underway.

Al Turner climbed onto the stage and stood behind a large cherrywood podium. After adjusting the microphone to his preferred height, he informed the audience about what they'd already heard, hitting home the reality of what they hoped was somehow not true. The college would be closed until further notice, although he hoped it would reopen by the end of the week. Notices would be posted in all the dorms, and the campus Security Office would serve as the control center for information. He advised people to listen to the college radio station, as well. Cries and sobbing pierced the silence of the crowd.

❉❉❉❉

The campus opened and classes resumed on Thursday, the week after Dr. Walpole's death. The department heads met with Dean Turner, who became Acting President of the college, and agreed it was best to start classes before the weekend, preventing a vast number of students from fleeing and extending their impromptu break. Dr. Walpole's funeral would take place in a few days, as yet unspecified.

Chapter Nine

On his way to work Friday morning, Sam made a stop at the small post office just south of his apartment. It was a cool day, but the sun shone bright and the air had a crisp fall tang to it. Sam usually enjoyed such weather, but today his mind was on other things, besides checking his mail, a task he neglected the day before.

After sliding out of his car, Sam heard a voice calling him. "Hey there, Sam. Tom West, remember me?" Yes, Sam did remember the big fellow who hosted the party Martha took him to just over a week earlier. Tom was positioned in a direct line between Sam and the post office, so there was no way to avoid him.

"Hello, Tom, of course I remember you and Bonnie. That was a nice party you had."

"Well, I'm glad you liked it. Of course, you and Martha didn't stay long. Things were just getting good. Say, how are you and Martha doing? Everybody said you two made a real cute couple." Sam kept walking while Tom paid his compliment. "Will we be seeing you two some more?"

The question stopped Sam in his tracks. "Us two? Oh, Tom, you've got it all wrong. Martha and I aren't a steady couple. In fact, I haven't been with her . . . out with her since that night."

"That's too bad, Sam. We hoped Martha had found her partner for . . . you know, these dance parties that we have now and then. We really like to have married couples or people with steadies at our dances. It makes for a more lively time, you know."

Sam nodded.

"About that night, Sam, I trust you and Martha had a good time after you left. We've known her for a long time and we know that she likes to be, shall we say, very generous with the guys. You know what I mean, don't you, Sam? Sure you do. Heck, we're not a couple of kids." Sam glanced at the ground. "Hey, don't get me wrong. We love Martha dearly. She and Bonnie go way back."

Sam thrust his hands into his jacket pockets. *If we're not a couple of kids, then why is this jerk talking like one?* "I understand, Tom. Believe me, I do. Let's just say it was a memorable night."

Tom shook his head with a childish grin. "There you go, Sam. There you go. Hey, I've got to be running. See you around."

Sam turned to watch Tom work his girth into a black pickup truck and back out of his spot, finally leaving. For a short conversation, it was the longest Sam had in quite a while. He hoped there wouldn't be any more surprises inside the building.

In the post office there were several students and a few townsfolk Sam didn't recognize. There was mail in his box, so he quickly worked the combination and extracted it. He flipped through the collection of small envelopes, like a dealer shuffling a deck of cards. His mind, however, drifted back to the party at Tom West's house.

They preferred steady couples and married ones to singles, an interesting comment. It made sense, if this was an adult swap club of some sort, as he had heard Seth Walpole say when arguing with Al Turner. It would be easier to maintain a level of secrecy if everyone knew each other and all had a similar level of risk. Singles could be too freewheeling with their conversations. *Loose lips sink ships.*

Maybe it was time to talk with Martha again. He expected to have a hard time getting information out of her about the club, but maybe there were ways to go around that, a sort of indirect line of questioning. Sam tucked his mail inside his jacket and hurried to his car. He noticed that many of the cars in the parking lot were left running while their owners went into the post office. It looked like people were returning to their trusting ways.

Gene Allen was at his desk when Sam entered the office, dutifully going about his business of checking invoices from film rental companies and preparing orders for other films to be obtained for faculty. Fred was away, working in the radio station with students, according to Gene. The quiet atmosphere in the office pleased Sam.

"I've got to take these papers to the Business Office," said Gene, as he gathered up his work, shoved the documents into a brown accordion folder and slipped into his jacket. "Be back in a jiff."

"Don't hurry on my account," laughed Sam.

"Okay, then I'll see you next week." They both chuckled.

With the room to himself, Sam decided it was a good time to contact Martha. He dialed her extension and waited a few rings before he heard her cheerful voice. "Hello. Nice day today, n'est pas? Who's this?"

"Hi, Martha, it's Sam. How'ya doing?"

"Well, love'em and leave'em Sam. It's been awhile."

Sam started to give an awkward reply, but Martha cut him off. "Don't sweat it, Sam. I'm just busting your balls a bit. I know the deal. Besides, casual sex is my specialty. What's up? You in the mood for some more?"

"Well, ah, boy, you get right to it. Okay, yes, now that you mention it. How about we take in a movie tomorrow night?" *Martha sure is a piece of work.*

"Yes, that would be nice, Sam, but you don't have to sugar coat it every time you need to get laid. I can meet you at your place for lunch, if you wish, or my place. Whatever. This sort of arrangement works fine for me."

"I'm not trying to sugar coat it, Martha. I really think it would be a fun thing to take in a movie together. What do you say?"

"Well, let me check my date book, Sam," said Martha, her voice trailing off at the end, as if she were researching her busy schedule. "Ah, turns out I'm free. What time?"

"I'll pick you up at five-thirty for an early dinner and then we can make the seven-thirty show in Concord." Dinner and a show, a very traditional date, was Sam's approach, even though he knew Martha would just as soon heat up a pizza and then hop in the sack for the night.

"That will be fine, Samuel. Don't work too hard. Save your strength."

"I will, Martha, I certainly will."

"You know, Sam, I wasn't kidding about lunch time today. I'll serve you the Sanborn special, something really satisfying. What do you say?"

Sam held the phone for a minute. He was tempted to accept, but feared an afternoon delight with Martha today would make the idea of going out with her tomorrow less appealing. Fun was fun, but the date with her for Saturday might produce something more than just sex. What was the phrase, pillow talk?

"I'll take a rain check on that, young lady. Check the paper to see what's playing. You pick."

"Okay, Sam, but I'm tempted to come up there and yank your crank right now. You are such a tease."

He had nothing more to say, so Sam hung up and hoped Martha wouldn't carry out her threat. Within seconds after hanging up, his phone rang again. After letting it ring three times, he answered. "Yay-ass," he said, expecting Martha again.

"Sam, it's Bob. Are you all right?"

Sam swallowed hard and composed himself. "Yes, yes, Bob, I'm fine. Ah, what's up?"

"I just found out that the funeral for Dr. Walpole will be Monday morning. There'll be a viewing Saturday and Sunday in Concord. The funeral will start at ten o'clock Monday, going from the funeral parlor to the cemetery in Hopkington. There'll be no classes that day. Pass this on to your staff."

Bob gave Sam the details, and he jotted them down. Again, the reality of Seth's murder hit Sam like a hammer. He needed to learn more about Al Turner. Was he capable of committing murder? Was public knowledge of his club damaging enough to motivate him to such an act? Was there someone else on campus with a reason to kill Seth?

Sam decided to check in with campus Security, to see if any news was forthcoming from that office. A phone call would have done it, but he opted for an in-person visit. Carl Mortimer, Chief of Campus Security, was standing next to the dispatcher's desk when Sam entered the small structure behind the Administration Building parking lot. Both he and Sally Worthington, the dispatcher who was seated, gave Sam a quick greeting.

"I just heard about the funeral arrangements," said Sam. "Anything new come in about the case?"

Carl was in his late fifties, tall and trim with sparse, graying hair. He retired a few years back from his position as captain of detectives in the Boston Police Department, and moved with his wife to Weare, New Hampshire. "Nothing new, Sam. I'll be sure to let you know if anything happens that needs to go out on the campus radio. You know, those kids do an awfully good job there."

"Thanks, Carl, I'll be sure to pass that on to them. Off the record, do the police have any leads, any idea at all who could have done this?"

"No," said Carl. "Not that I know of. I'd like to be more involved with this, but Cal told me to stick to Campus Security and leave the investigation to his people and the State Police. My job is to keep the campus safe, while he's got the whole town to worry about. So that's what I'll do. Of course, it can't hurt to talk to some students now and then, to keep an ear open to what they know, or think they know. Put it under the heading of the mood of the campus. I figure trying to stay ahead of what the student body is thinking will help me look out for them. You know what we don't want is students thinking they can play detective."

"Amen to that, Carl. I'll keep an eye out for the kids at the radio station. I want to make sure they just report the news, not become part of it. I'll see you around."

Sam thought the local police department might be ignoring a good resource by instructing Carl to stay out of the investigation. A veteran detective from the Boston Police Department was right here at Cal's disposal. It seemed to Sam that a lot of help would be needed.

Sam couldn't resist a quick trip to Carol's office. He wished he could see her every day, but he couldn't make that happen. She wasn't in her office when he arrived, but Doris perked up. He asked her to mention to Carol he'd come by, and Doris acknowledged his request with a nod and a grin.

The rest of the day was uneventful. He succeeded in staying out of the library and away from Martha most of the time by checking on audiovisual equipment stored in classroom buildings and by installing new screens in three of them during the afternoon. He brought Fred along to help and for small talk, dragging the work out as much as possible.

Saturday night arrived; time to pick up Martha and head into Concord. He liked her modest- length brown dress. Cut low at the neck, however, it revealed some attractive cleavage. She tucked a white cardigan sweater under her arm in case the evening air grew cooler. His straight legged gray slacks were paired with a light brown, corduroy sport coat over a yellow button-down, an outfit he rarely wore since his divorce.

The drive to a steak house on Main Street was not the time to question Martha, so Sam played the radio softly, picking up an FM station from Manchester. Martha was content to slide close to Sam, fighting the bucket seat and console in his car. Her left hand rested on his inner right thigh, a move he expected and didn't object to.

The couple was seated across from each other at a table for four, since it was early and the restaurant wasn't crowded. They each took red wine before their entrees. During the dinner, Martha tried to squeeze more information out of Sam about his youth in Poland, but he kept his answers short. He deflected most of them back to her, answering her question with another question.

"This game of verbal ping pong is resulting in a boring dinnertime conversation, Sammy old boy. What gives?" Martha tried to enliven things by sliding off one shoe and engaging Sam in some foot-to-leg rubbing. Her moves were rarely subtle, and Sam offered her a smile.

"Nothing at all, my lady, nothing at all," said Sam.

He didn't want to turn her off completely. He'd want her to be talkative later, but if he gave her too much silent treatment now, he might not get her back. "You know, Miss Martha, you've got all the moves and a good reach. I bet if I sat across the room, you'd still find a way to make contact."

"I'm not Plastic Woman, so I guess I'd just have to slide over there after you." Her foot moved higher on his leg and gently found his crotch.

"You might be a pretty good acrobat, Martha."

"You're going to find out later, buddy boy." Her light toe rubbing achieved its purpose. "Or should I call you . . . Spike?"

Sam was losing interest in seeing a movie, what with Martha's effective come on, but he wanted to stick to the game plan. Good thing the table cloth provided some degree of privacy. He slid his hand under the table, found her foot and tickled. Martha giggled and withdrew her weapon, sliding her foot back to the floor.

His dinner timing was working well and he persuaded Martha that dessert would have to wait. It was time to head for the theater.

"The heck with dessert, but I've only had one glass of wine, Sam. I guess that will have to . . . come later."

"I like your use of words, lady. Let's get going."

Sam paid the check and helped Martha out of her chair. She clung to his arm as they strolled out of the restaurant and back to his car, parked a few paces away on the curb. In a few minutes, they were off Main Street and arrived at the shopping center that housed a department store, a couple of small retailers and the movie theater complex. There were three cinemas, but only one with a film appealing to Sam. *The Sting* was more work for Paul Newman and Robert Redford, after their huge success as *Butch and Sundance*. He figured Martha would agree with him and elect the two heart-throb actors. That was a no-brainer.

Once inside, Martha grabbed Sam's hand and ushered him to the concession stand. "I'm a popcorn freak, Sam. Would you get me a large bucket, no butter?"

"You got it, kid. What about a drink?"

"Oh, yes," she said. "I'll take a large Coke. You can split it with me, if you like."

He was happy she said no butter, since he knew her hands would wander during the movie. He purchased her treats and they found their way through the dark and up the stadium seating to the last row, squirming to the center seats. It had been a long time since Sam enjoyed a night at the movies, not to mention being with an attractive and playful woman. He felt like a teenager again and let himself enjoy it.

The movie was about a couple of con men working to con a gangster, a very dangerous activity. Sam enjoyed its intricate plot and Martha enjoyed Redford and Newman. *People conning people. Was that what life was about, deception against deception? Wasn't Al Turner's adult club a deception against the college community? Was Martha a part of it or just someone always looking for a good time?* He thought of the tall doctor in the camp wearing a white coat while handing candy to the children, getting them to trust him like a kind uncle. *People conning people. Did it ever stop?*

Martha didn't wait to get back to her apartment before trying to arouse Sam. He would have been surprised if she had, so he made no effort to stop her wandering hands. It made for an interesting ride back to Henniker.

Martha's apartment was part of a two story duplex with a cozy living room, complete with brick fireplace. Once inside, Martha showed Sam where she kept the wine and liquor. "Open the red, would you Sam? There's a corkscrew in the drawer, the glasses are in the cabinet on the left, and I'll be right back." She disappeared upstairs while Sam opened the wine and poured two glasses.

Sam settled in the living room, standing near the fire-place, searching for the wood, when his hostess appeared, wearing a dark red, silk robe and slippers. Her legs were bare and he knew that the robe and slippers were all she had on. *She gets right to the point, this woman.*

"I was going to start a fire, but I don't see any wood," said Sam.

Martha stepped her way up to him, placing a hand on his chest. "Get comfortable on the sofa. I'll start the fire."

Sam did as told, placing the glasses on the coffee table in front of him, still puzzled. He watched Martha step to the wall beside the fireplace and push a button. In a second, an even row of flames shot up between the artificial logs, warming the air. "That's all you have to do with gas, Sam. Do I look like the type who chops wood?"

"I should have known," he said. "I'm familiar with gas-powered fires. I just wasn't thinking." But Sam was think-ing. He thought of gas fires from long ago.

Martha smiled and turned her back to the flames, bending over slightly and rubbing both hands over her buttocks. "Don't you love the way a fire warms everything, Sam?" She inched over to him and stood with her back to him. "Check it out."

With a smile, Sam rubbed his hands together, then slid them under Martha's robe, caressing each cheek. "Hm-

55

mmm, your theory is correct. But I have to say your ass is downright hot, lady. You're way past warm."

"Hey," said Martha. "How about some music?" Without waiting for an answer, Martha swayed over to a cabinet beside the fireplace, which housed a stereo unit, complete with AM/FM radio, turntable and eight track tape player on top. Speakers extended from each end of the cabinet top. She turned on the power and popped in an eight track, filling the room with the soft sound of Sam Cook. "An oldie, but a goodie."

Sam sipped his wine, going into deep thought. In a few seconds, Martha slid in beside Sam, holding her glass and nuzzling her face against his arm. "Say, didn't he get himself shot at a motel years ago?" asked Sam.

"Yes, I believe he did," replied Martha. "He was with some broad who ran out on him the morning after their playtime. I think she took his wallet or something. I'm not sure. I believe he forgot to put his pants on or something and the motel owner thought he had some crazy black guy on his hands, so he shot first and asked questions later. End of story. Too bad. I like his voice."

"Well, here's to a guy named Sam," said Sam, raising his wine glass.

"Good thing you didn't take me to a motel, Mr. Sam. No telling what might have happened in the morning, ha ha ha." Martha touched Sam's glass with her own and put down a healthy gulp of her wine.

Sam decided to pace himself, so he sipped easily, barely wetting his lips, and placed his glass down on the end table beside the sofa. "Is that what members of your club do, Martha, take their partners to a motel? That little place in Hillsborough must get a lot of regular business."

Martha held her glass in her left hand, freeing her right for any action she had in mind while positioned to Sam's left. She brushed the back of her hand against Sam's left leg, sliding it back and forth while humming along to the music. "What are you talking about, Sammy boy?"

"You know, that adult club that has those parties, like the one you took me to at Tom West's."

Sam watched Martha take another large gulp of wine, noting the level of liquid in her glass dropping sharply. He reached for his own and sipped from it.

"What a lot of hogwash. I've heard that talk, too. You don't really believe those stories, do you, Sammy?"

Something in her voice sounded almost sincere, but not enough to convince Sam. After his chat with Tom West, he was certain that Martha was a welcomed guest at that party and a prospective member in the club. But she need-ed a husband or steady boyfriend to join. He was her likely target as a ticket to membership.

"Okay," said Sam. "Let's change the subject. How do you feel about Al Turner as Acting President of the college? Will he do a good job?"

"Oh, Sammy, you're getting so serious. What are you trying to do, spoil my mood?"

"No, not at all, far from it, but we've got lots of time and I don't like to rush. I'm just making conversation while we enjoy the music and the fire. But, really, what do you think of Al?"

"Al, shmal. I don't care about him." Martha spoke while tilting her wine glass back and forth. The contents were low enough to not spill a drop.

"Your glass is almost empty, Martha, shall I get a re-fill?"

"That's a good boy. Bring that bottle over here."

Sam fetched the opened bottle, refilled Martha's glass and put a small splash into his own. He returned to the sofa, bottle in hand, and set it down on the end table. He looked at Martha, who had put her feet up on the edge of the coffee table, knees bent, allowing her robe to slide up, revealing her well-shaped legs. After enjoying the view, he settled in again next to her.

"Sounds like you don't like him much, pretty lady." Sam thought it best to keep the endearing comments com-ing her way. "How long have you known him?"

"Long enough. Let's just say he's not my cup of tea . . . or my glass of wine." Martha turned toward Sam, laughing at her own joke. He smiled, going along with her.

"There must be a reason. Is he a lousy Dean or some-thing, you know, professional?"

"No, it's not that. I guess he does his job all right. I just think he's a little snobby, that's all."

"How so?" Sam sipped his drink, watching Martha's expression. She looked at her feet, as if examining her toes.

"At parties, yes Sam, we adults do have parties, at parties he usually gives me the cold shoulder. One time, we were having a snowball dance and I picked him. Well, he said he had to take a leak, so he left me. He didn't come back until the song was over."

"No loss for you, right?" said Sam. "You must have had a partner . . . a date for the night."

"Yeah, yeah, but nobody you know."

"Martha, you can't blame the guy because nature called. When you gotta go, you gotta go."

"That wasn't the only thing." Martha took another large gulp of wine, as if she needed fortification before speaking again. "When he hosted a party, I wasn't invited. I found out about it when Tom West accidently spilled the beans one day. I saw him and Bonnie in town. He said he missed me at the last party. Bonnie looked like she wanted to club him. I think he wants to get into my . . . he wants to dance with me. I think I put a tilt in his kilt, if you get my drift."

"I get it, Martha girl. I get it."

"Speaking of which . . ." Martha put her glass down on the coffee table and snuggled up close to Sam. She placed her hand on his chest, toying with his shirt.

The contact pleased him, but Sam continued his questions. "Have you ever known Turner to lose his temper or get violent?"

"No," said Martha. "But I wouldn't be surprised if he did. I mean, he gets crappy sometimes, you know, making wise guy comments and just being a general asshole. Someday he's going to piss somebody off big time and then he'll get his."

"Does anybody else feel the same as you about him?"

"I guess he's got some friends. He and his wife started up this . . . you know, these dance parties, so he gets along with people okay. Maybe I'm the only one he has it in for." Martha's voice faded and she looked down at her feet again, as if her own words pierced her heart. A quiet spread across the room, despite the sound of the stereo. In an instant, Sam recalled man's inhumanity to man at the camp. Martha was a lonely woman and her pain was real, but not like his mother's had been.

58

Martha reached for her glass and gulped down more wine. "Geez, this wine tastes good, Sammy." Another gulp and her glass was empty again.

"I'll pour you another, Martha," said Sam, reaching for the bottle.

"No, no, that's okay, Sammy. I'm getting a little juiced as it is. I want to have some fun tonight and still be able to remember it in the morning. It's time for us to get down to the business of pleasure." Martha pushed herself off the sofa, into a standing position at Sam's feet, and with an easy motion, undid her robe and let it slide to the floor. She stood naked before Sam, like a sacrificial offering.

The music played in the background as Sam rose up to join her in the seduction. He took her hand and guided her away from the sofa. "That a'way, cowboy," said Martha, pointing toward the stairs. He wrapped his arm around her shoulder, pulling her to him, pleased that he was about to enjoy the fruit of the night's labor. Martha slid an arm around Sam's waist before easing it downward over his buttocks. She was pleased, too.

Martha hadn't revealed a great deal of information, but it was enough to confirm in Sam's mind that the adult club existed for more than just dancing. And Martha wasn't a full-fledged member because she didn't have a steady guy. Al Turner could be a jerk, but Sam wasn't certain that he could be a killer. Just the same, there was a killer out there.

Chapter Ten

SUNDAY, OCTOBER 13.

When Sunday morning came, Sam awoke, but Martha was in deep sleep. He avoided the temptation of a morning romp. Deciding not to wake her, he got dressed and departed without disturbing his partner. He scribbled a polite note on a piece of stationery he found on her kitchen counter, thanking her for the fun and saying he would see her later, whatever that meant.

His thoughts turned to Carol as he drove home through the quiet Henniker streets. How different it was to spend time with each woman. He could have all the sex he wanted with Martha. She was attractive and seductive and very available. Yet his time with her lacked the emotional satisfaction he felt with Carol, who intrigued him beyond words. Her physical beauty was matched by her intellect and warm personality. But she was not readily available, being married to Arthur, and that barrier nagged at him constantly.

By noon, Sam felt a tug in his stomach that was a call for lunch. He didn't feel like preparing his own food, not really knowing what he wanted, so he decided that a trip down the road to one of the local diners might be in order. He found a parking space available, parallel to the curb just past The Nook, a Main Street diner frequented by college people and townsfolk alike.

As he stepped out of his car, a dark blue Jeep Wagoneer pulled up beside him, HENNIKER POLICE painted in big white letters on the side. Chief Powers, smiling and looking very much at home in the new vehicle, leaned over to the passenger side, cranked the window down halfway and motioned to Sam. "Hop in, Sam. Let's go for a ride."

Sam stood with his hands in his jacket pockets. "I was about to get some lunch. Why don't you join me?"

"No thanks. This won't take long. I just want to chat for a minute."

Do cops ever want to just chat? Is there an ulterior motive? Sam looked around and drew his hands out of his pockets, opened the passenger side door and climbed in.

"Nice car, Cal. You look good in it."

"I feel good in it. It's got four-wheel drive and rides like a charm. I even get to take it home after work. I guess you could call it a company car."

As they eased away from The Nook, the police radio squawked, catching Sam's attention. Cal noticed Sam's look. "Nice being able to keep in touch with my people. I can even tune in on the channel used by the Staties if I want. When the snow falls, I'll be ready for it this year with this car. Thank you, taxpayers of Henniker. I like this a lot."

Sam noted Cal's approval of his vehicle and nodded, thrusting his hands back into his jacket pockets.

"How long have you been in Henniker, Sam, about three months?"

"Yeah, I got here in June, so that's almost four." Sam looked straight ahead as the Wagoneer continued out of town on the road going past the town dump and a field that looked like a former cow pasture.

"That used to be the athletic field for the college. I played lacrosse on that field when I went to NSC, a good ten years ago. What an experience that was, especially when they fertilized the field across the street. Wow."

"I can imagine."

"I guess you're not in a talkative mood, Sam, but that's okay. A lot of people are less talkative now, after Seth Walpole's murder. That's to be expected. I still can't figure it, Sam, why anybody would want to kill Seth. You hear anything that might help me?"

"Who, me? No. I'm the new guy around here. I'm the last guy anybody would talk to if they knew anything."

Cal slowed down as he approached an intersection with highway Route 202. There was a blinking red light hanging on a wire over the road. He stopped, looked both ways and proceeded across the highway and up a steep, winding hill road.

Sam looked at the old farm houses lining the road and the thick woods between the structures. The woods got deeper as they climbed the hill.

"The State Police say their investigation isn't going well, so they'd like me to stay on it and get back to them if I come up with anything substantial. Some of my officers have tossed about some ideas, you know, theories based on some small talk around town. One of them thinks Seth was connected to the government and was working undercover for the FBI. Now, ain't that a kick? Seth Walpole, an FBI agent. Well, anyway, this officer thinks that Seth was looking into some group of people who got together as a social club, but were really a gang of Communists plotting against the United States. Imagine that, a bunch of Commies right here in Henniker, New Hampshire. Not likely. I think my officer watches too much television. I'm not about to take that theory to the State Police."

"There is a social group of some sort, isn't there? I've heard about that." Sam wondered if he should have said that.

"Oh, I've heard about that, too. The word is that they have private parties now and then and everybody goes away with somebody else's wife, or husband, depending how you look at it. Nothing unusual about people who are friends having get-togethers once in a while. Hell, in rural America, that's been true for ages. But swapping wives, I doubt it."

Sam was beginning to feel uneasy about this conversation. He glanced at Cal and then looked away, peering out the side window. "I doubt it, too, Cal." He paused, before deciding to go on. "I was at a party not long ago. Martha Sanborn took me there. We had just been out to dinner and she suggested we swing by this place, so I could meet some new faces. They were dancing and having a good time, but I don't think anybody swapped wives. Of course, I couldn't, since I don't have one."

"Hey, you know what, Sam? I think my sister, Ellen, and her husband were at that party. She told me about Martha coming by with somebody she didn't know and they left early. That might have been you."

Sam held his hands in his pockets with fingers curled into a loose fist. He rubbed each hand against the inside of the pocket. "Yeah, that could have been the same party. Your sister, eh? What does she look like?"

"She's tall and nice looking, with long brown hair. Ring any bells?"

"No, can't say that it does." Sam thought of the woman who cut in on him during the snowball dance. "Nope, doesn't ring any bells." At the prison camp, Sam learned that lying was often the best policy. The Nazis never rewarded a Jew for telling the truth.

"You and Martha left the party early and wouldn't have been there, if and when, any swapping took place, so you can't really be sure, right Sam?"

"Hmmmm, I guess you're right."

"How do you think they'd pull it off, Sam? I'm just speaking theoretically, you know."

Sam looked at Cal, trying to figure out what he was getting at. "I really have no idea, since I didn't see anything happen."

"Oh, come on, Sam. Humor me. How do you think it would work?"

"Look, Cal, I really don't know."

Cal kept silent, but had a tight grin on his face, as if to say he wasn't going to stop until Sam gave him something.

"I suppose, let's see, I guess there'd be someone in charge of the thing. Any organization has a leader, could be a married couple. They'd run the show, I guess, but what they'd actually do . . . I have no idea."

"You know, Sam, I think you're right. Somebody would be in charge, would set up the parties, would lay out the rules, stuff like that. Boy, if that were somebody who worked at the college and the word got out, it could be real bad. I mean, it might lead to a big scandal, you know. They'd probably want to keep a tight rein on it, don't you think? So they'd want to keep this in a closed circle, I'd bet, just a bunch of people they could trust. That would probably mean couples only, preferably married couples, don't you think?"

"I guess that would keep me out, since I'm single. Whoever does their recruiting wouldn't have me on their list."

"You think they actively recruit people, Sam?"

"I don't know, I'm just saying . . ."

"Oh, I understand." Cal drove up the hill to where it leveled off near a pond. "You ever been up here, Sam?"

"No, this is new territory to me." Sam eyed the country landscape, a few houses and cottages sprinkled among the dense woods. Stone walls, in various states of disrepair, decorated the land. "Hey Cal, what's with all these old stone walls in the woods?"

"Once upon a time this was all farmland. The walls were built when they cleared it and dug out the stones. Once the farming stopped, it didn't take long for the forests to renew themselves. Nature's way, you know."

"This is a great place. Real Norman Rockwell land."

Cal nodded at the Rockwell reference. "Do me a favor, will you, Sam? If you ever hear something definite about such a club, tell me about it, okay?"

"Yeah, sure. You must really have an interest in this idea."

"Well, you know, Sam, like I said, it could become a big scandal. Seth, being the college president, would probably be very upset if he found out about such a thing. He might even have to fire somebody, if it turned out that the leaders were college employees. Losing one's job, and maybe destroying one's career, could be a strong enough motive for murder, see what I mean?"

The Jeep wound down a road that took them back toward the highway. After a few turns this way and that, they were back at the intersection with the overhead light.

"So, let's see Sam, you and Martha were there, at that party. Anybody else from the college?"

Sam swallowed hard. "No, not that I can remember. Of course, there may have been college people there who I don't know yet. I'm not sure. Say, why don't you ask your sister? Maybe she can help you."

"Okay, Sam, good idea, but she doesn't work at the college so she might not know everybody either. She didn't recognize you, after all. But I'll be sure to check with her."

Sam could feel Cal's gaze on him. "There's something else I wanted to mention, Sam. You know, I graduated from NSC and know a lot of the faculty and staff people, so we have many good chats. Some of those folks seem to think you and Carol Vasile spend a lot of time together. I guess you two are getting along real well."

"What do you mean, Cal? We're just friends, that's all. Arthur is very busy and takes trips out of town to consult on some kind of project in Massachusetts. Carol is a very social type, so she likes to talk with me at lunch or in her office, nothing big."

"You go to her office to talk?" Sam didn't like Cal's tone.

"It's business, Cal. I have to bring invoices to her for payment. That's part of our jobs. There's nothing sinister about it."

"Calm down, Sam," said Cal. "I didn't mean to suggest there was, I was just commenting, that's all. So, I guess they've never been to any of those parties, Carol and Arthur?"

"Look, Cal, I've only been to the one party I told you about, and no, I didn't see the Vasiles there. I don't know if there have even been other parties. Like I said, check with your sister."

The Jeep cruised down the long, straight road by the old athletic field and Cal pulled over to the shoulder once they were across from The Nook. Sam opened his door as soon as the Wagoneer stopped and slid out.

"Sam," called Cal, before Sam could close the door. "Thanks for taking this little ride. Really, I appreciate your giving me the time."

"Sure, Chief, sure." *Giving you the time? Seems more like you took it. Wonder why you didn't offer me candy.*

Sam lost his desire for a sit-down lunch in The Nook, so he got into his car and drove home. He'd had enough chatting with people.

65

Chapter Eleven

SUNDAY EVENING, OCTOBER 13.

Sam was at home Sunday evening, at his modest one bedroom flat in a two story, brick apartment building just north of town. He'd finished his dinner and was enjoying a cup of coffee when his wall telephone rang in the kitchen. He placed his cup on the counter near the phone and lifted the handle to answer. An unfamiliar voice called his name. "Schmuel, is that you?"

Who in the world could this be? He paused for a moment, trying to place the voice, to no avail.

"You seem to have me at a disadvantage, sir. Who is this?"

"Oh, I forgot," said the voice. "You are known as Sam in this country. I'm sorry, I'll try to stay up to date, but to me, you'll always be Schmuel. This is Eli, Eli Rosen. I hope you remember me."

Sam was stunned. He remembered his old friend from the camp. A feeling of joy raced through his veins, and the memory of his old friend nearly brought him to tears. "Eli, I'm so glad to hear from you. After we were liberated, I thought you were gone from my life forever. I'm so glad that you're in America, or, at least I assume you are. This call sounds like long distance."

"Yes, Schmuel . . . Sam, I'm in Washington, D.C., where I work. It's great to hear your voice, too. I hope you are well, my friend."

"Eli, how did you find me? It's got to be fifteen years since we last spoke. What are you doing for work? We must get together." Sam's enthusiasm grew as he spoke, replacing the pain of the last few days.

Eli's voice changed at the thought of getting together with his old boyhood friend. A serious tone took over from the joyous greetings. "Sam, I found you because I've made it my business to be able to find people. I've wanted to connect with you for years, but I must be careful not to get close to fellow camp survivors. It can interfere with my work."

Sam was confused by these words. *What kind of work was Eli in?* He hoped it was nothing dangerous or illegal. He didn't know how to ask his next question, but Eli anticipated it and gave the answer.

"Sam, I work for the United States government. I'm in a special unit within the Department of Justice. It's the OSI, the Office of Special Investigations."

"That sounds rather vague, Eli. Special investigations could be any number of things."

"Yes, I know. I guess that's why they gave it that name, to keep it mysterious. These are very, very special investigations, Schmuel. I work as a liaison to the Israeli Mossad. Together, we hunt for escaped Nazi war criminals. It's important work, and to succeed, we must be quiet about it."

"Good Lord, Eli. The war was a long time ago. You sound like you're still fighting."

"We are still fighting. Look, thousands of Nazis escaped from Europe after the war. There was an underground network called ODESSA that helped them. Only a few high profile Nazis were tried at Nuremberg. Many fled to South America, and we must find them. I hope you will help."

"Help?" said Sam. "I'm in New Hampshire, not South America. Besides, those Nazis would just bring back terrible memories. They already haunt me, Eli. I don't want to make it worse. What could I do? I work in higher education, and I like it. I don't want to join your organization, if that's what you're asking."

"No, Sam, that's not what I'm asking. Please, listen to what I have to tell you."

A silence interrupted the conversation, as if both parties were cautious of guards listening. How many times had they lowered their voices while talking as young prisoners?

"As you know, Eichmann was captured several years ago. Now, we are on the trail of Dr. Mengele, that rotten butcher."

Again there was a silence, as Eli gave Sam time to absorb his words. They struck home immediately, giving Sam a sick feeling. He remembered the doctor who gave candy to him and always sounded assuring and kind. He also remembered the times Mengele sent a guard for his mother, not knowing what that meant or why the guard stayed with Sam until his mother returned. It was years later that the puzzle came together as Sam matured and learned the way of things between men and women. He learned some men liked to use their power over women, manipulating them into submission. He remembered his mother was a twin, and that these doctors had a fascination with twins. He understood why he and his mother were given better food and living accommodations than other prisoners, why he was kept alive while other lame or infirm children disappeared forever.

"Eli, I know what you are saying. Mengele was a monster, but no amount of punishment can bring back our families. Can't we just let it go after all these years? Can't we just move on with our lives? I'll never forget my mother or her courage. She will always be a part of me. But I want to have happiness in my life, not sadness."

"Yes, Schmuel, we all want happiness. But these monsters took our happiness away. They are holding on to it and will continue to for as long as they live without punishment. I'm afraid, Schmuel, you can't escape it. It's already closer to you than you think."

"What are you talking about, Eli? I'm in this tiny New Hampshire town and they are in South America. What do you mean?"

"Listen carefully, Sam. Do you remember that Mengele had an assistant?"

"Yes, of course I do," said Sam. "He was very mean. I always thought he wanted to kill me. He once threatened to cut off my mother's hand if I dropped his lunch tray. It was Mengele who kept him from hurting us. Of course, back then I didn't understand why. Mengele got what he wanted, that bastard."

"Do you remember his name, that assistant?"

"Yes, I do. It was Dr. Rauf."

"Correct," said Eli. "Dr. Augustos Rauf. In our hunting for these men, we've learned that not all of them went to South America. Many stayed in Europe under false identities and many went to North America, a few to Canada and many to the United States. We have reason to believe that he is in the New England states, working at a college or university. He can't practice medicine for fear of drawing attention to himself. What's more, it would be too difficult for him to put together all the false credentials he would need for medical certification. But to become a college professor, say, of Biology or Physiology, well, he wouldn't be the first professor with questionable qualifications. Many institutions don't do a very good job of vetting such people. Once they get employment at a reputable institution, it may be all they need for a lifetime."

Sam thought about the horrible notion that Rauf could be nearby. Eli broke the silence.

"We have people looking into the major universities, but I have a hunch that Rauf would go small time and try to burrow in. He might be very close to you. I tracked you through the last places you worked before landing at New Sussex College and decided to seek your help. We don't have an endless supply of agents and it takes a long time to hunt at all the possible institutions. I'm taking a chance that you could at least help out where you are, to examine your faculty and those at the other small colleges near you." There was another silence. "Sam, are you there?"

Augustos Rauf. He could be a Biology professor. Arthur. Could it be Arthur Vasile? No, he's Romanian. Of course, he could have falsified his credentials and changed his name. What about Carol? Oh, my God. No, that can't be. This had to be just a coincidence, but one he wasn't ready to share with Eli.

Still, perhaps he should look into it and help his old friend, just to make sure Carol was safe. "All right, Eli, I'll check out our faculty and the other small colleges in the area. Give me a description of Rauf, you know, how he might look today. Let me know how to get back in touch with you in case I find something."

"That's very good, Sam. I'm glad you can help. There is another thing about Rauf. We know that while at Auschwitz, he cut his left hand badly, an accident perhaps or maybe a prisoner tried to attack him. Anyway, it did nerve damage to his hand and left a long scar. It's another reason why he can't try to practice medicine. He may have limited use of the hand. I'll send more information soon, things that will help you. How should I address them to you?"

Sam gave Eli his mailing information and work phone. Eli had more to say. "Sam, another thing, if you find anything, don't tell the police. This is very important. Sometimes when we find these monsters, there is no way to extradite them . . . through normal channels. Sometimes we have to do things . . . well . . . differently. We fight fire with fire."

"I understand, Eli. I understand."

They exchanged goodbyes. Sam felt twisted inside. What started as a wonderful surprise from an old friend turned into a troubling predicament. He would have preferred to say no to Eli, that he couldn't help him in this hunt for former Nazis. But if Arthur Vasile was really Dr. Rauf, Carol could be living with a monster. She had come to mean a great deal to him, so Sam knew he had to find out the truth. *First Seth Walpole is murdered and now there may be an escaped Nazi on campus. What more could happen?*

Chapter Twelve

MONDAY, OCTOBER 14.

It was a typical Monday for Sam, starting work with a high energy level. He never did get the business about it being *blue Monday,* with people grouchy about the start of the work week. It was best to get right to it, get it done and behind you. Besides, he liked his job and rarely felt blue about it, even though a murder had recently taken place. He learned long ago to move past death.

It was past one o'clock when Sam welcomed his young colleagues, Fred and Gene, back into the office after their lunch break. He usually camped out in the office until they got back. The young men settled in and Sam waved to them as he marched out of the room and down the library stairs.

"Hello, Sam," called a tall man at the circulation desk—Arthur Vasile. "Hold on just a moment, will you?"

"Sure, Arthur, what's up?"

"I'm just giving this lovely librarian a list of reading material to put on reserve for my students." The pretty, blond woman behind the desk smiled at Arthur and took his list. He gave her a wink and motioned for Sam to come near.

"Got to keep my students busy, you know. Have you had lunch, Sam?"

"No," he replied. "I was just about to grab a bite."

"Good. You can come with me. I was just about to have lunch myself. We'll go to The Nook. I'll drive."

Sam's pulse quickened. Was he going to lunch with Dr. Rauf? He swallowed hard, realizing that he had to learn more about Arthur.

They strolled out to Arthur's vehicle, a black Ford pickup truck with a cap on the back. Sam climbed into the passenger seat, recalling the phrase déjà vu.

"You know, Sam, I was just talking to Martha Sanborn. Interesting woman, that Martha. She said you have a Eu-

ropean origin, like me. Isn't that a coincidence? Polish, I
believe she said. Is that right?"

Sam began to answer but was distracted by Arthur's
method of steering his truck. He held both hands on the
wheel, but didn't grip it tightly with his left. He did all the
work with his right, sliding the wheel through his weak left
as it rested, curled in place. It was less than a mile to their
destination.

"Yes, that's right, Arthur."

"So you were in Poland during the war, perhaps? Where
in Poland did you live?"

"I really don't remember the town. We seemed to always be moving around." Dodging the Germans was a full
time job, his mother used to say. "I was very young. Frankly, Arthur, it wasn't very pleasant, so I don't talk about it
very much. You can understand that, I'm sure."

Arthur nodded, keeping his eyes on the road. "I'm sorry, Sam. I didn't mean to bring up bad memories. Yes, those
of us who had to leave Europe certainly experienced some
dark times. My family used to live in a beautiful little village
in Romania. It was a quiet place, very peaceful, until war
broke out. I won't bore you with it. Let me park this thing
and we can go enjoy our lunch."

Arthur pulled his truck, nose first, into a parking space
outside the large old market building beside The Nook. The
small, white clapboard structure was a stark contrast to its
much older two-story neighbor that housed two other retail
establishments: a hardware store and a clothier.

Once inside, the men looked around for agreeable seating. Arthur spotted an open booth at one end of the diner
and motioned for Sam to follow as he made his way there.
Menus and place settings awaited them on the table. They
eased themselves in on opposite sides.

"You know, Sam, I'm glad to see that you and Carol
have become such friends. You get along very well. There
must be, what do they say here, good chemistry between
you two."

Sam looked at Arthur and picked up his menu, giving
it a glance. "Yes, I guess we do. Carol is a very friendly person, and she seems to get along with everybody quite well.
She makes friends easily. I don't think I'm the only one who
has befriended her."

"No, of course not, Sam. You are quite right. She is a very popular person among the college community. But, she has spoken of you often, like the time she cooked dinner for you at our house. She said it was a very nice evening. You know, I suggested that she invite you, since I was going to be out of town. I hated spoiling her weekend by leaving, but I'm glad you were around to brighten her evening. Thank you for pleasing my wife."

What an odd thing to say.

They examined the lunch offerings and placed the menus back on the table. A stocky woman, in her mid-fifties, took their orders, carefully jotting everything down on her notepad. Sam ordered a turkey club; Arthur chose soup.

"Carol is a very attractive woman, don't you agree, Sam?"

"Yes, of course, she is quite lovely."

"What do you think of her figure, Sam? She's pretty well built, don't you think?"

"I agree with everything you're saying." Sam looked around to see where the waitress was. He realized it was only a minute since she took their orders. He couldn't expect the food to be ready yet.

"I'm sorry if I'm making you uncomfortable, Sam. I'm just making, you know, man talk. Say, I understand you go out with Martha. Now there's a woman I'd like to get on the examining table. What a chest."

"Yes, of course," said Sam, tapping his fingers on the table. "Say, why did you think of an examining table?"

"Oh, how silly of me. I was studying to be a doctor, you know, in Europe, but the war ended that possibility. I guess I was just thinking like a doctor. I'm glad you have her for a partner."

"She's not my partner, Arthur. We go out from time to time, but it's nothing steady."

"Oh, so she takes care of your needs. That's good. That way you can have a good friendship with Carol and go see Martha when you get the urge."

"Arthur, really, I . . ."

"It's okay, Sam. I understand your situation. I am a man, too, remember, and I've been around much longer than you. I know that when a man has urges it helps to have a good female he can rely on, despite whatever situation he is in. Believe me, I do."

Sam's face tightened. *Was this the man Eli was looking for? Was this Dr. Rauf, the assistant to Josef Mengele? Was he referring to Sam's mother, "a good female he can rely on?"*

"So, you were in medical school, Arthur. How many years?"

"Only one, then the war came and we had to move on. Once we got settled in the United States, I took all the biology, physiology and anatomy undergraduate courses I could, but it was too late for me to try medical school."

The food arrived, causing a break in the conversation. Sam attacked his sandwich with vigor, while Arthur slowly spooned soup into his mouth. A quick swallow allowed him to resume his talk, while Sam's mouth was occupied with turkey, lettuce and tomato.

"You are either very hungry or in a great rush, Sam. Slow down or you'll get indigestion. Oh, by the way, Martha also said you hurt your leg as a boy. I didn't notice your limp before, but now that I know about your injury, I can see it. Funny how that works. What happened, if you don't mind my asking?"

Sam struggled to finish a mouthful of sandwich before answering. "It was an accident when I was very small. I broke my left leg, the thigh bone."

"Yes, the femur. That can be so painful, but if someone knows to pull the leg straight out, the sections of bone line up, and it gives the patient great relief. Then the bone can be set in place properly, although the patient must be immobilized for months while it heals."

"I don't remember everything, but the bone was never set properly for me. They put a cast on my leg and I wasn't able to get around much for a long time. My mother said the doctor was in a great hurry when working on me, that he had an appointment and had to rush."

"Did this happen near your home or were you staying someplace else, Sam?"

"We were in a car. I don't remember where we were going and I was reading a book when the crash happened, so I didn't really see anything. I must have been knocked out for a short time."

"That's very sad. I'm sorry you had to endure that kind of pain, especially at such a young age."

"Yes, thank you, but there was a lot of pain for many people in Europe back then. You understand."

Arthur stared at Sam momentarily and slid another spoonful of soup into his mouth. He swallowed and swirled his spoon in the soup bowl. "You were married once, I believe. I think Martha said that to me. I'm sorry it didn't work out. Do you have children?"

Sam didn't like this probing, even if Arthur felt he was just making conversation. Then he got an idea.

"No, we didn't have any children, but, well, almost."

"Almost? What do you mean, Sam?"

"My wife was pregnant and we think it was going to be twins, but she had a miscarriage late in the first trimester. It was very rough for her, physically and emotionally."

Arthur let go of his spoon and let it slide into the bowl. He folded both hands in front of him, his elbows on the table. "Twins and a miscarriage. That can be very difficult, indeed. And it's very rare. The whole concept of twin births is quite fascinating, you know. I had a professor who made a deep study into the subject. I had hoped to be able to learn much from him, but, well, you know how the war made many things impossible, Sam. It's all so fascinating, how the human body is constructed and works so well., and of course, there are the oddities, like multiple births or deformities. These things require more study. We just don't understand enough about them"

Sam watched how Arthur perked up at the mention of twins. It was alleged that Mengele did unspeakable things to twins, in the name of medical research. He was a butcher. Could Arthur have been his assistant? Sam stared down at the table, avoiding eye contact with Arthur.

"What is it, Sam?" asked Arthur. "You seem to be far away. Come back to earth, my friend."

Sam fidgeted with his plate and pushed it away from himself. "You know, Arthur, I just remembered I promised the students in the radio studio something. I should be getting back."

"Surely you have time to finish your lunch. It's a shame to waste such good food."

"I've had enough, Arthur, believe me. You can have the sections I haven't touched. Go ahead." Sam worked his way out of the booth and straightened up, reaching into his pants pocket for money.

"No, no, Sam. I've got it. My treat."

Sam started to protest, but Arthur held up his hand. "Okay, Arthur, thank you. I'll have to return the favor sometime."

"Yes, sometime when you are not rushed, Sam. Perhaps I can drive you back?"

"No, Arthur. That's okay. I need some exercise, too. See you later. Say hi to Carol for me."

As he left, Sam sensed Arthur watching him all the way out of The Nook. *Arthur was full of questions about my background. I've got a few about him, too. Is Carol married to a war criminal?*

Chapter Thirteen

MONDAY, OCTOBER 14.

Arthur finished his soup after Sam left and decided to eat the untouched portions of the turkey club as well. Soup alone didn't fill the big man.

After finishing, Arthur took out a pen from his shirt pocket and a small notepad. He began scribbling a few notes to himself about Sam and the answers he received about Sam's background. At the top of the page he jotted *Letter to Leinhardt.* There was something about Sam Miller that seemed to echo from his past. He was from Poland, for sure, he had admitted that. He would have been a small boy during the war, like the ones Arthur knew from where he worked. The slight limp was especially troubling to Arthur. Wasn't there a boy with a limp? It was long ago and hard to remember with certainty. *Maybe there is something in the old diary.* Perhaps Leinhardt, his old colleague, could help.

Arthur put his notepad away, paid for the lunch and was about to get up from the booth when another man appeared and occupied the seat across the table. "Hello, Arthur. I see you were taking a late lunch with Sam Miller. You guys must be old buddies or something."

"Why, Al, how nice to see you." Al Turner was another Nook patron, ready for a late lunch. "Sam and me, old buddies? Not really, but he's an agreeable young fellow. You could say that Carol and I have struck up a friendship with him."

"So you don't know a lot about him, either?"

"No. Perhaps you should ask Carol. She spends more time with him than me." Arthur reached inside his coat, searching for his car keys. "I thought you hired him. You must have read his resume."

"No, I don't have time for that. Besides, I'm the Academic Dean, not the Chief of Personnel. Bob Hill, his boss, would know his background, I guess. I know he spends time with Martha Sanborn. Maybe he likes the ladies but stays single. That can put a guy in an interesting position. He can mess around and still look like everybody's pal."

Arthur straightened up in his seat, his head tilted slightly back, like he had just heard something he'd rather not.

Al read the non-verbal sign. "I'm not suggesting, Arthur, that Sam is messing around with Carol, although he probably wants to. You might not be so friendly with him if he succeeded."

"No, Al, I certainly would not. But Carol is not the type to play around with another man. And I would not take another woman. We aren't the type for that sort of activity." Arthur spoke the last sentence slowly, as if there were deeper meaning to his words, his back still straight and his head up.

"I can see that . . ."

"If you will excuse me, Al, I must be going. I'll see you around." Arthur gathered himself up and slid out of the seat. "Say, I guess your schedule is even busier than before, now that you've got the duties of the college president on top of your own. It's good that you can get away for a break now and then."

"That's right. This is a late lunch for me. Some days I don't get lunch at all, but right now my stomach is aching. I've got to be quick and get right back to the office. Jim Kirkson is in town, coming by to go over some of the plans for his building. Take care, Arthur."

The wind had picked up, so Arthur buttoned his coat when he got outside. Al Turner's words about the Personnel Office and Sam's resume came back to him. Perhaps a visit to that office would be fruitful.

The Personnel Office was located on the second floor of the Administration Building, a few doors down from Carol's office. He climbed the front stairs from the lobby and slowed his stride as he moved inside the office.

Mary Hall, a plain looking woman of forty-six, with dark hair and a warm smile, welcomed him as he walked in. She stood behind a reception counter, hands busily flipping papers in a folder before her. "Hello, Dr. Vasile, how are you today?"

"Very well, Mary, thank you. And please, it's Arthur. You seem very busy. Are you hiring or firing today?" Arthur grinned broadly.

"Neither, right now. But when we get that nice new building it should create a few new jobs. That's quite exciting, don't you think?"

"Oh, I suppose so. But I don't think about it much. I'm happy with the nice Science Building we have. What an improvement that is over the scrawny little excuse for a science lab we were using. Now we have plenty of room and up-to-date equipment. Speaking of up-to-date, that's why I'm here, Mary. I'd like to see my personnel file to make sure it is current. Could you get it for me?"

"Why, of course, Arthur."

Mary gathered up the papers in front of her, slid them back into the folder and scooped the whole thing up, turning and placing it on the desk behind her. It was a tiny office without much room, but comfortable enough for Mary and her assistant, who was out sick today.

Arthur noticed her effort to keep the folder away from his eyes. It was very discrete and professional of her. She reminded him of the clerical help he knew many years ago. He would have hired such a woman.

Mary ambled over to a row of file cabinets, going straight to the one containing Arthur's file, drew it from the drawer and returned to the reception counter. "Here you go, Arthur. Take your time." She placed it in front of him before going back to her desk and resuming her interest in the file she'd been working with.

While the woman worked at her desk, which was perpendicular to the reception counter, her back was turned halfway to Arthur. He flipped through the papers in his folder, making enough noise for Mary to hear. He spent a minute or so doing this before speaking.

"Thank you, Mary. I think my file is okay for now. I'm doing some outside consulting work and perhaps I'll add that to my file when the current project is finished." He returned his papers to the file and pushed it back to Mary.

"That sounds like a good idea. Let me know when you're ready."

"Yes, indeed, Mary, my lovely personnel officer, I certainly will."

Mary smiled at the flirty comment.

"Say, there is something else you might help me with. You know Sam Miller, don't you?"

Mary nodded.

"I've gotten to know him these last few months and he strikes me as being pretty well versed in science. I'm wondering if he'd be qualified formally for helping with my consulting work. Do you suppose I could look over his file?"

"Now, Arthur, I can't let you do that. These files are confidential. Why don't you ask Sam for a copy of his resume? I'm sure he'd be happy to hear about your idea of hiring him."

"Yes, of course, but I don't want to sound like I'm making a job offer if I'm wrong about his qualifications. That could hurt his feelings."

"That makes sense to me, Arthur, but rules are rules. I'm afraid I can't help you."

Arthur's face betrayed the pleasant tone of voice. "No problem, Mary. It was just a thought, that's all. Thank you for being so helpful. It's good that you are also a real professional in your work. I understand completely." He turned and exited the office, slightly peeved at Mary and her damned professionalism.

He decided that a quick visit to Carol would be appropriate, since she was just footsteps down the hall. Perhaps he could learn more about Sam from her. Yes, he would ask discrete questions, but that would have to wait until they were at home.

That evening, Arthur enjoyed a cocktail while Carol poured a glass of red wine. She was in the kitchen, about to start preparing dinner. "I had a late lunch, darling, so why not just make something for yourself. I'm not very hungry," said Arthur.

"Very well, dear. I'll just cook some rice and have it with the leftover chicken. There'll be enough for you if you change your mind." She took out a pot, measured some water into it and set it on the stove on high heat. She pulled a Tupperware container out of the fridge and placed it on the counter.

Arthur stood a few feet away from her, sipping his drink. "I know we talked before about your dinner date with Sam Miller, dear . . . I know, I know, it wasn't a date. I'm just having fun with you. But, I was wondering. Did he talk about himself? He seems like an interesting young man."

Carol eased up to her husband, pressing her bosom to his right forearm, which was across his body while holding his glass. "Well, yes, he's interesting, but not as much as you, my dear husband."

Though her breast was soft and the contact was pleasing, Arthur backed away. Seduction was not what he wanted. He saw her smile change to a frown. "Really, Carol, did he say anything about his upbringing, his education, things like that?"

"No, darling, he wasn't here very long. After dinner, I tried to have a conversation with him, including talk about his younger days, but he didn't seem to want to have that discussion. Other than acknowledging his broken leg as a boy, he didn't go into his past, and I decided not to push it. I guess I did most of the talking, telling him how much I enjoyed his friendship. I offered to teach him how to ski, but he backed away from that real quick. Why are you so interested in his past, Arthur?"

"Oh, just curious, that's all. Like I said, he seems interesting and he relates well to science and technology. I'm naturally interested in people like that."

"I can understand that, dear, so why don't you just talk to him?"

Arthur sipped his cocktail. "I did, today. We had lunch together and he was just as you've described. He admitted to being from Poland, so we have something in common, you know, both of us from Europe during the war years. But that's about all he would say. Although, he did say that his ex-wife was about to have twins, but she lost them. Twins. Imagine that."

"There you go again, dear, your fascination with twins. Sometimes I think you have an obsession." Carol turned away, walking to the stove to check the water in the pot. She poured out the rice into a measuring cup and set it next to the stove, waiting for the water to reach a boil.

"By the way, dear," said Arthur. "I may have to go out of town again this weekend. Why don't you invite Sam over again? I'm sure he'd like that."

"Wow, that would get people talking. It might start to look like a habit. When the cat's away, Carol Vasile seems to play, with a mouse named Sam. What do you want me to do, Arthur, get him into bed and make him talk . . . hah, hah."

"That's not what I meant, Carol. Don't even think like that."

"Hey, don't get excited, big guy. I was just joking, like you did with that date crack. Besides, he might have a date with horny old Martha."

"Then invite them both over. I bet that would be fun. Have a few drinks, dinner and a good chat."

"Sure, and watch Martha grope the poor guy right in front of me. I don't think that would be so much fun." Carol waved her hand, reinforcing her negative assessment of the idea.

"Okay, Carol, but it's okay with me if you change your mind. Just make sure it's Martha he gets into bed with."

"Boy, you're getting downright touchy about that. I was joking, Arthur, just joking."

Arthur refilled his drink and left the kitchen. "I have some work to do in my study. Enjoy your dinner, my dear." There was more to Sam Miller and he was going to find out what.

Chapter Fourteen

TUESDAY, OCTOBER 15.

On Tuesday morning, Sam signed a handful of film rental invoices with a smile on his face. These papers would give him a good excuse to visit Carol in her office. He wondered how she'd be dressed and looked forward to finding out. His urge to see her was stronger than the physical need he satisfied with Martha. He didn't want to waste a trip uptown, so he phoned her office first to confirm she was in.

"Hello, Sam. Nice to hear your voice. You must have some serious business to warrant a phone call. Normally, you just drift in."

"Well, yes . . . no, nothing really big. I've got to drop off some invoices and wanted to see if you were in, that's all."

"That's sweet, Sam. I'd be happy to see you, too. When are you coming by?"

"In . . . how many shakes of a lamb's tail is it?"

"I think it's three, but who cares? Come on over. You'll be happy to know that Doris is out today, so we won't have her glued to our every word."

"That is good news."

"Don't get me wrong. I like Doris and we're friends, but she seems to think we're an item."

"Imagine that, me and you an item. Be still my heart." The thought of it struck Sam.

He gathered up his invoices, neatly folded them and slipped them into a large envelope, staring at it like a container of love letters. Sam slipped into his fall jacket and skipped down the stairs, making his way past the circulation desk and into the parking lot. In moments, he was entering through the open door to Carol's office. He rapped his knuckles on the door frame as he entered.

Carol swiveled her chair to face her guest, rising to greet him. He wanted to hug her, but wasn't sure if he should. She ran her hand against his left arm and the contact thrilled him. Their eyes locked on one another for a second before Carol broke it by looking at the envelope Sam carried by his side.

"Are those for *me?* Oh, you shouldn't have." Carol took the envelope from Sam and hugged it to her bosom before placing it on her desk. She was dressed in tight, straight legged jeans with a yellow blouse, much to Sam's approval. "I'm glad you called, Sam. It's really good to see you."

Carol's tone changed quickly, speaking as she eased back into her chair. "Sam, Arthur tells me he had lunch with you yesterday."

"Yes. My, you sound like something serious is going to happen. Is something wrong?" Sam pulled a small chair up beside Carol's desk and dropped into it. "I was taken off guard by his invitation to lunch and he asked me a lot of questions about my background in Europe. I guess he was just making small talk."

"No, there's nothing wrong, Sam. Well, maybe." Carol stared at him. "But you're not comfortable talking about your early years, are you?"

Sam didn't speak, merely nodding in agreement.

"He asked me about our dinner together when he was away. Of course we talked about it before, so I didn't understand why he brought it up again. He's interested in you. He says you're a very interesting man and he likes that you know a lot about science."

"Well, my field is Educational Technology, not exactly a hard science like Biology or Physiology, but, yes, science appeals to me." This was getting to be intriguing. Not only had Arthur questioned him directly, but he followed it up by interrogating his wife later. Why did he have such an interest?

"I have to tell you, Sam, that Arthur's behavior of late has me concerned. He has this sudden interest in you, your childhood, and he goes out of town more often than before. And Sam, well, he's been very cold to me lately. I can't seem to get him interested in me. Maybe I should be jealous of you."

Sam stiffened in his chair. "That's a joke, right?"

"Oh, I didn't mean it like that. But it's like I'm not around, as far as he's concerned. Something is on his mind, has been for a while now. I can't figure it out."

Sam looked down, pausing, as if searching for a solution. "Maybe that consulting project of his is bigger than he expected."

"True," said Carol. "He does seem to be spending more time on it. He's always going into his study to work on it. At least that's what he says. It makes me feel shut out. And here's another thing. He said you told him your ex-wife miscarried twins. He was rather excited about that. It really got his interest."

"Yes," said Sam. "I told him that at lunch and his face livened up as if happy to hear the news." *Arthur has more than a family interest in twins. Didn't he say he wanted to learn more about multiple births with a colleague in Europe?* He couldn't tell Carol he had made up the story about his ex-wife.

"Please don't mention this to Arthur, okay Sam? One day when I was home alone, I was straightening up the place and went into Arthur's study, just off the living room. The door was closed but unlocked. He usually locks it. He said it was just an old habit he'd developed as a young man, so I tried to forget about it. I never liked that. I'm his wife, after all. Well, I went in there and a picture album was lying on his desk, a thick brown album. I flipped it open out of curiosity and there they were, lots of pictures of twins, most of them were children. I know he said the ones on the walls are family, but this was a whole album with many pictures of twins. Sam, they couldn't all be family members. It was really freaky."

Sam leaned forward, pausing in deep thought. He couldn't reveal his suspicions about Arthur being an ex-Nazi. "He told me he studied to be a doctor, at least he was pre-med. He had a professor who did a study, research I guess, into the phenomenon of multiple births, mainly twins. So that might account for the photo album. Perhaps he had those family members and the subject always fascinated him. Perhaps the twin thing is like a hobby for him."

"Maybe you're right, Sam," said Carol. "Still, I think it's kind of creepy for some reason I just can't explain. And

I hate that he usually locks the study door. I wonder if he has other secrets in there."

Her comment resonated with Sam. Yes indeed, other secrets could be hidden in Arthur's study. Perhaps there was a way of getting in there. Was there Nazi treasure tucked away? Or something that would prove Arthur Vasile was, in fact, Dr. Rauf, assistant to the infamous Dr. Josef Mengele? Was this the man who once threatened to cut off his mother's hand and laughed about it?

Carol was a troubled woman. What he'd thought was an idyllic marriage upon first meeting the couple was, in fact, one full of insecurities. Of course, that was not unlike millions of American marriages. In his heart, Sam hoped it was a seriously troubled marriage that would end, freeing him to pursue Carol openly. Fat chance. Carol loved her husband and tolerated his habits, work and actions, no matter what he did that bothered her. She was searching for answers, not a parachute. Her eyes showed concern and disappointment, not fear or hatred that would make her want to get away from her husband.

"Arthur said he might have to go away again this weekend and I should invite you to be with me again. Do you believe that? He said even if you have a date with Martha, I could invite you both over. Too bad we don't have those old switchboard phone systems in Henniker. I could call you up and really get the old party lines buzzing."

"I admit that I don't have a date with Martha, or anybody else, but that's not such a bad idea. We could have a good time. There's a college drama production on Saturday. We could have dinner and take in the play, all three of us, presuming Martha is available. That would be cool, me out with two babes. Yeah, I guess I've still got it." Sam pounded his chest, grinning from ear to ear.

"At ease there, lover boy. Your male ego is showing." They both laughed.

"There you go, Carol. I much prefer to see you laughing than wearing that frown you had on a minute ago."

She reached out, placing her hand on Sam's forearm. "You're a sweet guy, Sam. At least there's one guy around here who thinks nice thoughts about me. I'll tell you what, you go ask Martha out for Saturday night and we'll do what you suggested."

"What if Arthur doesn't go away? You said he might be, not is."

"Then we'll include him. I'll tell him I took him up on his suggestion and already made the plans, so we can't back out. He'll have to go along.

Sam smiled. He didn't like the idea of having Arthur along, but perhaps it would provide an opportunity to learn more about him, just as he was trying to learn more about Sam. Yes, this also would be an opportunity to spend more time with Carol. He couldn't give up on her.

Chapter Fifteen

TUESDAY, OCTOBER 15.

Martha was at her desk when Sam walked in, a smile masking his true intentions. He was seeking a date with her to spend time with Carol. Sam felt a twinge of excitement from the deception. It didn't hurt that sex would be a sure thing that night.

"You're looking rather roguish, Mr. Miller. What gives?" Martha wore a tight blue turtleneck that emphasized her assets. Her legs crossed under a simple, red skirt. She brought out a totally different feeling in him than the tug on the heartstrings that Carol produced. Lust versus love, that's what it was. He once felt them both for the same woman, now his ex-wife. Could that happen again?

Sam chose the corner of Martha's desk for his resting place, his right leg draped over it, his left foot still on the floor. "I've got a proposition for you, Miss Martha. Here's the deal . . ."

Martha listened to Sam's offer while rubbing his inner thigh on her desk. She accepted without hesitation. After the date was set, her hand continued the gentle, enticing movement, and Sam found it difficult to break away.

"Saturday is a long way off, Sammy boy. I don't think you're going to make it. You'd better meet me at my place for lunch. I'll be happy to ease your suffering."

Sam found the strength to back away from Martha's caress and stood up straight. Martha chuckled at the bulge in his pants and handed him the folded newspaper lying on the left side of her desk. "Here's a shield, Don Juan. Now get back to work. I'll see you at lunch time."

Sam accepted the shield and proceeded to his work place, looking about for watchful eyes all the way. Fred and Gene were at their desks, going about their business. Sam was pleased he had two reliable young staffers. They seemed like free spirits, yet took a professional approach to their jobs. Somebody was always sure that the department had coverage in case a library patron, such as a faculty member, came by.

"Glad to find you all here together. We've got something important to discuss." Bob Hill rarely appeared on the second floor, usually opting to buzz Sam on the phone, but he was in the flesh this time, a big grin on his face.

The words and the demeanor of the Library Director puzzled the three men, considering recent events. He walked into the middle of the space between them, rubbing his hands together, like someone about to take on a great task.

"Gentlemen, a great challenge is before us, one from which I know you will not shrink," said Bob. He waited a moment, allowing the suspense to build. "Dean Turner and I were just on the phone discussing . . . business. In the course of that discussion, he challenged the library staff to a co-ed, twenty minute basketball game against the administration team, tonight in the gym. The stakes are high, gentlemen. The losing team must host a dinner party on Friday night. We can use the Sussex Room as the venue, since the library will be closed at that time. What say you, sportsmen? I trust you are up to this great challenge."

Gene raised his hand, like a student in a classroom. Bob clasped his hands together, extending both index fingers toward the young man. "You did say co-ed, didn't you?"

"That's correct, Gene. Martha and the other ladies on the library staff have already agreed to play. Dean Turner has several women from the administration on his team. There must always be one, but not more than two women on the court from each team at any time."

An image appeared in Sam's mind. He saw Martha in shorts and T-shirt, running about a basketball court, her bosom bouncing to the great distraction of the male players. *Even if she knows nothing about the game, Martha could be a useful team member.*

"This sounds interesting, Bob," said Sam. "What brought this on?"

"We usually have some faculty and staff teams in the intramural league each year, which doesn't start until January. This will be a kind of warm-up to the season. I asked

Al if the administration had a team for this year and the conversation went on and on, with him talking trash about how they could kick a library team's ass. Well, I couldn't let him insult our pride like that, so I suggested an early match, with a social event after. He came up with the dinner party idea on Friday and I agreed. So, my good fellows, what's the decision? Are you in?"

"Tonight, you said?" asked Fred. "That sounds okay to me."

"Sure, count me in, too," said Gene.

All heads turned to face Sam. He felt like the accused in an Agatha Christie novel, when all suspects are garnered together in one room for the thrilling climax.

"You all realize my chance of scoring any points in a basketball game are somewhere between slim and none? I'm not too good at sports."

Bob stepped closer to Sam and spoke like the wise old coach, trying to motivate his players. "That's not a requirement, Sam. You just need to show up and give it your best. We'll all be pulling for you. What do you say?"

Sam felt the pressure of the moment and the heat of all eyes peering at him. "It's not often one is confronted with situations like this," he said. "The gravity and importance of this challenge does not escape me. Therefore, I am in."

All hands came together in applause, "That-a-boy, Sam," said Bob. "I knew I could count on all of you. Of course, if you didn't say yes, you'd be fired. I'm just kidding. This will be great fun. So, be at the gym at seven for some warm up time. Bring it in, boys, bring it in." Bob held his arms out in front of himself, clasping one hand on top of the other. The others followed suit in the familiar sports team gesture. "Ready, say Go, Library!"

All four repeated the phrase, "Go, Library!"

The group dispersed, and Bob hustled away, pumping a fist in the air. "I'll call Al with the good news. Thanks, men. See you tonight. Oh, by the way, wear white T-shirts."

Sam looked at his young colleagues. "What have I gotten myself into?"

The three men looked at each other with tight smiles and nodding heads. Gene broke the silence. "This should be fun. I haven't played a co-ed basketball game before. Do you think it's better to foul or to be fouled?"

"Oh, be fouled, definitely. That way you get to stay in the game no matter how many times you are the foulee. The fouler gets five and he's out, but that shouldn't be a problem in just twenty minutes."

"I've got a question, guys," said Sam. "Basketball, is that where the ball is kind of pointed at the ends?" Fred and Gene paled. "I'm joking, guys, I'm just joking. I'm not that bad, you'll see."

Almost in unison, Sam's colleagues replied, "Oh, my God."

After a private party with Martha at lunchtime, the rest of the day went quickly and without further surprises. Fred worked with some students in the radio studio, helping them make pre-recorded public address announcements. Gene set up and ran a film for a professor in the basement level classroom. And Sam did paperwork in his office, resisting all impulses to call or visit Carol again.

By seven o'clock, people began appearing at the gymnasium. The thumping sound of basketballs hitting the court floor got louder and louder, as more and more players arrived, found practice balls in the equipment room, and took to the court.

Sam parked his car and entered the gym through the lobby. He felt a chill, wearing old gym shorts he had from his school days and a light jacket over his white T-shirt. He spotted Bob at one of the team benches, sitting down and lacing up a new pair of sneakers. Other library staffers, including Gene and Fred, were on the court taking practice shots. Bob saw him and waved. Sam strolled across the court, intending to greet Bob.

As he walked among his teammates, Sam paid no heed to the multiple basketballs flying through the air. He smiled at his library colleagues, hands in his coat pockets, strolling without haste. "Heads-up," called Gene, to no avail. A ball bounced off the back rim of the hoop and took a long rebound, striking Sam in the back of the head. He grabbed his head where the ball struck him and realized, to his great relief, he wasn't hurt.

"You okay, Sam?" called Fred, the shooter. "Sorry!"

"No problem, I'm okay," said Sam, rubbing his head.

Gene ambled up to Fred, holding a ball in his hands, spinning it slowly. "Something tells me this is going to be a long twenty minutes." Fred agreed with a grin.

Chapter Sixteen

TUESDAY NIGHT, OCTOBER 15.

Sam held a basketball under one arm while standing at the foul line, watching with amazement as several people in street clothes entered the gym. Spectators! Among them was Seth Walpole's secretary Irene, who now worked for Al Turner. He also recognized Ian Barnstead, but there were many unknown faces. Carol arrived to watch the game, much to his delight. His enjoyment at the sight of Carol diminished when he saw Arthur right behind her. He waved to them, nonetheless, and they returned his gesture.

A tapping on his shoulder got Sam's attention. He turned to find Bob holding a bunch of yellow sleeveless shirts with blue numbers on them. "Here Sam, take one and put it on. Turns out they have these pullovers for us. We get yellow and Al's team gets red with white numbers. The numbers go in back. Go yellow." Sam did as instructed and the rest of Team Hill did the same as Bob passed them around.

Balls flew about at random, crashing into the rim and backboard and caroming every which way. Team Turner's group engaged in similar behavior at the other end of the gym. The noise level in the building grew steadily as all the players arrived and took to their warm-ups.

Martha bounced a ball as she skipped up to Sam. "Hey, hot shot, try to take the ball away from me." She bounced the ball rhythmically with her right hand, turning her left side slightly to face Sam. He lunged toward her, swiping at the ball, and his right hand grazed her shirt front. "Hey, watch what you grab, mister. Didn't you get enough today? I said take the ball away." Martha switched hands from right to left, dribbling away from Sam as he awkwardly lunged again, missing his target completely.

"You seem to know what you're doing, Martha. How did you learn to do that?"

"I grew up with three older brothers. We had a hoop in the driveway and they needed a fourth to play two-on-two with them, so I had to learn. The youngest of them, Zeke, took pity on me and taught me some basics."

"He taught you well, I can see. Where does he work? Maybe we can recruit him for the intramurals."

Martha held the ball on her hip and her expression changed briefly. Sam knew instantly he'd said the wrong thing.

"We lost him in '67 in 'Nam." Just as quickly, she resumed her dribble, bent her knees as if ready to make a move and waved for Sam to chase her. "Hey, it's okay big boy. What's past is past. Get back in the game, Sammy. Focus, focus."

Could Martha really be over the loss of her youngest brother? Maybe this was her secret. Maybe this was why she took men as her adult playmates but never got too close, why her attempts at marriage failed. His mind flashed back to the camp and those young boys who were his playmates for a few days, or weeks, and then disappeared. He didn't have any siblings, so he could only imagine what it must be like to have playmates right in your own home. His friends at the camp became his brothers, until they were gone.

You're not the only one here who knows about war. Dumb, Schmuel, dumb.

Sam forced a smile and took another lunge at Martha. This time she turned her body, backside first, at Sam. His front struck her, as he placed a hand on her back to soften the blow.

"Well, well, my boy, seems like you've got some moves of your own," she said, as their bodies came into contact.

"I think you pulled a fast one on me, Martha. You're pretty slick. Guess I'd better watch out for you. It's a good thing we're on the same team. I think I'm warmed up enough."

Sam strode over to the bench and took a seat next to Bob, who was placing some papers onto a clipboard. There was a diagram of a basketball court on the papers and Bob wrote something across the bottom of each one.

He noticed two people walking from the equipment room, one with a whistle around the neck. It was a young woman, mid-twenties, whom he'd seen around campus, but never met. The other was Dan Zumowski, the manager of the college bookstore. He carried the apparatus that plugged into the large scoreboard mounted on the wall between the benches. A referee and a score keeper. Boy, this looked serious.

Sam said hello to Dan, whom he'd met at the College Pub a couple of times. Dan introduced him to Audrey Nagle, the referee.

"Nice to meet you, Sam," said Audrey. Sam looked her up and down. She wore a short-sleeved, blue and gray jersey with a basketball emblem patched to one arm, a classic official's jersey. She had tight, navy blue slacks and black sneakers, low cut.

"You look very official, Audrey. I guess you do this sort of thing a lot."

"Yep. I referee girls' games at both the high school and college level. And I coach the women here at New Sussex. How's your game?"

"What game?" asked Sam. "I haven't tried this in years. My leg doesn't like it when I run."

"Maybe my husband should check you out. He's the athletic trainer."

"I'll be okay. I usually avoid any rough stuff."

"Suit yourself. Okay, we're about ready to go." Audrey turned to Dan and he nodded affirmatively. He gave the buzzer a blast and the players grabbed the practice balls and carried them to their benches. She waved to Bob and Al to bring it in.

After hearing from the ref, Bob came back to his players and gave some instructions. The coaches agreed the game would be thirty minutes, not twenty, with two fifteen minute halves. Bob, Gene, Fred, Martha, and Gloria Schmidt, a library employee, would start. Sam felt relief and hastily took a place on the bench.

"Hey, Sam, get back here," said Bob. "We're not done." He rejoined the team as they stood in a circle. "We'll play a zone defense, Martha and Gloria outside. Don't you two get any deeper than the foul line. I'll take the middle, Gene and

Fred play forward. Everybody hustle back on defense and keep both hands up. Okay, hands in."

Bob put his hand out, arm fully extended. The others did the same, touching their teammates, one hand on top of another. "Ready," said Bob. "Let's win!" The players repeated the yell.

"Okay, Sam. Now you can sit," Bob said with a smile.

The game started at a quick pace, with Team Hill taking an early lead. Much of the success was due to Martha's swiftness and expert ball handling. She stole the ball from Team Turner's Mary Hall twice while Mary dribbled carelessly and flew to the basket for easy layups. The group of spectators emitted high-pitched cheers of delight at Martha's skill.

Bob's instructions to his team were well understood and they took their defensive positions quickly and effectively. As Team Turner's players passed the ball around the perimeter, Team Hill's defense slid from side to side, following the ball with their hands up high. After a few seconds of this, the Turner players would grow impatient and toss a feeble shot at the basket, usually missing. Five minutes into the game, Team Hill was building a substantial lead.

When a foul was called on a Team Hill player, it was time for a substitution. Bob jogged to the bench and motioned for Sam to enter the game.

"You play the corner position for Fred. He's going to slide into my position at center. Just concentrate on defense, hands up, and try to stay out of trouble on offense. You'll be fine."

"Glad you think so, Coach," said Sam. "Here goes nothing."

As he reached the free throw lane where the other players had assembled, Gene pointed to where Sam should stand. "You gotta wait until the ball hits the rim or backboard before you can step over this line," said Gene, pointing down at the line that marked one side of the free throw lane. "Then go for the ball. If you get the rebound, pass it to Martha or me."

"Got it," he replied with false confidence.

As the game progressed, Team Turner made a comeback. On one play, however, Martha stole a cross-court pass aimed at Al, and she sped toward the basket. Turner caught up with her just as she was leaving her feet for a layup. He managed to hook two fingers over the waistband of her gym shorts and they came down as she went up. Her legs tangled in her shorts, which slipped halfway down her thighs, and she tumbled face down on the floor. The spectators made noise, half laughter and half worry, as Martha slid to a halt, her pink panties on full display. The ref's whistle screeched.

Turner offered a hand to Martha as she jumped to her feet and pulled her pants back up. "Sorry about that, Martha." He offered no explanation as to how it happened.

"Geez, Al, if you wanted to get in my pants, couldn't you at least wait until after the game?" The ref heard the remark and chuckled as she checked to see if Martha was hurt.

"I'm okay, ref. No harm done. I just didn't expect to do a strip show while playing basketball."

The players assembled at the free throw lane, and Martha stood at the line, awaiting the ball from the ref. Audrey held up two fingers and called, "Two shots. First one's dead." She flipped the ball to Martha, who made both.

At the halftime break, Team Hill held a ten point lead over Team Turner. Sam had played more minutes than he expected and performed above expectations. His teammates congratulated him, and Sam's spirits rose, a feeling of minor accomplishment boosting him.

Bob told a startled Sam to start the second half, giving Gene a break. Bob explained to Sam what to do at the jump ball that started the second half. Sam watched with flat footed amazement as the ref tossed the ball up between Fred and Al and play resumed.

The teams traded baskets for a few minutes, with Team Hill's lead staying intact. Sam followed his instructions, concentrating on defense, and held his own against the opposition. Then he got a rough taste of what Martha had experienced.

At his defense end of the court, Sam was in the corner, to the right of the basket. The man he was guarding sprinted toward the middle, down low, an area vacated by Al Turner, who moved to the high post. Sam's man went past the middle, just outside the free throw lane, took a pass and immediately threw up an awkward shot. The ball skimmed the top of the rim and bounced off. Sam reacted to the opportunity to grab a loose ball, since nobody on Team Turner was near. He ran to the basket and leaped up for the rebound, clutching it with both hands.

A shot of satisfaction bolted through Sam like lightning, as he captured the ball. The sensation was short lived, however. As his feet landed simultaneously, he felt the weight of another body slamming against his own. The impact of the collision thrust him violently forward, his body gaining momentum from the hit, and he crashed into the end wall of the gym, about twelve feet from where he snared the loose ball. Sam's body lurched and his head struck the wall first, followed by the rest of him. He dropped to the floor like a sack of cement, dazed but conscious, thankful for the gym mat hanging against the cinderblock wall for human protection.

The referee blew her whistle. Play stopped while teammates and the ref rushed to check if Sam was injured. Martha pushed past her teammates. She helped him to his feet and escorted him to the team bench, his knees wobbling all the while. Bob replaced him in the game. Al Turner faced the scorer's table and raised his hand, signifying that the foul was on him. He offered no apology or sign of concern about Sam.

Audrey trotted up to the scorer. "Backcourt foul; two shots," she proclaimed and walked over to Sam. "You have to take the shots, Sam, unless you can't continue."

"Yeah, okay," he said, trying to shake off the effects of his collision with the wall. He ambled back out on the court, and Bob returned to the bench. At least he'd get two shots where nobody could block them or hit him. Some consolation.

Uncertain how to shoot from the foul line, Sam did his best to imitate the other players. He placed his right hand behind the ball, but it felt heavy in his hands. Spinning it, he grasped the ball with both hands, bent his knees and pushed the ball away from himself, like trying to discard a piece of garbage. The sphere flew upwards toward the basket, where it missed the rim, whacked against the backboard and sank back into the cylindrical opening. The referee gathered up the ball, dribbled it once while saying "This one's in play." She handed the ball gently to Sam who repeated his shooting technique. This time the ball took a higher arc to the basket, neatly dropping into the cylinder without touching the rim. Sam smiled as he heard the sound of the ball speeding through the netting of the basket. Swish!

Bob called an *injured player* timeout and motioned Sam over to the bench, a big grin showing his delight at the points Sam scored. As Sam walked to the sideline, he heard Martha's voice. "Way to go, Sammy boy. Nice shooting." He felt the sting of her hand spanking his butt with gusto. Her last strike ended with a tender grasp of the same area. "Way to go, big boy."

The game resumed with Sam sitting on the bench, still woozy, but improving. Players jogged past him, including Al. Sam looked up in time to see Al staring coldly back. It was a look without compassion or caring, a look he'd known a long time ago.

Team Hill held on to its lead, as Team Turner made a run at it. They trimmed the lead to four points, but a nifty defensive move by Martha, stealing another errant pass from the opposing bunch, secured the win for the library crew.

Friday dinner would be on the administration team.

Chapter Seventeen

TUESDAY NIGHT, OCTOBER 15.

Victory in hand, Team Hill gave each other high fives and pats on the back. Martha saved a special congratulations for Sam. She approached him and ignored his upright hand, opting for something warmer. She threw both arms around his neck and gave him a big kiss, holding it beyond Sam's comfort zone. Sam held her momentarily, but broke his grip while Martha prolonged the kiss. "I gotta catch a breath," he said as he pulled her arms, forcing her grip to relax.

"You did great tonight, Sammy boy, just great. How's your head? Why don't you come over to my place for some good medicine? I promise to make you feel better." Martha's hands slid down his sides and rested on Sam's hips.

"Let's go to the Pub for a cold pitcher," said Bob. "A victory beer is in order for my team, and I'm buying."

The members of Team Hill gave a cheer and everyone agreed with their coach. "A little celebration is appropriate tonight," said Gene.

"That's a big ten-four," said Fred, using the CB radio term for affirmation. The idea gave Sam a way out of Martha's proposition.

"My head's still ringing, but maybe a quick one will help," said Sam. "I'm in."

The players of both teams moved slowly toward one another, meeting in front of the scorer's table. They extended their hands for high fives and handshakes. Sam noticed Al was not among them, and nowhere in sight.

Having donned his jacket, Sam moved toward the exit when he felt an arm grab him around the waist. "Way to go, Sam." It was Carol, with Arthur right next to her. "You're a much better athlete than you give yourself credit for. I still think I could teach you to ski." She held onto Sam as they moved toward the exit, patting and rubbing his back like a jubilant cheerleader.

Sam was startled by her embrace in Arthur's presence and resisted the temptation to touch her. His arms hung limp at his sides. "Thanks, Carol, but this was rough enough. I'm not ready to tackle a mountain just yet."

"Al Turner gave you quite a bump, didn't he, Sam?" said Arthur. "That wasn't very nice." Arthur's voice was monotone and didn't sound very consoling to Sam. Perhaps Arthur enjoyed the injury somewhat.

"Yeah," said Carol. "What's with him? First he practically strips Martha, knocking her to the floor and then he tries to send you through the wall. That's dirty play, if you ask me. I've never seen that side of him before."

Sam stared at Carol, appreciating her concern. "I guess that's how some people are with sports. What does that guy say on TV, the human drama of athletic competition? I guess Al is highly competitive and overly dramatic about it. Hey, the team is going to the Pub for a beer to celebrate. Want to join us?"

Carol, her arm still around Sam's waist, looked at her husband and got a nod. "Sure," she said, turning back to Sam. "Let's go."

They walked a few more steps toward the exit before Carol released her grip on Sam. He wished she could've held on longer. He glanced at Arthur, who walked a few feet away, his face blank as if he didn't care about Carol's friendly embrace, or perhaps his mind was elsewhere.

Once outside, everyone made their way to their own vehicles. As Sam approached his, he noticed a lone figure standing next to it. "Nice game, Sam," he said. It was Chief Powers, leaning against the passenger side of the car.

"Thanks, Cal. Glad you enjoyed the game. I hope you aren't planning on another little ride. I'm committed to a victory celebration with my team at the Pub."

"No, nothing like that. I'd just like a word or two with you, that's all. Mind if I get in?" Cal waited for Sam to climb into the unlocked car before he took the passenger seat.

Sam wasted no time in starting the engine and turning on the headlights. He wanted some warm air to start flowing as quickly as possible since the evening was getting chilly. He sat with his hands folded, resting on the steering wheel and let Cal start the conversation. Never assume what's on the mind of a man in uniform.

"I just thought I'd tell you I took your advice and spoke with my sister about the party she went to. You know, after that conversation we had last Sunday?" Cal looked at Sam and waited for a response. None came. "Well, she said she knows who Al Turner is and that he was also at the party. Funny, you didn't mention that to me before, that Turner was at the party."

"I must have forgotten about him. Now that you mention it, I do recall spotting him from a distance as we were leaving. We didn't even speak. I was focused on whatever Martha had in mind for us. She's good at distracting a guy's mind."

Sam gazed at Cal, not sure if the Chief was buying Sam's story or not. He didn't want to implicate Al, but after the things the guy did to him and Martha in the game, he was reconsidering that position.

"I hear you, Sam. You're a single man and Martha is a single woman, with a lot to offer a guy. If I were in your position, I guess I know what I'd be thinking about, too."

Sam took a breath. He liked Cal and wanted to help him, but he was confused about what the right course of action was. As a boy in the camp, he learned that keeping one's mouth shut was a good survival tactic. Maybe this was different.

"Cal, there is something you should know about Al."

Cal sat relaxed, not shifting his position in the passenger chair.

"Look," said Sam. "Maybe it's nothing, but there was an incident back in September. Turner and Seth Walpole had an argument, a pretty heated one. We had just finished a meeting where Seth announced the large donation from an alumnus that was going to be used to build an important new building, something that would become the centerpiece of the campus. It was great news, and everybody was very upbeat afterwards, except Seth and Al. Seth took Al into his office after everybody else left. I still had other business in the building, so I was there for a while and then I was reading the bulletin board a short way down the hall from Seth's office. I couldn't help but hear them go at it."

"Hmmm, that's interesting, Sam. Go on. Could you hear what they were talking about?"

"More like shouting," said Sam. "It sounded like Seth was accusing Turner of being involved in something that could be a big scandal for the college, something that could jeopardize the plans for the new building."

"Sam, I want you to think very carefully about this. What could cause such a big scandal that would get Seth so upset?"

Sam paused, collecting his thoughts. "It was something about that wife swapping club." Sam did as Cal instructed. He thought carefully and decided he'd said enough. "I couldn't make out any details beyond that." Sam left out the part about Seth threatening Turner's career and turned his head away from Cal, indicating he was through. He felt like he had just confessed a great sin of his own and somehow felt purged, the feeling of relief overcoming one of guilt. He also felt fear. Was he getting in too deep?

Cal turned to face the windshield and both men were quiet for an awkward moment. The chief spoke while both kept looking straight ahead. "Thank you, Sam, for sharing that information. You realize, of course, that you've just suggested Turner might've had a motive for killing Seth. If Seth believed Turner was involved in something that could be damaging to the college, it would make sense he might fear some sort of discipline, that his job and career could be threatened. Of course, I'm going to have to question Turner about this."

Sam was relieved Cal reasoned by himself the part of Turner fearing for his career. At the same time, however, he was chilled that Cal seemed to know the answers to his own questions.

Sam snapped his head toward Cal. His face gave away his worry.

"I don't need to tell Turner where I heard this, Sam. From the way he treated you in that game tonight, I gather he doesn't like you much. There's no need to add fuel to the fire. I'll leave your name out of it, but if there is something to this, you may have to make an official statement. I hope you understand."

"Yeah, sure, Chief, I understand." *I understand Turner will want to get his hands around my neck.*

Chapter Eighteen

SATURDAY NIGHT, OCTOBER 19.

On Saturday night, Sam picked up Martha and took her to the Vasile house for an early dinner. Carol had let him know Arthur had a change of plans and was not going out of town. She said he seemed delighted with the plans for the two couples and would cook the dinner himself. A college theater production also suited his taste.

The four people gathered in the kitchen, watching Arthur, wearing a white chef's apron, go about his culinary chores. They enjoyed their drinks while chatting. The women sipped red wine and the men agreed to start with Woodford Reserve Bourbon, neat.

"So, how was your dinner celebration last night, Sam?" asked Arthur as he put a pot of water on the stove and cranked the heat up high. "I hope Al behaved himself better than he did in the game."

Sam stood at the kitchen isle, as if it were a bar, with Martha sitting on a stool beside him, to his right. She wore a blue miniskirt over black tights, with a white, high neck blouse. Even with Carol standing at his left, he couldn't help but steal an occasional glance at her legs.

"Heck, Turner was a different person last night. He was almost jovial, you might say. What did you think, Martha?"

Martha sat with her hands folded in her lap and legs crossed. "Oh, absolutely, he was a perfect gentleman. He never once tried to pull my pants down."

Everybody laughed and sipped from their drinks, almost simultaneously, except Arthur, who kept busy, pulling the ingredients together to make a meatloaf. "I don't suppose he apologized to either of you for his rough play," said Arthur.

"I said he was jovial, not contrite," said Sam. "I saw no point in bringing up the rough stuff and we just let that go."

Arthur assembled the package of meat, two eggs, and a can of breadcrumbs on the counter, next to a large bowl. "I hope you like meatloaf, everybody. It goes quite well with pasta and a salad." His face turned to a frown as he stared at the items before him. Sam wondered what the problem was until Arthur turned and searched through the food cabinet again. Something was missing.

"Arthur makes a great meatloaf, you guys. You're going to love it, unless you're vegetarian, of course," laughed Carol. "Sam, pay attention, you might want to make this for Martha some night."

Sam forced a grin and sipped his drink. *There they go again, putting Martha and me together as a couple.*

"How dumb of me," said Arthur, slapping his forehead as he searched in vain through the cabinet shelves. "I should have checked my food inventory. I'm missing a key ingredient, the diced tomatoes." He turned off the heat under the water pot, untied his apron and slipped out of it. "Not to worry, people. I'll make a quick run to Howard's Market and get what I need. I believe he's still open. Carol, why don't you put out some crackers and cheese for our guests, so they don't starve? I'll be right back."

Arthur was gone in seconds and Sam was left in the company of two lovely women, one of whom filled his sexual needs and the other of whom occupied his thoughts. His eyes consumed Carol in an instant, but not fast enough to escape Martha's notice. "Hey handsome, come over here, will you?" she said, motioning Sam with her arm. "My neck feels a bit stiff. How about giving it a rub, the shoulders, too?"

Sam obliged while Carol smiled. He sensed she fully understood the sexual politics going on and admired her quick grasp of the situation, as well as Martha's maneuvering. A rush of male ego shot through him, but was quickly cooled by a practical shift in his thinking.

"Martha," he said, leaning over her shoulder, his hands still kneading her gently. "It seems Arthur has several sets of twins in his family."

"Really, Sam? Is that right, Carol?"

Carol nodded, staring at Sam. "That's right. He has some pictures on the wall."

Sam found his opportunity. "Carol, didn't you tell me he has an entire photo album with twins in the pictures? I'd love to see that. It must be quite interesting. Where did you say it was?" He watched her intently, looking for non-verbal signs. Her face took on a very serious demeanor, perhaps even a bit worried. He hoped she'd cooperate. There was little time before Arthur would be back.

The trio meandered through the rooms where the pictures were displayed. Martha took an interest in the old photos on display, taking her time to observe them. Carol and Sam moved on toward Arthur's study, where Carol tried the door. It was locked. "I'm sorry, Sam, I guess we're out of luck. Arthur is back to locking up his study. Why are you so fascinated with Arthur's thing about twins? I don't get it."

"Later, Carol. Hmmm, maybe our luck can change," said Sam, as he reached into his pocket, extracting his key ring with several items on it, including a small Swiss Army knife. He opened it and found a slender, pin-like piece. Sliding it into the old fashioned keyhole, Sam maneuvered it until he heard a click. A twist of the knob and he had the door opened.

"Geez, Sam, you're breaking into Arthur's study. He's going to be furious!"

"He'll never know," said Sam. "Just tell him he must have forgotten to lock it. Maybe that's why it was opened before. You look like the cat that swallowed the canary. Stop worrying. We'll just be a minute. Where's that album you told me about?"

"That's it, still lying on his desk," said Carol as she pointed to it.

Sam moved around the desk, standing beside a big, padded chair. His eyes opened wide as he flipped open the cover, revealing the first page of old, black and white photos of nothing but twins. Another flip and he had two pages opened at once, with the same result.

"This is amazing, absolutely amazing," said Sam. He continued flipping. His face went cold when he recognized the background in some of the photos. The pictures were taken indoors at what looked like a hospital, but it was small and dingy looking. There was a woman standing beside two girls who must have been about six or seven years old. Her face seemed familiar, but he wasn't sure. Could this be Auschwitz where he and his mother were imprisoned?"

"Sam, hurry up. I think Arthur just pulled into the driveway. We'd better get back into the kitchen." Carol closed the album, almost catching Sam's fingers.

They were about to exit and close the door when Martha appeared, blocking their way. "Hey, what's in here, more family photos?" She pushed past Carol and Sam, tickling his stomach as she went by. "Wow, this is a really nice office, or study. I guess that's what you'd call it. Must be Arthur's favorite room." She gazed about, noticing items on the walls, including a framed map of Europe.

Sam and Carol turned toward each other as they heard a car door slam shut outside.

"Yes, this is Arthur's study," said Carol. "I think I just heard his car, so let's get back to the kitchen and freshen up our drinks." Carol and Sam moved through the opened door, signaling Martha that it was time to go.

She didn't move, standing in front of the desk and grabbing the photo album. Sam went to her and took her by the arm. "Come on, Martha dear. Let's go."

"Hey, what's the rush? If that's Arthur coming back, maybe he can tell us about his old pictures."

Sam took the album from Martha and placed it on the desk. He held Martha's arm and eased her out of the room while Carol waited for them to move past her so she could close the door. He leaned his head down to her ear and whispered to her. "Martha, you must not, under any circumstances, tell Arthur that we were in his study. Do you understand?"

"Christ, Sam, what's the big deal?"

"Look, he's very touchy about it. That's what Carol told me, so do us all a big favor and don't even mention it, okay?"

"Okay, okay, but you two are acting pretty strange about the whole thing," said Martha. "Is the study where you two get it on?"

"Stop it, Martha, just stop it." Sam tried to hurry her along when he heard a thud on the front porch. He pulled her by the arm, away from the study and back into the kitchen. Carol was right behind them. They gathered near the counter as Arthur emerged through the front door.

When he entered the kitchen, he was holding the can of tomatoes in his bare hand. "Clumsy me," he said. "I dropped the can on the porch. I bet the whole neighborhood heard it. Well, now I'm ready to do some cooking. I'm very sorry about the delay."

"No sweat, Arthur," said Sam. "No sweat at all." He grabbed Martha by the shoulders and resumed massaging them. "Easy with the grip, big boy," she said. "This is supposed to be a massage, not a torture session."

Sam noticed Arthur look up from his chore when Martha used the word torture. It was just for a split second, and perhaps, meant nothing. Maybe Sam was just seeing what he wanted to see. Or maybe the word struck a chord with Arthur.

The photo album intrigued Sam. The twins depicted in the photos were very possibly victims of Mengele and Rauf. The settings were hauntingly familiar to Sam, and he was sure that some pictures may have been taken at Auschwitz. He wanted to know for certain. He had to get that album.

Chapter Nineteen

MONDAY, OCTOBER 21.

The following Monday, Ian Barnstead was in the library around ten in the morning going over film orders with Gene. He was boisterous in a happy way, always raising the energy level in a room.

"Gene, hand me your *Time Life* catalog, will you? I want to see if they have anything new on Black History. There was a great documentary on TV last year and I hope it's available."

Gene did as asked and Ian stood near his desk, flipping the catalog to the contents page. "These guys have a lot of great material. There are other good sources, but I think *Time Life* is the best. I don't know."

"They're certainly one of the biggest distributors, that's for sure, Ian," said Sam from behind his desk. "What have you been up to? Haven't seen you around for a while."

Ian continued to browse the catalog while he spoke. "Well, besides imparting knowledge and wisdom to my students, not much. How about you?"

Sam summarized his weekend to Ian, who lifted his head out of the catalog. "I'll bet that was a fun night," he said, referring to the Saturday evening with Martha and the Vasiles.

"As a matter of fact, it was." Sam's wry smile gave Ian the answer he expected.

"Well, speak of the devil," said Ian, looking around after hearing footsteps. Arthur was coming through the door, which he closed behind him, before striding up to the two men.

"Good morning, gentlemen. I trust you are all doing well." Arthur's eyes swept the room, including Gene and Fred in his greeting. They responded accordingly. "I was downstairs when I heard Professor Barnstead's rich baritone, so I thought I'd come to say hello."

"I hate to leave a party, but I've got to go down to the studio. See you later," said Fred. He grabbed his toolbox and scooted past the others.

"Sam was just saying what a great time he had Saturday," said Ian.

Arthur turned from Ian to Sam. "I'm glad you had such a good time, Sam."

Sam made a boyish nod to one side. "The dinner, the company and the play were all terrific."

"Yes, and I'll bet the after party was great for you, too, Sam, eh?" Arthur was making *man talk* again. "That Martha is a hot little number in a miniskirt."

Sam ignored the remark and directed his eyes at Ian. "Found that film yet, Ian?"

"No, it's not in here. I guess they haven't released it yet to *Time Life*. Maybe it'll be out next year. I don't know." Ian exhaled and dropped the catalog onto Sam's desk. "You know, maybe Seth Walpole was right."

"What?" asked Sam. "What do you mean?"

Arthur said nothing, but glared at Ian.

"Last summer, we were out playing golf. Boy, could he smack the ball, real long off the tee. Didn't have a great short game, though. Anyway, he told me I should put together a course on World War II, focusing on the Holocaust. He said he'd taken an interest in it and a lot of information was coming out. He had a cousin in England, another academic, who told him the Brits were a couple of years away from declassifying a lot of World War II information. You know, he said the Brits had broken the German code real early and always knew what Hitler was planning. How about that?"

"Ah, that is so much nonsense," said Arthur. "Look at the pounding they took from the Luftwaffe. Do you think for a minute that Churchill would have let his cities, like Coventry, be destroyed if he knew the attack was coming? And what about the V2 rockets? Wouldn't he have built a defense weapon to stop the attacks? I think Dr. Walpole's cousin must be terribly misinformed, or off his rocker."

"Who knows," said Ian. "Just because they knew what was coming didn't mean they had the resources to defend against it. Churchill needed Roosevelt to bail him out."

"Roosevelt, ah yes, now there's a case of American aggression, plain and simple. He wanted to forge a new imperial power in the world," said Arthur, inching closer to Ian.

"Aggression? You want to talk about aggression, do you?" asked Ian. "What about trying to exterminate an entire race of people? That's a high level of aggression, if you ask me."

"You're talking about the so-called Holocaust, Ian? You know, there are many, many scholars who say it never happened; that it was just a product of Allied propaganda."

Before Ian could respond, Sam made an effort to cool down the escalating tension. "You know, guys, there are those who don't believe that we ever sent men to the moon. Some even joke that it all took place on a Hollywood back lot."

"Ian, don't take this personally," said Arthur, "but history can be manipulated. I believe Churchill said history was going to be very good to him because he was going to write it himself. Perhaps that is what the British are going to release as formerly classified. That would give it great credibility. You see, after a war, the history is usually written by the winners. That doesn't make it all true."

Ian spoke as his face reddened. "History is the accumulation of the facts by qualified experts and scholars. Auschwitz, Dachau, Gross-Rosen are not fabrications. They were liberated with thousands of survivors giving testimony to the atrocities carried out there. People were starved, medical experiments carried out on living patients, executions in gas chambers and bodies dumped into mass graves. Even Eisenhower and Patton saw these places in person. I know of no qualified scholars, as you claim, Vasile, who have denied the Holocaust. It is very dangerous to a society when its people fail to learn from history, and even worse when they deny it."

As Ian spoke, Sam felt as if he had been transported back in time. He heard the screams of people from the deepest regions of the camp. He saw the children he played with, even the ones who called him names, like the word that was new to him—collaborator. He smelled the odor of what he learned later was burning flesh. He saw his mother's face when a soldier came to fetch her for Mengele., and worst of all, he heard her sobbing at night. He felt the pain he shared with her, from the unanswered question—why was this happening?

Arthur slipped his hands into his pockets. "It is hard to separate truth from lies during wartime. Do you think the Allies were pure as the snow? Hasn't the world learned a lot from the Vietnam War about what American soldiers are capable of, herding villagers into a pit and shooting them all, old men, women and children?"

Ian's voice came back to Sam. "I'm glad you brought up the Vietnam War, because that refutes your remark about history being written by the winners. That war is still going on, so there is no declared winner yet. But we know about the My Lai massacre and it is part of the history of that war. It's an ugly part, but history, none the less. The truth always comes out eventually, only now it doesn't have to wait for decades. We see it on the six o'clock news and there's no denying it, Vasile."

Arthur gritted his teeth, as if holding something in his mouth. His eyes stared into a blank space. "I can see you're not in the mood for an objective discussion, Professor Barnstead. I'm sorry if I disturbed your morning. Well, I have to get ready for my next class. Good day, gentlemen." Arthur brought his feet together, as if he were about to click his heels but caught himself in the act. He spun around and marched out of the room.

Sam saw that Gene had buried his face in his paper work. He motioned with his finger to Ian to follow him out of the room and around a corner to a nearby restroom. Once inside, Sam checked to see that they were alone. "Ian, I'm going to share something with you, in strict confidence, please."

"Okay, sure, Sam. I can keep a secret."

Sam stood tall, bringing himself up to his full height, like an old bull elephant trying to impress a younger male. "Ian, I am a Holocaust survivor."

"What? Sam, I had no idea. Then, you understand what I was saying in there to Vasile, the creep. Why didn't you back me up? He really got defensive about the Germans. He usually blows off the whole discussion, or tries to change the subject, praising German technology. I must have touched a nerve. Boy, you'd think he was one of those Nazis, you know. Romanian, my foot. I think that guy's a German, probably an ex-soldier. I had him on the ropes, there, for a while. Sam, why didn't you let him have it? You were there. You saw it."

"I'm sorry, but I have my reasons. My name was Schmuel Milowitz. My father changed our name to Miller before he died. I was very young when it happened. My mother never told me the details of his death. She and I were sent to Auschwitz. I was among those liberated by the Allies, but my mother didn't make it."

"Oh, Sam, I'm so sorry."

"You used the term ugly history a minute ago. Yes, it can be very ugly. That's why I prefer not to talk about it." Sam swallowed hard.

"Geez, Sam, this sure is crazy. I'm having an argument over the existence of the Holocaust with this ass Vasile and there's you, a Holocaust survivor, standing right next to me. It's crazy, man. I don't know." Ian spun around like a dog chasing his tail.

Sam stepped closer to his friend. "Ian, I must repeat, do not ever tell anybody about this. Perhaps someday I can talk more freely, maybe even address one of your classes." He broke into a tight grin and then it was gone. "Really, Ian, I can't talk about it yet, but someday . . ."

The burly professor held his mouth open as he nodded. He looked at the floor for a second. "Sam, you're starting to scare me, what with this news about you being in the Holocaust and all this need for secrecy. It's starting to sound like something out of a spy novel, or something. I don't know. You're really serious."

"Yes, Ian, and somewhere along the line, I may need to ask you for a favor."

Ian's eyes opened wider.

"No, no, my friend, it's not like in The Godfather." Sam eased out a smile.

"Oh, oh, you had me worried there for a minute, Sam. But you're into something, aren't you?"

"Maybe, Ian; maybe not. But tell me, what else did Seth Walpole say to you about his interest in the Holocaust?"

"Nothing much, just that he'd taken an interest in it and was trying to learn more about it."

"Was he doing any formal research into it, Ian?"

"No, not that he mentioned," said Ian, tilting his head up, as if trying to look into his own head. "No, just that he was taking an interest, those were his words. He said I should put a course together, like I said, focusing on the Holocaust. Seth said most courses dealing with World War II were too general, lacking clear focus. This could be a high level course, for History majors only and he would help me find good source material. He would make sure Dean Turner approved it."

Sam took in Barnstead's words. He was struck by the fact that others took such a deep interest in that horrible experience. He had spent years trying to forget about it, but to no avail. It just wouldn't go away. Now, with his promise to Eli to help in his search, he was facing that hard fact head-on.

"I don't mean to be getting so melodramatic, Ian. Thanks. Let's wrap this up."

"Sam, look, I know you and Carol are good friends. I hope it's not about . . ." Ian held up both his hands, palms out. "None of my business, none of my business."

Sam patted Ian on the back as they made their exit and said farewell. He felt some assurance that he might have an ally if he needed one in his effort to help Eli Rosen.

Chapter Twenty

MONDAY, OCTOBER 21.

It was late Monday afternoon. The day went smoothly after the heated exchange between Arthur and Ian. Sam was back in his office after a meeting with the students who ran the college radio station. They had an executive cadre: a Station Manager, an Assistant Manager, a Music Director, a News Director, and a Sports Director. Fred sat in as the technical advisor.

When his phone rang, Sam grabbed a tissue first and spat a wad of gum into it, before answering. Sam had taken to chewing gum more often lately.

"Hello, Sam Miller here."

"Hello, Sam, it's Al Turner. Have you got a minute? Actually, can you come to my office? I'd like to chat with you, if you're free."

This was a rarity. He didn't often get a casual call from Al.

"Sure, no problem, Al. I'll be right there."

Sam stood up, grabbing the windbreaker he'd slung over a file cabinet. "Got to go see the big boss, fellas. Take care of the farm while I'm gone."

Fred looked up from the collection of metal things on his desk. "Dum, de dum dum," he uttered, mocking the theme from the old TV show Dragnet. "Watch out, Sam. He might try to drive you through a wall again."

"I doubt it. You saw him at the dinner. He was a real pussycat. That stuff was just in the heat of competition. There's nothing to worry about."

"Not until the next game," said Fred with a laugh.

Sam withheld comment and moved on his way, but a question repeated in his head: *What is this all about?* In a matter of minutes, he was uptown and found a parking spot behind the Administration Building. He left his car and entered the rear of the building, making his way toward the president's office, where Al usually stationed himself these days. It was an inner office, with Irene parked at her desk in the outer space like a guardian. *Too bad nobody was serving as guardian the night Seth was murdered.*

"Hi, Sam, go right in," said Irene, motioning Sam toward the open door to the inner office. Al sat in his chair, looking very businesslike with his sport coat on, his collar buttoned and his tie straight. Sam figured it was the way an acting college president should look. Al rose up without speaking as Sam entered and pointed to the door on the far wall that led to the conference room. Sam obeyed the non-verbal direction and followed Al inside.

"Take a seat, Sam." Al broke the silence, watched Sam ease himself into a chair at the table and closed the door after him. He chose a seat directly across from Sam.

Sam's thoughts raced back to those times in the camp when he was summoned by Mengele and Rauf. He didn't speak until spoken to, so now he decided to forego any meaningless pleasantries with Turner. Both men sat back in their chairs, eyeballing each other, waiting for the other one to blink.

Eventually, Sam leaned forward, resting his elbows on the table and folding his hands together, but he still didn't speak. He opened his eyes wider and tilted his head slightly, making a silent inquiry: *What's up?*

Turner remained back in his chair. Sam thought of a tennis analogy, another game he liked, but didn't play well because of his bad leg. Turner was deciding to return Sam's volley from the baseline, rather than charging the net. "I had an interesting visit from Chief Powers today, Sam, very interesting."

If Turner was expecting a scared reaction from Sam, he didn't get it. Sam saw Turner as a bully and wasn't expecting anything less, so he kept a stoic expression while Turner made verbal shoves.

"He said he knew that I had an argument with Walpole in the president's office just after our meeting about the major alumnus gift. He said he had reason to believe it was a heated argument and he wanted to know more about it."

Sam just nodded his head. His silence irritated Turner, whose voice grew louder. "Now, where would the Chief of Police get the idea that there was such an argument?"

Cal had promised not to mention him by name, but Sam figured that Al would recall seeing him in the hallway after the session with Seth.

"Who could have told Powers about such an argument, Sam? Walpole told Irene to excuse herself from the office while he spoke to me and everybody else left after the meeting." Turner stopped talking, inviting a reply from Sam.

He was done with the cat and mouse game. "I guess you figure it was me, Al."

"Yeah, I figure it was you. You were snooping around outside his office, doing some eavesdropping. I saw you when I left."

"I wasn't eavesdropping, Al, but if I was, you sure made it easy for me. Your voices were getting pretty loud. I'll bet people upstairs could hear you."

Turner's face showed a shadow of doubt, but he stayed on his course. "No, it wasn't anybody from upstairs who talked to Powers. It was you. Where the hell do you get off accusing me?" Turner slapped his hand on the table.

"Whoa, Al, take it easy. I didn't accuse you of anything. Did the Chief?"

Al glared at Sam. "No, of course not. Just because I had a . . . disagreement with Seth Walpole doesn't make me a murderer. I don't know what you think you heard, but you'd better be careful about running off at the mouth . . . to anybody."

"Look, Mr. Acting President, I didn't run off at the mouth. Chief Powers approached me. He's grilled me a couple of times. He's just doing his job. I didn't tell him about the argument the first time he spoke to me, but I decided that I shouldn't withhold that information. It's pertinent to his investigation, you know, the one about Walpole's murder."

Turner stood up. "So, you do think that I killed Walpole?"

"It doesn't matter what I think, and frankly, I don't care if you did it or not. What I care about is not getting my own ass in a sling because I withheld information. For all I know, Irene Preston could have done it. If Chief Powers talks to me, I've got to be straight with him. I thought I could be evasive with him at first, but I can see he's going to be persistent." Sam rose from his chair, sensing victory.

Turner shifted his head from one side to the other, as if searching for words. "You just better be careful, Miller. Don't forget, I can fire your ass in a heartbeat."

"Oh Al, how would that look? It would look like an accused man killing a witness, so to speak. I think that would only draw more attention to you."

"Just the same, I'll be watching you, Miller."

Sam let Turner have the last word, and walked out of the office. They only made Al look weaker. Sam smiled to himself. Game, set, and match to Miller.

Chapter Twenty-One

MONDAY EVENING, OCTOBER 21.

Daylight was long gone by the time Al got home. He waited for the garage door to open after pressing the remote control clipped to his car's sun visor, tapping his hand, palm down, on the steering wheel.

Entering the house, he smelled the aroma of sauce simmering on the stove and saw his wife, Elaine, standing over it. "Hi, hon," she said. "You're just in time to lend a hand. Would you please fill the pot with water for the pasta?"

Al rubbed his hands together, his head shifting from side-to-side. "Sure, dear, but let me go change first. I don't want to spill anything on these clothes."

Elaine shook her head. "Oh Al, it'll only take a minute and you're just going to handle water. While it's coming to a boil, you can go change."

"Damn it, Elaine, I'll do it when I'm back." He spun away, leaving his perturbed wife to the task.

When he returned, he saw that the water was boiling, but offered no apology for his abruptness. He pulled a glass and a bottle of single malt Scotch from the cupboard. The whiskey splashed into the thick-bottomed tumbler. Al took a quick drink. He liked it neat.

As he drank more, he saw Elaine glance at the opened bottle of Merlot on the kitchen counter and expected her to make a comment on his liquor choice. Without speaking, she topped off her wine glass with the red beverage. That was her way of commenting on the better match of liquor to dinner entrée.

He strode into the living room, parking himself in an easy chair, still grasping his Scotch. He had an important message for Elaine, but decided it should wait until she had finished preparing their dinner. She needed to understand fully the significance of his words.

The Scotch went down quickly while Elaine toiled in the kitchen, so he poured a second. His wife set the table in the breakfast area of the kitchen, without losing sight of the dinner's progress on the stove. Her wine glass remained full. Al returned to his seat and his thoughts.

Elaine served dinner, including a green salad, which Al declined. He brought his Scotch to the table, earning him another look of chagrin from his wife. They were a couple of bites into the meal when Al began.

"Hon," his voice was subdued from earlier, "I know we've spoken about this before, but I have to bring it up again."

Elaine looked up. "Yes, dear, I'm listening."

Al swallowed more Scotch. "It's now more important than ever that we say I was home with you the night Seth Walpole was murdered."

Elaine looked at him. "Yes, dear, I understand. We have gone over that before."

"No, you don't. Something happened that you don't know about."

"Well, okay, I'm listening. What could possibly have happened?"

Al took in a breath, trying to keep his tone calm. "I had a visit today from the Chief of Police. Somebody told him about my argument with Seth and he thinks I'm a suspect now."

"Oh my goodness, Al. That's ridiculous. You wouldn't hurt . . ."

"Don't interrupt, Elaine. He thinks I have a motive for killing Walpole. The fact is, as you know, his death has given me a career boost. I'm now the Acting President. Even if I don't get the permanent position, it's still a good ticket punch for me. It can help me get to a better job at a university someday. We can't jeopardize that chance."

Elaine looked at her husband, anxious to speak. He gave her the chance. "Al, why can't we just tell the truth, that you were with friends that night planning a club party?"

"Don't be ridiculous, Elaine. If I'm implicated in the running of the club, it would be like throwing fuel on the fire, adding to the chief's suspicion. You have to stick to the story that I was home with you all night. You can't waiver from that position. *I was home all night.* Our future is at stake."

A long breath escaped from Elaine's nose and she clutched her hands together on the table. "I guess I understand. But I feel uncomfortable having to lie."

"What are you talking about? You've . . ." He struggled to control his tone. "You've enjoyed the club as much as I have and you've been . . . excellent in keeping quiet about the whole thing. How comfortable will you be if I get arrested? You can do this. I know you can. Be my strong girl, okay? Besides, there'll be another party soon. That should take your mind off this murder affair, eh?"

Elaine nodded, drank from her wine and reached across the table to touch her husband's hand. He felt assured his wife would obey, and that would include covering for him again tonight, when he'd go out again.

Chapter Twenty-Two

MONDAY, LATE EVENING, OCTOBER 21.

The bedroom clock radio said 11:45 p.m. while the phone rang and rang. Sam couldn't believe his eyes. Who'd be calling at this hour? He usually hit the sack around ten and had been in a deep sleep before this interruption. Martha, perhaps? He wouldn't put it past her. She was the most sexually aggressive woman he'd ever known. Maybe she was looking for a treat.

As he grabbed the bedside phone, he heard a voice on the other end before he could pull it to his ear. "Sam! Sam! Sorry if I woke you, but you won't believe what's happened. This world is really going crazy. I don't know. Are you there, Sam?"

Ian Barnstead's voice disproved Sam's first suspicion. His feeling of relief was quickly replaced with puzzlement. What could be so important ... no, crazy was the word ... to warrant this late call?

"Ian, is that you? What the hell are you talking about? I was asleep, for Christ's sake. What's going on?"

"I don't want to talk about it on the phone, Sam. I'm coming over to your place right now. I'll be there in a few minutes. Turn on channel nine."

The phone went dead after the click when Ian hung up, and in an instant, the silence was replaced by a dial tone. Sam returned the handset to the cradle on his nightstand and fell back onto his pillow, staring up at the ceiling. He wiped a hand over his face, hoping to feel more alert. It didn't help much. *What the hell is Ian up to?*

Sam labored to pull his body into a sitting position on the edge of the bed, resting his hands on his knees. A couple deep breaths later, he reached for the lamp beside him and switched it on. The brightness made him blink. He pushed himself to his feet and slid them along the floor to the bathroom. After some quick relief and a face wash, he changed into a pair of jeans and a sweatshirt. No need to get spiffy for Ian.

A trip into the kitchen was Sam's next move, where he had a half pot of coffee left over from the morning. He poured enough water into his Mr. Coffee and spooned some grounds into a filter to freshen it up. There'd be enough for Ian, too.

With a semi-fresh cup, complete with milk and sugar, Sam sipped the hot liquid, still working his way from dreamland to full consciousness. His sips got bigger. What did Ian say about a channel? *Turn on channel nine.*

He made his way into the tiny living room and flipped on the old Westinghouse TV. Before it could warm up and reveal an image, the doorbell rang twice. Never letting go of his coffee, Sam opened the door and was nearly trampled when Ian rushed past him. "Where's your TV, Sam? Did you put on nine?"

"It's right over there," said Sam, directing him to it. Ian sat down on the sofa facing the Westinghouse. Sam parked himself beside the big man and they stared at a man with an apron on, holding a package of toilet paper in what looked like a supermarket aisle. "That's it, Ian? You woke me to watch a commercial with some guy squeezing toilet paper? Weird hobby."

"No, no, Sam. It's the news. It'll come back on in a minute. There's been another murder, this time in Manchester."

"You want some coffee, Ian?"

"No . . . no, thank you."

"Ian, what's so special about this murder? Why are you so upset about it?" Sam swallowed more coffee.

"Geez, Sam. It's Dr. Ike Wirth. Don't you know who that is?"

Sam shook his head and drank more of his coffee.

"Brandeis Junior College in Manchester. Dr. Wirth is . . . was the president of the college. Don't you see the significance? Another college president has been murdered in New Hampshire, within a couple of weeks of each other."

The image on the TV changed as the news broadcast came back on. The reporter was the same fellow Sam noticed at the press conference in the lobby of the Administration building. Once again, he was impeccably groomed and smooth in his delivery. As the reporter talked, Ian broke in.

"Aw, they're saying the same stuff over and over," said Ian.

"What same stuff?"

Ian went on to provide the details faster than the TV newsman. "He was shot earlier tonight while in his home, just after dark. He was sitting in a chair watching TV when, boom, a shot came through a window and got him. He never knew what hit him. A neighbor called the police after hearing the shot and the sound of the window shattering. His house is near a wooded area, and they think the shooter got away through the forest. There's a road on the other side of the wooded lot, and they figure a car could've been parked there. He might've driven himself or he might have had an accomplice. I don't know. Geez, this is crazy."

Sam stood up, wrapping two hands around his coffee cup. He inched closer to the TV. "This has to be a coincidence, right, Ian? Two college presidents murdered within weeks and in the same state? This guy was shot by somebody outside his house. The methods aren't even close to the same, you know, this and Seth's murder." He held out a hand, palm up.

"Sam, come on, coincidence? Really?" Ian rubbed his hands together rapidly. His shoulders shook.

"You're really spooked by this. There's more to it, isn't there?"

Ian got up and paced the floor in front of Sam, like Ralph Kramden in front of his wife Alice. "Do you remember what I told you about Seth and me playing golf? When he told me I should work up a course on the Holocaust? Remember that?"

Sam nodded.

"He said he wouldn't go into detail at that time, but he mentioned Ike Wirth as a friend and somebody who taught him things he didn't know before about that history. They gave a quick bio of Dr. Wirth on the news and said he was a Holocaust survivor, a freaking Holocaust survivor, Sam."

A fear he hadn't felt since he was a boy returned to him, chilling his bones. Could this man, Dr. Wirth, have been targeted because he was a Holocaust survivor? Was that why Ian was trembling? Was he afraid for Sam?

"Ian, you think that's a connection? That the murders aren't coincidence at all? You think it has to do with Holocaust survivors and maybe Seth Walpole because he was close to one?"

Ian didn't respond, but looked hard and cold at Sam. His face gave Sam his answer. I think we should tell Chief Powers about this. He should know."

"Absolutely not, Ian. We can't tell anyone just yet. Besides, we could be dead wrong about this idea. I happen to know Chief Powers has other information. There could be a totally different reason why Seth was murdered. It has nothing to do with the Holocaust."

Ian looked stunned. "Really? What is it, Sam?"

"I'm sorry, but I can't share that with you yet."

Ian spun around, flapping his arms against his sides. "Oh, shit, Sam, there you go with more secrets. This whole thing is crazy. I don't know."

"Take it easy, Ian. I have my reasons. You have to trust me. Besides, the less you know, the better for you. Think about it. If there is some sort of conspiracy going on here, you don't want to get caught up in it. I don't want that either."

Ian clenched his hands together in one big fist in front of himself. He tapped his fist against his mouth. "I guess you have a point. Okay. I'll keep quiet, but I have to tell the wife why it was so important that I came over here and not just talk to you on the phone."

"Just tell her it was a misunderstanding and you overreacted. Okay?"

"Yeah, I overreacted. She says I do that a lot anyway."

"Go home and get some sleep."

"Okay, I'll try." Ian made his way out, and Sam heard him start his car in the parking lot and drive away.

Sam put his coffee cup in the kitchen and headed for the bedroom. *A late night phone call, a cup of coffee near midnight and news of another murder, one that might involve Holocaust survivors. Sleep?*

Chapter Twenty-Three

TUESDAY, MID-MORNING, OCTOBER 22.

Only the sound of his own movements echoed through the hallway on the second floor of the Administration Building. He heard none of the usual background laughter among coworkers, as was often the case. Sam found his way to Carol's office. It was as if something had stunned everyone in the place, much like in the days immediately following Seth Walpole's death.

Sam approached the open door and rapped on the frame as he walked into Carol's office. She turned away from her desk and faced the sound. Her coworker, Doris, did the same. "Oh, good morning, Sam." Carol jumped from her chair to greet him, stopping short of an all-out embrace. "Are those invoices?" She pointed to the clutch of papers in his hand. "Here, I'll take them." She placed them on her desk, very businesslike.

After releasing his grip on the papers, Sam scanned Carol from top to toe, enjoying the visual trip. She wore tight-fitting jeans, flared at the leg and without hip pockets. A white turtleneck sweater clung to her torso. White tennis shoes over white socks completed the outfit. All of it met with Sam's approval.

"Ah, hum, good morning, Sam." Doris injected a greeting while rising from her chair. She knew the drill. "I've got to go see . . . Irene, for a minute. See ya later."

Carol and Sam remained silent until Doris was gone.

"You know, sometimes I think she expects us to be screwing here on my desk when she comes back. She can be a real busybody." Carol shook her head.

"She won't ever find that happening . . . here," smirked Sam. "This building is awfully quiet today."

"You saw the news, didn't you, Sam?"

"Yes, of course. Now Brandeis Junior has a mystery to solve, an unbelievable mystery." He decided not to tell Carol exactly how he learned of the murder in Manchester.

Carol wrung her hands together and nodded from side to side, as if she were searching for words, but couldn't find any. Her feet remained firmly in place in front of Sam. She appeared on the verge of tears.

"Did you know Dr. Wirth, Carol? You seem very upset. Why don't you sit down?" He took a step forward, meaning to help her to her chair, but she moved toward him, leaning her hands and her head against Sam. He engulfed her in his arms.

"This is so strange. How could this happen? How could two college presidents be murdered within weeks of each other, and so close to one another?"

Sam repeated his question. "Did you know him?"

"No, I didn't know him, just of him." She held herself against Sam as she spoke. His arms held his embrace until he released one and brushed the back of her head. The embrace thrilled him, warmed him and he closed his eyes, still stroking her head. He wished this moment could last forever, but in an instant, it was over, as Carol pulled away.

"Sam, Arthur was away again last night. He went to Massachusetts again, you know, for his project. It scares me there's a maniac running around out there and Arthur isn't home. I'm worried about him. What kind of psycho is out there? Is he just after college presidents, or could professors be on his list, too? Oh, Sam, it's just awful." She turned and sank back into her desk chair.

"Whoa. Don't jump too far ahead on this thing. We don't know that there is any connection at all to Seth's murder, or that it's somebody's twisted act against educators. It looks like it's totally separate from Seth's murder. The methods are completely different. It could be a disgruntled student or employee, or somebody Wirth knew before. Forget it. Let the Manchester and State Police worry about it. It's their problem."

"You think so, Sam? Do you really think they're unrelated?"

Carol sat with her hands on her desk, looking straight ahead. Sam took a position behind her chair and placed his hands on her shoulders. "Yes, I do. There's nothing we know yet to suggest otherwise. Let the police do the worry-ing. Just relax."

His hands began kneading her shoulders in a gentle, slow motion. His fingers pressed against the top of her shoulders while his thumbs began to dig against her back. After a moment, he released his grip and slid his hands down her back near her spine, repeating the motion. He noticed Carol tilt her head back in a positive response to his touch. His lips curved into an unconscious smile and he repeated the motion.

"Oh, Sam," she whimpered. "That feels so good."

He continued caressing her and his thoughts raced for-ward in a daydream.

"I wish Arthur could be so thoughtful."

The daydream crashed and Sam ceased the massage. "What? Oh, you said he was away again, didn't you?"

"Yes. He's still working on that project. It seems like it's become more important to him than anything else, even me. And he's so secretive about it. I fear I'm losing him, Sam."

Her words dug deep, and Sam crashed back to reality. She still loved her husband. Her affection for Sam was real, but more friendship than romance. How could he change that, if it was possible? *She may be married to a monster. When can I tell her?*

"Don't be worried about Arthur's safety, Carol. He sur-vived World War II Europe. He can take care of himself. It's you I'm worried about."

"That's so sweet of you. You're such a good friend."

There she goes again. Her statement of friendship was confirmation of her continuing love for Arthur. His chest tightened.

Carol spun out of her chair and rose to face Sam. She pressed close to him, raising one hand to caress his face while planting a kiss on his cheek. "You know, Sam, a lot of people around here—Doris I'm sure—think we're having an affair. What a bunch of old twits." She pressed against him again, repeating the caress and gentle kiss.

Sam struggled to keep his arms by his side. The feel of her body against him was warm and exciting. He knew it was time to leave, but not before he returned her kiss with one on her forehead.

"It's a good thing Doris didn't see this," he said, as he reluctantly withdrew his arms and turned away. Carol smiled and watched him leave.

In a moment he was out of the building. But he didn't go directly back to his office. He drove the loop that Chief Powers had taken with him, questions racing through his mind all the time he was driving.

Chapter Twenty-Four

TUESDAY, MID-MORNING, OCTOBER 22. NORWOOD, MASSACHUSETTS.

Arthur stood at a desk in the second story bedroom that served as an office. It had file cabinets against the walls, each with locking devices running through the drawer handles.

Arthur took special pleasure in visiting Otto Leinhardt. It reminded him of his youth and the days they worked together at the camp. And Otto was a good asset to have in communicating with their colleagues in South America. He could call them directly, a task that would be too dangerous for Arthur to do from home. He didn't want to risk having Carol overhear such a conversation.

Otto settled into the work with him. "Otto, were you able to call Chile for me and ask them to look into that issue that I wrote to you about? I felt it would be safer for me to ask you about it in a letter, rather than call on the phone."

"Why, yes, I did. I asked them about the Jewish woman, the one with a boy, who worked with you and the doctor. I told them you wanted to know if the boy survived his time at the camp, and if so, where did he and his mother go after the camp was disbanded. They said they'd check into it. Their names might show up in records if they were transferred elsewhere before the end of the war. They'll get the information and airmail it to you right away. You should be getting a letter soon."

"To me? You gave them my address? Otto, you should have had them send it here."

"I'm sorry, but I didn't see the harm. Perhaps you are right. I should have had them send it to me."

Arthur grimaced and curled his hands into fists, as if he wanted to hit his friend. He quickly calmed down and shook his head. "I shouldn't have snapped at you. That was

silly of me. If my wife sees the letter, I'll just explain that we
have people on the project in South America."

"What if she opens it?"

"She's a good wife. She never opens mail addressed to
me. It will be fine." Arthur walked over to his friend and
placed a reassuring hand on his shoulder. "It's a great trag-
edy that the war didn't take us where we should have gone,"
said Arthur. "Our world would have been a great one."

Otto stared into Arthur's eyes as if looking into the
past. "Yes, my old friend, I recall those days very well. Ah,
we had a good setup, thanks to the doctor, didn't we?"

Arthur stiffened his posture.

"Oh, come on Arthur, you took some pleasure, too,
with that Jewish woman, the one you talked about in the
letter, didn't you?"

"There were times, I admit, but only because I am a
man and must occasionally satisfy manly needs. Enjoy
what they have to give and move on with one's work."

Otto smirked. "Oh yes. That woman had a lot to give,
as I recall. Too bad she had that boy at her heels all the
time, the feeble one with the bad leg."

"Yes," said Arthur. "I took x-rays of him to assess his
potential. There wasn't much, since he'd suffered a broken
femur sometime earlier. It didn't heal well, so he didn't offer much in the way of working ability. He was useless and
should have been gassed."

"His mother was a smart woman, Arthur. She knew
what power she had over the doctor. As long as we kept her
boy alive and safe, she helped us in many ways, not just in
bed."

"Do you remember their names, Otto?"

"Yes, I believe she was called Sadie. But, no, I can't
recall his name."

Arthur rolled his eyes, as if searching for the name in
the sky. The name would come to him.

"This project is just a start at rebuilding our world. It
will take time, and we may be too old to see it all the way
through, but we will be remembered among those who gave
it life," said Arthur.

He filled his briefcase with the documents from his
colleague. They'd worked late into the night, sorting and
organizing documents and photographs Otto prepared for

him. His briefcase merely held the overflow. The bulk of the paperwork rested in four cardboard file boxes, each marked with the words *Project Phoenix* followed by a number: R0001, R0002, R0003 and R0004. The boxes bulged at their sides, thus the need for slipping some into Arthur's case.

"This is quite a load you have given me, Otto. I will have to start another box when I get back home to New Hampshire. Too bad you don't have any more empty ones."

The short but stocky Otto piled the boxes onto a hand truck, ready to move them to Arthur's car. "Yes, our colleagues have collected quite a lot for us. The past few months have seen several shipments from many places. It makes me feel good to know that we are enlarging our circle of influence. The project is growing in scope. That is good."

Otto lived in a modern townhouse, part of a complex in Norwood, near the Westwood line, about fifteen miles southwest of Boston. The complex occupied several acres, with six clusters of four attached townhouses. A reserved parking area sat close to each unit for residents with a large visitor's section further away from the building, for guests like Arthur. With such a parking arrangement, visitors could come and go and rarely be noticed. That was fine for Arthur and Otto.

"Your associate did a fine job last night, Otto. He is a most capable young man. I may have further work for him in New Hampshire."

Otto smiled at Arthur as he loaded the last box onto the two-wheeled hand truck.

"I must get going now. My lovely wife will be worried if I'm not back soon. Besides, I have an afternoon class. I hope someday you will meet her, Otto. She is a sturdy woman and very bright. She is serving me well, being the dutiful spouse, not nagging into my affairs. I think I will have to perform my husbandly duty on her tonight, eh? I've got to keep her reasonably satisfied. You get my drift, of course."

Otto smiled again. "I envy you. My wife was weak, even if she was physically well done. She couldn't be counted on. Too bad she passed on, but my work requires much of my time, and I think it is safer to live alone. I don't want another wife. There is no chance of someone prying into my affairs. You are different from me in that way."

Arthur snapped his briefcase shut, grasping the handle as he lifted it. Otto moved his stack of boxes out of the room and toward the stairway, where they looked down and made a decision.

"We are not young men anymore. I think we'll have to carry the boxes down one at a time and reload them onto this hand truck down there."

"I was looking forward to watching you perform that task, Dr. Leinhardt, but I agree with you."

They went about their chore and soon had all of the boxes in Arthur's big car, all of them fitting into the trunk. The rear end dropped noticeably.

"Have a safe drive, Arthur. I'll talk to you again, soon."

"Yes, indeed. Our project is moving along nicely, but we have much more to do."

Arthur saw Otto begin to raise his right hand in an old salute, but his frown convinced Otto to refrain. He simply waved with his left hand, his arm at waist height. Arthur smiled.

Chapter Twenty-Five

TUESDAY, EARLY AFTERNOON, OCTOBER 22. HEN-
NIKER, NEW HAMPSHIRE.

After driving around Henniker, trying to sort things out
in his mind, Sam decided to go home to his apartment and
make a quick lunch for himself. There were leftovers in the
fridge, which he nibbled while preparing a can of soup in a
small pot on the stove. Chicken noodle would do.

What was going on in this tiny town? There had probably never been a college president murdered in the state's
entire history. Now there were two in a matter of weeks.
They couldn't possibly be connected, but the coincidence
was just too much to believe.

Sam knew he had to focus on his mission to help Eli
Rosen find a Nazi war criminal, but it was impossible to
extract his mind from the murder cases. If his suspicions
were true, Al could be a prime suspect because of his argument with Seth, which Sam had witnessed. Although he
had no direct connection to the murder of the man in Manchester, it didn't feel that way.

He finished lunch and decided to run an errand at the
little department store in town. A nose-in parking space
was open right in front of the store, and Sam jumped at
the chance to grab it. As he opened his door and slid out,
he saw Chief Powers' police car parked a few yards away
in front of The Nook. It wouldn't hurt to check in with the
Chief.

When he got closer to the little restaurant, Sam saw
Cal's tall frame emerge. As the chief made a casual look to
his left, Sam waved to him. "Hi, Cal."

Cal strode out to the sidewalk and stood tall, hands on
hips. "Hi, Sam." It was a short greeting, but Sam expected

more. Perhaps Cal wanted Sam to take the conversational lead. He usually did.

The two men met on the empty sidewalk. "Can we talk for a minute, Cal?" The Chief pointed to his car and Sam understood. He climbed in on the passenger side while the chief slid into the driver's seat.

"What's up?"

"What's up? Is that all you've got to say, considering what happened in Manchester?"

"Well, you're the one who said you'd like to talk, so I'm ready to listen."

"Oh, yeah, I get it. You can't talk about this new case. I get it."

Cal took the steering wheel in his hands and slid them up and down the circle. "Actually, I can talk about that all you want, since it's not my investigation. If I hear anything, I'll share it with the Manchester Police, but so far I haven't heard anything. Is that about to change? Is that why you're here?"

Sam shook his head and looked down, rubbing his hands in front of himself. "No, no, Cal, I hope I haven't given you the wrong idea." *Boy, this has gotten off to a bad start.* "I just think that this second murder of a college president is really weird, you know?"

"I agree with you there. It certainly is. What are the odds of something like that happening? You know, I don't think a Hollywood writer could have thought it up. But, like I said, it's not my case. Good luck to the Manchester PD with that one."

Sam looked straight ahead. He was afraid his expression would give his real feelings away, the feeling that he didn't buy Cal's indifference one bit. *He is one cagey guy, Cal Powers. Cagey Cal, that's what we should call him.*

"I actually wanted to tell you that I had an incident with Al Turner."

Cal's head snapped up a bit, then he relaxed and turned toward Sam. "What kind of an incident?"

"He called me into his office and took me into the conference room, just the two of us. He told me about you talking to him. He thinks I've made him into a suspect because of my talk with you. He was pretty angry."

"I never mentioned your name, Sam. I told you I wouldn't."

"Oh, I believe you. I'm not surprised Turner would draw that conclusion. He's a big bully. I learned that at the basketball game. But I'm not afraid of him." Sam paused and took a breath. "I've dealt with worse than him, much worse."

"I think you're right about Turner being a bully and I'm sure you can handle yourself, but if he ever does something stupid, like getting physical, you tell me about it, okay?"

"Oh don't worry about that. Like I said . . ."

"I mean it, Sam. This isn't a sixth grade school yard. I won't say any more other than you've got to tell me if he tries anything. Tell that to your friend, Martha, too. Okay?"

Sam heard the authority in Cal's voice. It went beyond concern. Perhaps he really did suspect Al Turner.

"I read you loud and clear. Anyway, Turner just huffed and puffed a bit, you know. He sort of implied he might fire me, but I think he knows it would only look bad for him."

Sam looked down and both men were quiet.

"What is it, Sam? You look far away. Is there something else on your mind I should know about?"

Sam took a deep breath, as if he were about to start a long speech. "No, no, that's all. I just had to get that thing with Al Turner off my chest. I hope you find Seth's killer soon, real soon."

"Me too. You know, in a crazy way, maybe the Manchester killing will help the Henniker townsfolk to relax a little. They've all been on edge. Maybe the killer isn't from around here."

"So you do think that there may be a connection? You said the Manchester thing wasn't your case."

Cal started up his car, letting Sam know their talk was over. As Sam eased onto the pavement, Cal looked him in the eye. "It isn't, Sam. It isn't." The Chief had a curious smile on his face.

Chapter Twenty-Six

TUESDAY, LATE AFTERNOON, OCTOBER 22.

Seated at her desk, Carol startled when she heard her name. She turned toward the office entrance and smiled, surprised and relieved to see Arthur strolling in. She rose, eager to greet her husband.

"Oh, Arthur, I'm so glad you're home. I was worried about you."

"Worried about me? Why on earth were you worried? I was just in Massachusetts working on the project." He stood in front of her and they stared into each other's eyes for a moment before she threw her arms around his neck and kissed his cheek. Arthur hugged her, causing her to stretch up onto her toes. He eased his grip, and she slid down onto her feet.

"Haven't you heard about what happened?"

Arthur held his hands on Carol's sides. "You mean the murder in Manchester? Yes, of course I heard about it. I haven't given it much thought. I got back in town in time to make my afternoon lab and have been busy."

Carol rested her hands against his chest, maintaining the mutual contact. "Don't you think it's creepy, another college president being murdered so close by?"

"Like I said, my dear, I haven't had time to concern myself with it. I suppose it is a terrible coincidence. I'm sure the Manchester Police will take care of it."

Carol was puzzled by Arthur's ambivalence about the killing, but said nothing further. She turned her head to one side and nuzzled against him. She felt warmed as he wrapped his arms around her, a feeling she hadn't received from her husband in a long while.

"You know, my dear, I've worked up a healthy appetite. I got back before class in time to go to the house and unload a few boxes of files from my project, then I had my lab. I'm starving. What do you say we go out to dinner as soon as you finish work?"

Carol looked up at him, smiling, still holding her hands against him. "That sounds wonderful, Arthur. I've only got about twenty minutes left and I'll be right home."

Arthur released her. "Excellent. I'll see you then." He kissed her on the lips—a quick, goodbye kiss, and he was gone.

She gently touched her fingertips to her mouth. She wished he kissed her with more passion, but she knew Arthur wasn't much for public displays of affection. She felt grateful for the affection he gave her.

"I sure wish I got as much male attention today as you have."

Carol snapped out of her momentary trance at the sound of Doris's voice from across the room. She had totally forgotten about her coworker. "Huh? What did you say, Doris?"

"Well, first Sam and now Arthur. You're getting your share today."

Carol twisted her face without speaking, pushing her palm through the air as if waving Doris off. She returned to her seat and pulled in close to the desk. She couldn't recall the last time Arthur took her to dinner, just the two of them. A smile crept across her face.

Carol approved of Arthur's choice for dinner. The Wurst Haus on Main Street was the only German restaurant in Concord. They hadn't been there in over a year. The interior was decorated in Bavarian style, with exposed wooden beams and stucco walls. She could see from his expression Arthur was happy, too. He eyed the young waitresses in their snug fitting cotton lederhosen, adorned with cream-colored embroidery. They wore button-down white blouses and black leather shoes with buckle closures. She took Arthur's arm as they were led to their table for two.

They ordered a bottle of Liebfraumilch, an inexpensive but tasty white wine. While waiting for it, they peered over the menu and began to chat. "You seem to really like this place, Arthur. Perhaps we should come here more often."

Her husband smiled and looked around. "Yes, my dear, I always feel good in a European atmosphere. You know, we had relatives in Germany and often went there to visit, so I feel very much at home here."

"I don't remember you ever mentioning relatives in Germany."

"Oh well, I'm sure I must have said something about it, but that doesn't matter. Let's just enjoy the evening."

Carol reached across the table to touch Arthur's hand. "You seem to be in a happy mood, dear. Is it because of the project?"

"Yes, the project is coming along nicely. In fact, we have identified a number of people who might be able to make valuable contributions, so that is a big step forward."

"What kind of contributions, dear? You've always been so quiet about it, but now I'm really getting interested."

Arthur took a large gulp of wine and looked around before speaking. "It is getting exciting, my love, so I'll tell you this, but you must keep it in strict confidence." Carol nodded. "The project involves building a new training center. It is a small, but highly successful chemical company. The training center will include the most modern labs and equipment, with overnight facilities for the people who come there. I have been involved in designing the labs and searching for other potential contributors." Arthur drank more wine.

"That does sound interesting. Where is this training center located?"

"The company hasn't decided for certain, but they are looking at land in northern New Hampshire. Isn't that wonderful? "

"Arthur, are you suggesting you'd go to work there and we'd leave Henniker?"

"No, no, dear, not at all. But a facility less than two hours away could mean long-term opportunities for me as a consultant. That would be quite good, don't you think? And I wouldn't have to deal with the Boston traffic."

Carol looked into her wine glass. "Yes, I guess that would be good." *It would be good for him,* she thought, *but it might also mean more nights alone for me while Arthur goes off to the place with overnight facilities.*

"Enough about me and the project," said Arthur. "What about you?" His smile disappeared after another mouthful of wine. "Have you seen Sam Miller lately?"

"Yes, as a matter of fact, he came by my office today."

"Good. I'm glad you two are friends. What did you kids talk about?"

"The murder in Manchester, of course. It has everybody stunned."

"Oh that. Yes, well, I hope you don't dwell on it, my dear. Think about the good things going on in our lives. You two must surely discuss other things, too."

Carol paused before answering. "Oh, we usually just make small talk."

"Does he ever talk about where he's from?"

"No, he never has and I haven't asked. Isn't that funny? It's usually the first thing people talk about."

"So, you didn't know he's also from Europe?"

"Why no, I didn't. Like I said, it never came up. What part of Europe?"

"I think it was Poland. He was very young when he came to the United States, which is why he has an accent that is barely noticeable. Perhaps, you should ask him about it."

"But if he doesn't talk about it, there may be a good reason. I don't think I should pry."

"On the other hand," said Arthur, "it might be helpful for him to open up about his childhood with someone he trusts, like you. You could be doing him a big favor."

Carol looked into her husband's eyes, as if trying to see into his brain. "I guess that's one way of looking at it. Perhaps you're right."

The couple enjoyed their dinner, but skipped dessert, as Carol was getting tired. She gazed around the restaurant as they made their way out. She had told Sam that Arthur was drifting away from her. For whatever reason, tonight he was back. She savored that feeling.

Arthur took his wife home and performed what he had called his *duty*. He hoped occasional lovemaking would keep her happy, but it was not uppermost in his mind. Other issues were more pressing and deserved his attention. The project was too important.

With Carol in bed, Arthur decided to stay up for a while. His day was not done. He entered his den and closed the door behind him. Seated in his comfortable old chair, he reached into a side drawer and lifted a small, metal box. Placing it on the desk, he slid a key from the center drawer into the front slot, unlocking the box, and grasped a thick diary: the box's only contents. He opened the diary, laying it down on the desk, and carefully flipped through the pages. The paper was old and some of the ink was faded, but he was able to find the passage that he was looking for and read a few pages. After a while, he put the diary back in its box, which he locked and returned to the side drawer. He smiled at the information he found. The woman was indeed named Sadie. The boy was Schmuel.

Chapter Twenty-Seven

WEDNESDAY, LATE MORNING, OCTOBER 23.

Sam grabbed his office phone quickly when it rang. He had left a hand-written note in a sealed envelope on Ian Barnstead's desk, while Ian was in class. By eleven, his class would be over, and Sam hoped he'd go directly back to his office. He grew anxious awaiting the return call.

"Hello, Sam Miller."

"Hi, Sam. I got your note. What gives?"

"Let's talk in private someplace. My guys are out right now, but will be back soon. Let's drive over to the old athletic field and park off the road. The trees will shield our cars from view and we can talk."

"Sure, Sam. When?"

"Right now is good. See you in five minutes."

"Got you. Five minutes."

The former athletic field was located just east of town along the old main road. It wasn't used anymore, although the college still kept the grass cut. A typical old stone wall, about three feet high, bordered the field along the road, and a few trees and bushes blocked the view along the wall.

Sam arrived first, pulled his car onto the field and slid in next to the first group of trees. He got out of his car and paced the ground. He hoped Ian could find some free time today to help him pursue an idea. Within a minute, Ian drove up and parked his vehicle next to Sam's. He eased his bulk from the car and walked toward Sam, who was hustling his way over to Ian.

"What is it Sam? It must be important if you think we need to meet like this."

Sam had his hands thrust down into his jacket pockets as he talked. "I saw Carol Vasile yesterday and she said something that's been bothering me. She said Arthur was away overnight when Dr. Wirth was shot. She said she was worried because these two murders involving college presidents were just too coincidental and she brought up a point I hadn't considered. She said this maniac could also be looking at other faculty members as well as administrators. What if Arthur were a target? He's a department chair, after all. She felt afraid while he was away."

Ian scuffed his foot against the ground. "That sounds like a stretch. I don't know. But, hell, I'm the History department chair. If she's right, I could be in trouble, too. What do you think we should do?"

"I also talked with Chief Powers about it. He kind of stonewalled me. He said it was not his case and the Manchester Police would have to take care of it."

"I thought you didn't want to talk to him."

"I had something else to talk to Cal about. The Manchester case came up, but we didn't talk much about it. Like I said, he was stonewalling it anyway."

"So he doesn't think there's a connection," said Ian.

"Well, he said that, but I don't buy it. I think he's just not ready to let us know if there is a connection or not. It was something about the way he talked. He strikes me as a very thorough cop, and he's not going to just turn his back on Manchester. I think there has to be a connection of some sort, but we're going to have to find out for ourselves."

Ian crossed his arms in front of himself and grabbed at his chin, pondering the situation. "Well, you've sure done a turn-around. I think there has to be a connection, although I think Carol's idea is from left field. I repeat my question. What should we do?"

"Do you know anybody at Brandeis Junior College who we can talk to?"

Ian nodded. "Yeah, sure, John Grossman, the head of the History department. We've met on a few occasions: symposia, conferences, things like that. Of course, you realize that the campus is probably closed today."

"I know, but it's too soon for the services so maybe you can reach him. Ian, what did you do the day you heard about Seth?"

Ian shrugged. "I was shocked like everybody, but I couldn't just stay home. I went into my office for a while to catch up on some . . . hey, there you go! I wouldn't be a bit surprised if John is in his office, even though classes are canceled. I'll give him a call."

"Great. See if he has time for us to pay him a visit. We've got to talk to him right away. When are you free?"

"I've got a two o'clock and then I'm supposed to have office hours until five."

Sam made a face. "How about you cancel your office hours, assuming we get in to see Grossman?"

"Okay, I can do that. What are you thinking?"

"I've got a hunch. You said Seth was interested in the Holocaust and wanted you to develop a course on it."

"That's right," said Ian.

"You also said that the news report said that Dr. Wirth was a Holocaust survivor and that he and Seth were friends."

"That's right, but you're still a long way off from a reason to kill them both, and remember that the methods were totally different."

"I know, but that's why we have to talk to somebody close to Dr. Wirth. Maybe he can shed some light on this thing. There's got to be a lot more to this than we know so far. This is a big puzzle, and we've got to start finding the pieces."

Later in his office, Sam got the call he was hoping for from Ian. Grossman would meet them in his office at three o'clock. He said he'd notify campus security about the visitors so they'd have no trouble getting onto the college grounds. Ian would pick Sam up at the library and they'd take Route 114 down to Manchester.

Sam's calendar was clear for the afternoon, and he told Bob Hill he needed to leave work at two o'clock. He slipped into his jacket and went to the parking lot beside the library so Ian wouldn't have to get out of his car. He only had to wait a couple of minutes before he saw the yellow Pontiac rumble into view. It was a large, four-door sedan, fitting for the size of its owner. When the car stopped, Sam opened the passenger door and jumped in.

"This is starting to feel a little spooky, Sam," said Ian. "What are we—amateur sleuths, or educators? I don't know. It's exciting and scary at the same time."

They sped off out of the parking lot and swung over to Route 114, an old two-lane blacktop that wound southeast through the small towns of Weare and the larger Goffstown. Traffic wouldn't be an issue for them, unless they got behind a large truck with a full load. The route was marked by many open fields, tall trees and expansive stone walls, similar to the type found throughout rural New Hampshire. No mortar was used in constructing these walls, made of stones dug when the land was originally cleared for farming. Some sections were marked by stones that had fallen out of place over many years. Now and then, rusted-out farm equipment could be seen among the trees.

"I think it's very significant that Dr. Wirth was a Holocaust survivor. We need to find out more about that. I know it may seem inappropriate under the circumstances, but I hope we can also get to meet his wife. I don't mean today, but perhaps soon."

Ian shook his head, his two big hands clutching the steering wheel in the "ten and two o'clock" positions. He leaned slightly forward in the driver's seat, as if trying to push his car along. "Based on what you told me before, about being a Holocaust survivor yourself, I can understand your position. If there is a connection between these murders, the Holocaust seems to be a common denominator. But I never got an explanation from Seth about why he was so interested in me developing a course about it. I mean, he certainly wasn't Jewish. He came from old Yankee stock. Maybe he just found it intriguing, what with his friendship with Wirth. I don't know."

"I'll tell you this. If we see a possible connection that way, it can't be lost on the cops, certainly not the State Police, and not Chief Powers."

"Then why don't you want to talk with Cal about what we find out?" Ian exhaled a loud breath.

"I suppose that we'll have to talk to him at some point, but I have to ask you again to trust me. I won't let you get into trouble over this, but I have a very good reason for not bringing any of what we learn to Cal just yet. Are you okay with that?"

"Hmm. I never thought about us getting in trouble. You mean like withholding evidence or something? Geez, I just thought I had to worry about my wife. I think there's something big going on here, but I can't figure you out on this one. Like I said, it's both exciting and scary. Boy, I don't know."

Chapter Twenty-Eight

WEDNESDAY, LATE AFTERNOON, OCTOBER 23.

They reached the college just before three o'clock and stopped at the main entrance, where they were met by two security guards. Ian and Sam showed their identification and the guard checked his clipboard with a list of names to be allowed onto the campus. He then presented the visitors with a small campus map and indicated where they would find Professor John Grossman.

"Those guards must be pushing eighty, wouldn't you say, Sam?"

"Yeah, I guess that's where we'll be someday, spending retirement working the day shift as security guards at some college. Boy, is that scary." The two laughed with a hint of worry.

"Nice campus, don't you think? All the buildings are red brick, colonial architecture and neatly landscaped. Looks like all the buildings are close to each other, too, not spread all over town like you-know-where."

"True, true," said Ian, "but someday soon our campus is going to be more compact and handsome. When that new Student Center is built, just wait. That's going to really anchor the campus. It may not be this good, but it'll be a big improvement. I'm really looking forward to it. So was Seth."

Sam thought back to the argument he overheard between Seth and Al. Seth understood the importance of the new building and didn't want anything getting in the way. In the same way, Seth's knowing about Turner's dirty little secret was a threat to Al's future. It could be a motive for murder, but the killing of Dr. Wirth didn't add up. Turner wouldn't have any reason to be connected to this one, but someone involved in the Holocaust could be. Sam wanted answers.

Ian parked the car, and the two men found their way to John Grossman's office. It was on the top floor of a two-story structure which had classrooms all along the ground floor and faculty offices above. There was some noise from other offices. Apparently several faculty members decided to work this day, but there were no secretaries or staff visible. Ian knocked on the open door.

John Grossman was a thin, balding man of about forty-five, wearing a black sweater vest over a white shirt. He looked up from his seat at a desk facing the door. "Hello, gentlemen, come in. Good to see you again, Ian."

"Thanks, John. Sorry about the circumstances. This is Sam Miller, our Director of Educational Technology."

"Nice to meet you. Please sit."

Sam and Ian eased into two chairs facing the desk. "How can I help you, Ian?"

Ian sat forward in his seat, his big hands folded in front of himself. "I'm sure you see how bizarre this situation is, what with the two college presidents being murdered. Sam and I think there might be a connection, one that the cops either don't see or don't want to talk about. We think it has to do with the Holocaust."

John leaned back in his upholstered, high-back chair. He tapped his fingers on the chair armrests and gazed at his visitors. Without speaking, he spun out of the chair, walked to the office door and closed it, returning to his seat.

"Before we go on, I'm afraid I have to ask you, Sam, why are you also interested in this? Ian has told me that Seth Walpole spoke to him about the Holocaust, but how do you fit in?"

"That's a fair question. I generally don't like to talk about my past, but I felt it necessary to share something recently with Ian. I'll share it with you, too, but I must insist you keep it in strict confidence."

John nodded. "You have my word anything we discuss here today will not leave this room."

"Good. I am also a Holocaust survivor. My mother and I were in Auschwitz thirty years ago. It was a terrible time, and my mother didn't make it out. We got separated and I don't know exactly what happened, but I think the Nazis took her away just before the camp was liberated. I was among those found by Allied soldiers, but my mother was gone. She must have been used by the escaping Nazi doctor who ran the camp hospital. He took favor with my mother and used her for his pleasure and for getting information about other prisoners. I realized many years later that she did whatever she had to do to save me. With my bum leg, they might've gassed me. I don't even know where she died, but I'm sure he killed her when she no longer served his purpose."

Ian leaned toward Sam, his face pale as a ghost. "Sam, you never told me that part. I'm so sorry. That must have been horrible. How can some people be so cruel to other people? The whole world seemed to be crazy at the time."

"I, too, am very sorry to hear all this. I'm honored to meet you, Sam." John spoke softly and reached his hand out to Sam, who took it. John clasped both his hands over Sam's in a gesture of bonding. "It's terrible that you have to relive your pain because of what's happened recently. What I have to say won't make it any easier. I'm sure you're aware of Seth Walpole's friendship with Ike Wirth, and that Wirth was a Holocaust survivor. It was on the news. What you may not know is the depth of their friendship and their mutual interest."

Sam gazed at Ian before turning to Grossman. "We know Seth was very interested in the Holocaust and wanted Ian, here, to develop a course on it. He seemed very intent on that. I can understand Dr. Wirth's interest, but I'm not sure why it became such a cause for Seth."

Grossman wiped his face with one hand, carefully considering his next words. "Gentlemen, you know that many Nazis fled Germany after the war. There was an organization called Odessa that functioned like an underground railroad for them."

"Yes, of course," said Sam. "I guess its general knowledge now."

"True," said Grossman, "but what people don't know is just how vast a number of Nazis got away. It may have run into the thousands. And not all of them settled in South America. Many are right here in the U.S."

"Still here?" said Ian, sitting up quickly.

"That's right. And here's the shocker. We know that many of Germany's best scientists, doctors, engineers and technicians were brought here by the U.S. government and were placed in jobs working for government contractors."

Ian looked dumbfounded. "What? We know many scientists ended up here, like Von Braun, that son of a bitch. But I never realized the government brought them here and gave them jobs."

Sam shook his head. "It sounds like that thing they do for gangsters who testify against the mob. You know, they change their identity and give them a new life someplace in exchange for their testimony. The good is supposed to outweigh the bad, but I don't know if it always works out that way. To think there are Nazi bastards among us! I know there are Nazi hunters who chase down the big ones, like Eichmann, but if there are thousands, as you say, then hunting them all down is an impossible task."

"Yes," said John, "and this leads to Dr. Wirth's area of interest. I can't say with certainty, but I think he planned to aid those in the Nazi hunt. There was something he might have learned from Seth Walpole. They seemed to meet frequently over the past year. Dr. Wirth spoke to me now and then and seemed to be trying to pick my brain for any knowledge I might have. But I doubt I knew more than he did. Perhaps he checked with me to make sure nothing fell through the cracks. He's the one who spoke to me about the many Nazis brought into this country, but he never named names."

Sam felt his blood pressure rise. He wanted to shout out what he'd been told by Eli Rosen. He wanted to scream the name Augustos Rauf and tell everyone he might be hiding as Arthur Vasile. But he knew that in order to help Eli, he had to keep quiet. If Vasile was an ex-Nazi and a war criminal, then Eli and his people might have to take him secretly, as was done with Adolph Eichmann. He also didn't want to risk putting anybody else in conflict with the law. For that reason, Ian and John couldn't know what Sam and Eli knew—not now, anyway.

Chapter Twenty-Nine

Sam had been working in the old theater building known as The Barn, located off the old Route 202, on the way to Hillsboro. He and Fred installed new stage lights. He was glad the job went quickly, because the old wooden building looked like a fire trap to him. Sam packed his tools in his trunk, and they headed back to the library.

"So, Sam, when do you think the old place will go up?"

"Don't joke about that, Fred. The possibility is too real, and very scary. The theater faculty convinced Seth it would be a great building for theater, and it came real cheap. I never liked the idea."

As they approached town, Sam noticed a Manchester PD car in front of the Henniker police station.

"That's interesting," said Fred. "I'll bet the Manchester police are checking with Cal Powers about a possible connection between the two murders. It couldn't be anything else."

"Why not? There could be any number of things going on that involves the two departments." Sam kept his eyes on the road and tried to sound convincing. Fred kept quiet, but Sam feared the young fellow didn't buy it.

Later that day, about half past two, Sam got a call from Cal that validated Fred's statement. "Can you come down to the station for a few minutes to talk?"

Sam agreed, but he was in no hurry to go.

Once at the station house, Cal brought Sam into his private office and shut the door. The chief took a seat at his desk; Sam sat across from him. "Sam, I found out something today I want to share with you. I feel you need to hear this, since you told me about the argument between Seth and Al Turner, and that it's put you in a sticky situation with Al."

A sticky situation. Yeah, one could call it that. Sam fidgeted and scratched his neck.

The chief leaned forward in his chair and folded his hands together. "I learned something that has me changing my approach to the murder of Ike Wirth in Manchester. A Manchester PD detective came by my office this morning to talk and compare notes. He was fishing for anything that might possibly connect the two crimes. I learned Dr. Wirth was shot with a .30-06 caliber rifle. I told him there are an awful lot of hunters between here and Manchester with such weapons, so that's not much of a connection. He agreed with me, but emphasized he was checking all possibilities. I told him we'd check our gun registrations, but didn't expect to find anything out of the ordinary."

Sam crossed his legs, trying to look relaxed. "And did you find anything?"

"Nothing out of the ordinary, but there is one tiny coincidence," said Cal.

Sam made a face, tilting his head like a dog trying to understand his master's commands.

"Al Turner owns a .30-06. It's legally registered, and he has a hunter's license, so it looks all on the up and up."

"That's not much to go on. But it sounds like you're growing more and more suspicious of Turner."

"You're right, it's not much. But when you add together his argument with Seth and his threatening you, he just looks too suspicious to ignore."

"But how does that connect him to the murder of Dr. Wirth? Just because he owns a .30-06 is nothing."

"That's true, but I want him to account for his whereabouts the night Dr. Wirth was killed. Look at it this way, Sam. If someone from Henniker killed Seth and wanted to throw the police off his tracks, then killing a college president in another town would be logical."

Sam looked at Cal. "Well, it sure has everybody in a tizzy. It's just too weird."

"Look. Al Turner has a possible motive, based on that argument with Seth, and he's shown a tendency toward anger and violence against people whom he sees as a threat. I know his ownership of a rifle with the same caliber as the Wirth murder weapon is not much in the way of evidence, but those are things that add up against him. So, as of now, I can't just ignore him."

The room fell silent. Sam agreed with Cal's logic, but was certain he was wrong about Turner. Sam had his own prime suspect, but he couldn't share it with Cal. Cal needed to know more about Turner. Maybe Sam did, too. If he could be certain that Turner didn't commit these murders, then he could concentrate more fully on Arthur Vasile.

Chapter Thirty

Sam finished a frozen dinner in his apartment, accompanied by a good, cheap wine. How was he going to get more information on Turner? The evidence against this unlikeable man was way too thin, even if Sam would have liked to see him get arrested. After meeting John Grossman, he felt the Holocaust was the connection between the murders, and it was bound to lead him to Arthur Vasile. But Chief Powers was leaning toward Al Turner, and Sam couldn't afford to let Cal know what else was going on. That could jeopardize Eli's mission. He topped off his glass with more wine. It couldn't hurt.

He didn't have many allies in this effort, not ones he could trust with the Holocaust connection, outside of Ian. Maybe Martha could help him to find out more about Al. He gave her a call, and she eagerly accepted his request to pay her a visit.

When he rang her doorbell, it took only a second for her to open the door. She was wearing an NSC tee shirt and nothing else, as far as he could tell. "Come on in, lover boy," she said. "It's good to see you. Been awhile."

"Good to see you, too, Mar . . ."

His words were cut off by Martha throwing her arms around Sam's neck and planting a hard kiss on his lips. It took a while before he came up for air. "Easy, Martha, we have to talk about something."

"There are a lot of things we can talk about, but that can wait." She threw her arm around Sam's waist as they walked into her living room. She tried to steer him to her stairway, but he stopped to face her. "Really, Martha, dear, this is important."

Martha dropped her hands to her side and stood in front of him. "Important, huh? Okay, so you've got something on your mind and you want to be serious. Well, here's the deal. Whatever it is will probably be a mood killer, so let's hold off on your serious talk." She ran her hands across the top of Sam's pants, then took hold of his zipper pull and started moving it slowly, down and up. The downward stroke brought a smile to his face. "First, Sammy, we're going upstairs to take care of the business of pleasure. It's been too long since your last visit."

"Hey, it's only been since Saturday."

"Like I said, it's been too long."

Her caress was too much for him to ignore, so Sam agreed to Martha's terms and followed her up the stairs. She ran a few steps ahead of him, and Sam was able to confirm his suspicions about her outfit. Serious talk could wait.

Their lovemaking was terrific, as usual. Martha came up with a few new moves that had Sam gasping for breath. How did she learn that stuff in just four days? Sam climbed back into his clothes after a trip to the bathroom. Martha slid fresh panties underneath her tee shirt, which barely covered them. That was all the getting dressed she cared for.

Once downstairs, Sam went directly to the sofa, while Martha skipped into the kitchen. "How about some wine, Sammy?" Her voice carried a faint echo.

"Yeah, okay, but make it a small glass," he answered.

Sam sat at one end of the sofa, leaning forward and rubbing his hands together. He wasn't surprised at Martha's seduction. He'd grown used to her sexual assertiveness and enjoyed it, but now more serious thoughts returned. Sex first with Martha was a good thing. Now maybe her mind was clear for a discussion.

She brought the drinks with her, handed one to Sam, and snuggled up to him on the sofa, pulling her legs up together onto the cushions. "Okay, lover, what's this serious talk you have in mind?"

"Chief Powers doesn't have much to go on, but he thinks Al Turner might've had a reason to kill Seth."

Martha sat as close to Sam as she could get, her hands clutching her wine glass. "Really? That's cool. Does he have something that can hang the son of a bitch?"

Sam put his glass on the end table. "I can't tell you, but, like I said, it's not all that much in the way of solid evidence."

Martha sipped some wine and asked Sam to put her glass on the end table next to his. She resumed her posture next to Sam's right and let her one hand paw his chest. "So that's why you came over, to tell me there's something you can't tell me?"

"No, no, Martha, of course not. Cal is looking for more solid evidence and maybe there is a way for us to help him find it. Maybe if we look more closely, we'll see something more damning about Al. I don't know what it could be, but we've got to try."

Martha's hand stopped moving on Sam's chest. "I keep hearing the word we, but I think that's a misspelling. You really mean me, don't you?"

Now it was Sam's turn to be charming. He turned toward Martha and caressed her face. "I was thinking about how you said that Tom West has a keen interest in you."

"He has a keen interest in my body, that's for certain."

"Good. I hope you can use that to our advantage."

Martha squirmed. "So, what, you want me to hump the guy?"

"No, no, not that." Sam tilted his head side to side. "What I mean is, maybe you could just flirt with him a little, maybe get him to take you to lunch, and get him to talk about Al and their club. Do you think you could do that?"

Martha put both feet flat on the floor and folded her arms across her chest. The erotic part of the night was over. "Getting that horny bastard to pay some attention to me won't be hard. I can always accidently run in to him at the post office, or something like that. I suppose I can get him to take me to lunch. He'll think it's a come on and set something up that will get his wife out of the way. If this can lead to something that will hurt big Al the asshole, I'm in."

"That's what I wanted to hear. I knew I could count on you. Now, look, this isn't a game. Remember that. If Al is a killer, you've got to be careful. Even if he didn't do it, we know he's prone to violence, if that basketball game is any example."

"Don't worry, Sam. I'm not interested in getting my head bashed in like Seth. Give me a little time and I'll let you know what I come up with. I think I deserve some compensation for my effort. How about Saturday night?"

"Okay, you've got a date for Saturday."

They held each other as they walked to the front door, stopping for a last kiss. Sam enjoyed the feel of her body against him. Earlier, she looked quite sexy and seductive in her tee shirt-only attire. Now, as he looked her over, she seemed small and vulnerable. He hoped he wasn't sending her into a bear's den.

Late Friday afternoon, Sam's office phone rang while he spoke to Fred. He didn't pay attention to it at first, distracted by the conversation about the radio station. After five rings, he decided to pick up. He heard a female voice before he could speak.

"Were you taking a nap, or is Carol in your office?"

"I'm sorry, Martha. I was in conversation with Fred."

"Well fine, but I thought you might like to know something related to our little talk the other night."

"Yeah, yeah, of course. Come on up."

Sam hung up the phone, walked out of the department office. He took up a spot next to where the library's collection of long playing records occupied several waist-high bins. Martha appeared within a few seconds, climbing the nearby stairs and spotting Sam immediately. He gestured with his finger for her to follow him as he moved to the side of the library that housed four audio listening rooms. Each one had a small window in the upper half of a solid oak door. All were vacant, with the doors slightly ajar. Sam claimed the last room, waited for Martha to catch up and enter the tiny room that had a turntable and cassette player built into a counter top, along with an earphone jack. There was only one chair, so Sam offered it to Martha. He squirmed onto the open part of the counter top after closing the door to the sound-proofed room.

"That smirk on your face tells me you've got something interesting."

She jabbed a finger against her chin and swiveled her chair back and forth. "I did as requested, Mr. Sam, and it didn't take much doing. I saw Tom West this morning outside the post office. I had to stake it out for a while, but he showed as expected. I think it's a daily routine for him, along with a lot of other people who don't like the idea of their mail sitting in an unlocked box at the end of their driveway, *Mayberry RFD* style. Anyway, I followed him inside and turned on a little charm, with these." She pulled her finger away from her chin and wiggled it across her ample chest, which was covered by a tight, blue turtleneck.

"You do have your, shall we say, tools of the trade," said Sam with a laugh. "Did you arrange for a lunch sometime?"

"Hell, we already had it. I agreed to meet him at that little deli in beautiful downtown Weare. You don't see many NSC folks there, so it was nice and private."

"You certainly work fast. How'd you make out?"

"Bad choice of words, Sammy. Anyway, I got him to talk about Al Turner all right. He's not all that happy about Al's controlling their little swap club, especially the part that doesn't let me stay at the parties. Tommy West wants a good shot at me. It's like I'm a magnet, and his you-know-what is made of iron. He'll follow me anywhere."

Sam looked down. Something inside him hoped Martha didn't plan to satisfy Mr. West's lust.

"Here's the big news. You told me Al's wife gave him a solid alibi for the night Seth was killed. Well, it's not so solid after all. It appears Al met with Tom early that night to discuss the club. When they got together, all Turner could talk about was the so-called Seth problem. Walpole had some information that could be damaging to the club's existence and to Al's career at the college. Tom said Al was getting more and more heated as he spoke about it, pounding his fist into his hand."

"Martha, did Tom say what time they ended their meeting?"

"Yes, he said they met between eight and nine o'clock."

Sam jumped off the counter, folded his hands in front of himself and bent toward Martha, as if he was about to kiss her. "Seth was killed after nine fifteen. I remember at the press conference that Cal said the campus security officer saw Seth Walpole in his office at that time. So, Elaine Turner lied to protect her husband. Holy shit."

He went quiet for a moment, realizing Cal Powers might not be wrong about Turner after all. This confused the issue for Sam, but he wrestled with the idea of telling Cal. On the other hand, how could he not tell the police chief?

Chapter Thirty-One

Sam noted the typical enthusiasm for the start of a weekend in the energy emanating from his young colleagues, Fred and Gene, as they prepared to leave work. "I hope you guys behave yourselves this weekend," said Sam while all three men were still in the department office. "I don't want to bail you out of jail."

"Very funny, boss," said Fred. "I'm planning to start my weekend with a visit to the pub. Anybody else care to go?"

"I'll see you there," said Gene, as he gathered up his coat, threw it over his shoulder and headed out.

"I've got to finish up a couple of things here, but I don't plan on a pub stop. Have one for me," said Sam.

"Will do," said Fred. He put on a jacket, grabbed a small tool box from behind his desk and waved goodbye to Sam. It puzzled Sam as to why Fred clung to that tool box so much, like his security blanket, but so be it.

When he finally had the room to himself, Sam knew he needed to call the police chief. He stared at his desk phone for a moment before dialing. How much could he tell the chief without giving away too much? He assured himself he had his approach under control and made the call.

Cal Powers agreed to see Sam, even though it was late in the day. A murder investigation took priority over all else.

Sam was at the station in a couple of minutes. He walked into Cal's private office and took a seat opposite the chief's desk. He eased himself into the chair as Cal closed his office door and returned to his desk seat.

"I assume you've got something interesting for me, Sam, this being a late hour on a Friday afternoon."

Sam rubbed his chin a couple of times, as if still figuring out how best to start his talk. He finally dove right into the whole story of Martha having a conversation with Tom

West and Tom's taking pleasure in having lunch with her. He held his hands in his lap, his fingers interlaced. His grip grew stronger as he spoke, telling the chief about the apparent discrepancy in Al Turner's alibi on the night of Seth Walpole's murder.

"Let me get this straight," said the chief, leaning forward in his chair. "Tom West is part of this club that Al Turner controls, and West has the hots for Martha, but she's not allowed to participate in the swapping because she doesn't have a partner. Turner has the final say in that, so Tom is all pissed off at Turner because he wants to bed down with Martha. So she and West meet for lunch and he blows off some steam, talking about a meeting he had with Turner the night Seth was killed. And their meeting broke up before Seth was murdered, giving Turner plenty of time to go to Seth's office."

"He took a chance that Seth would be there, but Dr. Walpole did that sort of thing frequently, and his Academic Dean would probably know that, since they worked so closely together," said Sam.

"Yes," said Cal, looking off into space. "It makes sense. Not too many people would know Dr. Walpole's work habits, but Turner certainly would be likely to know that sort of thing. It's not hard proof that Turner is the killer, but it throws a lot of suspicion his way, and that suspicion is mounting. Why else would Turner have his wife lie about his being home that night?"

Sam paused for a moment before answering, although he knew the question was rhetorical. "Turner needs to keep a very low profile on his club, so maybe he didn't want anyone to know about his meeting with Tom. It was a bad decision by Turner to have his wife lie. He could have any number of reasons for meeting with Tom, but perhaps he got panicky and decided to hide that, too."

"At some point, I'll need to have Martha Sanborn come in and make a statement. If I can arrest Al Turner, she'll have to testify. Is there anything else?"

"No, that's it. I thought you should know about it."

"Thanks. It was the right thing to do. I'm going to have another talk with Al Turner. I'm going to repeat myself to you, Sam. Go very carefully with Turner. He might have killed two people and we know he doesn't like you one bit."

"If you're trying to scare me, you're doing an excellent job. Don't worry. I'll be very careful around that guy."

Chapter Thirty-Two

SATURDAY AFTERNOON, NOVEMBER 2, 4:15 P.M.

As soon as Sam arrived at her place for their evening together, Martha poured two glasses of wine. He'd been easily persuaded to come over early for a start on the activity, which was pretty much still undecided. She wore tight jeans and a white, three-quarter-length tee shirt with red arms, the kind jocks wear when practicing. Even with it hanging loose at her waist, her shapely figure came through, much to Sam's pleasure. Sam's outfit consisted of brown slacks, a yellow, long-sleeved shirt and a green sport coat.

"I hope I'm not overdressed for tonight. You seem to be favoring a casual look," said Sam.

"Don't worry, old boy. You look great. Besides, I won't let you stay overdressed for long."

Sam accepted his glass of wine, and they took up their usual spots on the sofa. He proceeded to tell her about giving a statement to Cal Powers and she said she had no problem with that. Her dislike for Al Turner made it easy.

Sam rested his wine glass on the end table and eyed Martha. Their minds were in total synch. He reached for her with one hand and caressed her cheek. Martha instantly reciprocated by placing her hand on his thigh. He felt the warmth of her touch through his slacks as he kissed her. He slid his hand down to her chest as the doorbell rang.

The couple halted their foreplay and looked at each other, like teenagers upset that parents had returned home. Sam felt a tingle when Martha squeezed his thigh before she rose to answer the door. "It better not be Girl Scout cookies," she said. "I already bought some."

Sam reached for his wine glass and took a sip. He was gliding into a Martha mood and didn't appreciate the interruption. His arousal faded, but soon was replaced with another type of stimulation when he heard Martha's shriek.

"Tom, oh my God! What happened to you? Come in, come in!"

Standing up as Tom West entered the room, Sam saw Tom's embarrassed and confused look. He also saw the black and blue around Tom's left eye and the swollen lip.

"Hello, Sam," said Tom. "I'm sorry, I must be interrupting you and Martha, you know, your evening. Maybe I'd better leave."

He tried to spin away, but Martha grabbed his arm. "Oh, no you don't. You need to tell us what happened. I'll get you some wine."

"No, don't bother. I'd have trouble drinking anything right now, with this lip. Really, I should go."

"You came here for a reason," said Sam, "so just relax. You're safe here and among friends. You're here to see Martha and I'm sure it's to explain whatever just happened to you. If anyone should leave, it's me."

Martha let go of Tom's arm and gripped Sam's arm instead. "You're not going anywhere either. We both need to hear Tom's story."

Sam and Martha locked eyes, a silent communication. They shared the same suspicion about who might have done this to Tom. Martha broke contact and eased Tom into a soft chair, diagonally across from the sofa. She and Sam took positions closest to Tom's chair, their bodies on the front edge of the cushions.

"Are you sure you don't want a drink, Tom?"

"No, really, I'm okay. Just give me a minute." Tom sat back in the chair, his hands gripping the armrests, as if trying to steady himself.

Sam folded his hands together, resting his forearms on his knees, his body bent forward. "What happened? Take your time, but tell us everything."

Tom threw his head back and stared at the ceiling, trying to gather his thoughts and clear a path through his still-dizzied brain. When he leaned forward, he saw Sam and Martha sitting side-by-side in almost exactly the same body posture.

"It was Al Turner," he said. "He did this. That son-of-a-bitch, I thought he was going to kill me."

Sam and Martha again glanced at each other in another silent communication, this time confirming their suspicion.

"Go on, Tom," said Sam. "We're here to help you, so tell us everything."

"He came to my house about ninety minutes ago. Thank God Bonnie wasn't home. He was in a rage, a real blow up. He burst through my front door and caught me off-guard sitting in front of the TV. He was screaming, calling me a stupid bastard and other things. When I stood up, he pushed me back down and hovered over me. He said Chief Powers visited him last night and practically accused him of murdering Seth Walpole, and implied he killed that guy in Manchester, too. He said Chief Powers had reason to believe Al's wife had lied about his alibi the night Seth was killed when she said Al was home all night with her. I didn't know anything about all that until Al started ranting and raving about it at my house. I said I didn't know what he was yelling about."

Sam saw Tom's hands trembling as they gripped the chair. "Martha, get Tom some water. I'm sure his mouth is going dry." Martha did as Sam instructed, and Tom didn't refuse it this time. Tom sipped some water, putting the glass to the side of his mouth that wasn't swollen. He continued his story.

"Al said I was the only one who could have told the chief about our meeting that night when we talked about the club. I swore to him that I didn't talk to Chief Powers. He didn't believe me, so he pulled me out of my seat and punched me in the eye. Then he hit me again in the mouth and kept yelling at me. I told him I didn't talk to anybody. He hit me again in the gut. Martha, I never told him about our lunch talk."

Tom held his mouth open as he looked at Martha and Sam, glancing back and forth from one to the other. They dropped their heads slightly in a contrite way before looking up again.

"I'm sorry for all this," said Sam. "I asked Martha to talk to you and to try to get you to open up about Al. Don't blame her. I put her up to it."

"Oh, shit, Sam, stop being so noble. It's true, I used you. That was as much my doing as Sam's. I'm sorry if I hurt you, but it was for an important reason."

Tom looked like a teenager who had his heart crushed for the first time. "So that flirting with me, that lunch date we had, that was all just an act?"

"Yes," said Martha. She reached for Tom's hand but he pulled it away. He tried to get up, but Sam placed a gentle hand on Tom's chest and stopped him.

"Tom, listen to me, you've got to come to your senses now," said Sam. "It was bad enough that his wife lied to give him an alibi, but now he's assaulted you because he knows you ruined that alibi by telling somebody the truth. I think you should call Chief Powers and press charges against Turner. I know the chief pretty well. I'll help you."

"Holy shit, no," said Tom. "That would only get him more pissed off at me. What could the police do? Turner would be in jail for less than an hour before getting out on bail. Then he'd come after me, for sure, and who knows what he'd do? I know he's got a gun, he talks about hunting enough. Well, I don't have one. Jesus, if he really is the killer, he wouldn't hesitate to blow me away. My wife, too."

Sitting back on the sofa, Sam inched forward. "Cal Powers does suspect Turner, but he hasn't had much to go on as proof. Knowing the alibi is false is good reason to suspect him and now this assault on you is even more reason. It isn't hard evidence. I mean, him beating you up doesn't mean he killed anybody. It certainly proves he's a dangerous asshole. You've got to tell Chief Powers."

"No. Absolutely not. I'm scared, for crying out loud. What about Bonnie? I have to think of her, too. Please, I beg you, don't tell Chief Powers. You have to promise me."

Sam took a deep breath and puffed it out. He looked at Martha. "Okay. We won't tell anybody about this. What about Bonnie, how are you going to explain this to her?"

Tom swung his head from side to side. "I don't know, but I'll think of something. Maybe I got into a road rage situation and got punched by a mad driver."

Sam walked Tom to the door, trying to assure him that things would be okay and that Turner wouldn't hurt him again, that he was only helping to build the case against himself by getting violent. Sam wasn't sure his tactic was working, but it was all he could do.

After Tom left, Sam returned to Martha and fetched his wine glass. They stood silently for a moment in front of the sofa, simultaneously sipping wine, hoping it would calm them. "This is getting awful, and very confusing," said Sam, who started to pace the floor.

"Awful, yes, but what do you mean confusing? I don't understand that part. It's starting to look pretty bad for Al Turner. I mean, this isn't like roughing you up in a basketball game, for Christ's sake. He assaulted poor Tom today in the guy's own home. His alibi is shot and he's all pissed off about it. He's going to want to know who Tom talked to. What if Al goes back to Tom and beats it out of him? He might turn on me, or you, for that matter."

Sam looked at Martha, feeling his heart rate increase. "I won't let Turner hurt you, Martha. I'll be right here with you tonight. Don't worry." Sam's thoughts raced back in time when he said words like those to his mother at the camp. But he was a grown man now, not a boy. A ten year-old couldn't really protect his mother from the evil she was subjected to. Sam felt a lump in his throat. Now, this woman who had become his lover faced a threat from another kind of evil. He wasn't sure how he would protect her. He just knew that he would, whatever the cost.

"Look, Sammy boy, I can take care of myself. But don't forget Mr. Turner doesn't like you too much, either."

Sam gazed away from Martha, as if he weren't in the same room. When his mind returned to the present, he put down his wine glass and grabbed Martha gently by the shoulders, guiding her to the sofa. He saw the look on her face change. "You said you didn't understand why this is confusing for me. Martha, Al Turner isn't the only suspect in Seth's murder. Up until a few days ago, I was certain it was somebody else, but then I got a call from Cal Powers and we talked about Turner. I didn't think he had much on him, but I decided to ask you to help me learn more. I really didn't expect you to find out anything, but, boy, you sure did."

"Who else do you suspect? I think Turner looks pretty bad right now."

Sam thought for a moment. Would it be wise to tell Martha his suspicions about Arthur Vasile? "I can't tell you who, not right now. Just trust me that I have very serious reasons to think there is somebody else on campus who might've done it, and here's the confusing part, it ties into the killing in Manchester."

"What? Who else could possibly be involved?"

"Never mind," said Sam. "There's something else going on here that might be very big and complex. Just trust me on this. I've already gotten you too involved with Turner, and I don't want to get you mixed up in the other thing." They went quiet.

Sam let go of Martha and bolted up to his feet. "Hey, I'm getting hungry. How about we go over to Hillsboro and get some dinner?" It seemed like a good time to change the grim mood threatening to engulf them.

"Yeah, okay. We'll get dinner." Her voice was soft and without the emotion she'd shown earlier.

"There, that's better," said Sam.

"I'll be right with you." Martha eased herself off the sofa and went upstairs. When she returned, she was holding a small, rectangular black purse, zippered across the top. Its contents made a bulge in the sides.

Sam noticed the purse and thought it odd for Martha. "I don't think I've ever seen you carry a purse before."

"Oh, just a new accessory. It's a girl thing. Let's go."

Chapter Thirty-Three

SATURDAY, LATE AFTERNOON, NOVEMBER 2.

Arthur Vasile was in his kitchen, preparing dinner for Carol and himself. Standing at the counter next to the fridge, his back to the room, he was about to split a whole, baby chicken by cutting out the backbone and pushing the bird into a *butterfly* position, making it better for roasting. He steadied the bird with his weak left hand and used kitchen scissors to extract the bone. Cutting into animal flesh always gave him memories of his earlier days in medicine.

"There you go again, practicing surgery in our kitchen," said Carol, entering the room. "You do seem to relish it so."

"Ah, just good fun with a practical purpose. Then again, maybe your observation is correct, my dear," he said, smiling back over his shoulder at her. When he turned back to face the bird, his smile disappeared.

"Well, you go about your task, Dr. Vasile. I'll check the mail."

"Very funny," said Arthur. "Perhaps one day I'll operate on you."

"Why Arthur, do I detect some kinkiness in your words? That would certainly be a new you. Maybe we will discuss that after dinner."

"Go. Scoot, woman, and lift your mind out of the gutter." Arthur feigned a laugh as he looked over his shoulder again, catching a view of his wife leaving the room. Her gentle movement, with hips swaying just a little, gave him a stir. This American woman served his needs well, needs he ignored as a young man in Auschwitz, when work was more important to him. The years in America had taught him that manly pleasure was an acceptable pursuit.

Arthur placed the bird in a roasting pan, laying it over a bed of sliced onions, red potatoes, and carrots. He seasoned the mix with sea salt, garlic powder and black pepper and set the oven to four-hundred and twenty-five degrees. He washed his hands at the kitchen sink and was toweling them dry when Carol returned with several items of mail in her hands. One, in particular, caught her attention.

"You got an airmail letter from someplace in Chile. What is Colonia Dignidad?"

She slipped her fingernail under the flap of the envelope and began to work it open. Arthur dropped the towel and rushed to his wife's side, snatching the letter from her hands.

"You know better than to open my mail! I don't want you prying into my letters!"

"Arthur, for goodness sake, you don't have to attack me. I was curious, that's all. I was just trying to help by opening the envelope for you. I wasn't prying. We're both right here in the kitchen and . . ." Carol gave up her attempt at explaining herself.

Arthur saw a tear develop in his wife's eye as she turned and ran out of the kitchen. He folded the envelope in half and stuck it into his back pants pocket, then took a deep breath before striding to his wife, now seated on the living room sofa, sobbing. He stood in front of her, searching for the right words.

"I'm so sorry. I didn't mean to hurt your feelings. I was thoughtless. Please forgive me."

"You did more than hurt my feelings. You scared me! I've never seen you react like that to anything. Why? What's so damned important about that letter?"

"It wasn't that particular letter. It's just about the project. But you know I am a very private person, especially about my work. Please, forgive me."

Carol nodded and eked out a feeble, "Yes," still sniffling.

"Why don't you rest here while I finish preparing our dinner? I'll pour you a glass of wine and bring it to you. Would you like that?"

Carol nodded again.

"Wonderful," said Arthur. "I'll get it for you right now." He rubbed his hands together and gave his wife an enthusiastic smile before turning his back to her, returning to the kitchen. He ground his teeth together as he walked.

Although the letter seemed to vibrate in his pocket, it would have to wait. He had drawn too much attention to it and had let it become a crisis issue with Carol. It would be best to let her cool down, have dinner and wait for her to retire for the night. Then he could see what his people in Chile had come up with.

It was a quiet time at the dinner table. Carol only spoke when Arthur asked her for something. Arthur could see that her mood didn't improve, so he let her wallow in her anger and tried not to give any more fuel for her fire. He suggested a second and third glass of wine, which she accepted.

They tried watching television for a while, an exercise Arthur found distasteful and tedious. Nonetheless, he kept quiet and indulged Carol, although it always tested his patience to sit through programs that Americans called comedy. The least offensive to him that evening was *The Mary Tyler Moore Show,* because she was an attractive woman and her boss, Mr. Grant, was strong and forceful, a characteristic he liked. The other characters were fools, weaklings and imbeciles.

By eight-thirty, Carol was fading. "Arthur, I'm going to go to bed. I just can't stay awake," she said and left the room without waiting for a reply from her husband. He gave none anyway. This was the time he'd been waiting for.

Arthur hadn't felt such anticipation over a letter since his days as a prospective university student, awaiting a letter of acceptance. Long, quiet strides took him into his study, where he closed the door behind him, pulled the letter from his pocket and eased himself into his chair. His nimble right hand fingers controlled a letter opener, but they worked in contrast to the clumsy, half-useless left hand that could only pin the envelope to the desk. The opener sliced through the envelope flap, and soon the letter was in Arthur's hands, unfolded.

The researchers in Chile had done excellent work. They found record of the doctor leaving Auschwitz-Birkenau and being sent to the camp at Gross Rosen. Since Arthur had been transferred out earlier, he had known nothing of the doctor's whereabouts at that time. The report said the doctor had a woman with him, but it was not his wife. She was listed simply as Sadie, and served as his assistant. When the Red Army approached, he made use of the Odessa network to escape to Bavaria, and eventually, Argentina. But he arrived in Buenos Aires alone, reporting that his female assistant died during their travels.

Yes. It made perfect sense to Arthur that the doctor would take Sadie with him, since he enjoyed her favors so much. Perhaps he had to kill her along the way, however, since escaping Europe through Odessa left little room for error. Or something else happened. There was no mention of the boy named Schmuel.

Arthur clasped his hands together in triumph. Now he knew exactly what had happened to the Jewish woman. Surely the doctor would have reported to Odessa what had become of the boy, if he had been eliminated. Because there was no such report, Arthur felt it quite possible that Schmuel could have survived. Skimming his diary, Arthur found note of seeing the boy often in the company of another, a teenaged boy named Eli Rosen. Perhaps with that one's help, Schmuel might have lived until the Soviets liberated the camp. That was it. It had to be. Sam Miller was the right age. He had a limp from an injury as a very young boy. He was Polish and escaped Europe. Arthur was convinced. Sam Miller was Schmuel, the young son of Sadie and someone who should have been gassed. He was a threat to Vasile, someone who might expose his true identity and imperil the project. He was a problem in need of a final *solution.*

Chapter Thirty-Four

SATURDAY EVENING, NOVEMBER 2.

Martha and Sam enjoyed a good dinner at Govoni's Restaurant in Hillsboro and were selecting dessert. The good food helped them forget momentarily the events of the afternoon.

His feelings for Martha were in a state of flux. She was a strong-willed woman, and certainly knew how to assert herself sexually. But ever since the basketball game, he'd seen a degree of vulnerability in her. She'd revealed that she lost a brother in Vietnam, someone very close to her, and he sensed she still hid the true depth of her pain. Sam was certain Martha feared developing a real relationship with a man because of that loss. It was logical she might want to protect herself from suffering the pain of ever losing a loved one again. Now she was caught up in bizarre events happening in what was supposed to be a pleasant, peaceful place. He put her directly into the line of fire of the man who might be the police chief's leading, maybe only, suspect. Sam had to protect her.

"What's the matter, Sam, can't make up your mind about dessert?"

Sam peered at the dessert menu like a student trying to select A, B, C, or D on a multiple choice test. He bit lightly on his lip and swayed his head from side to side.

"For me it's easy. Remember, from The Godfather movie? 'Leave the gun and take the cannoli.' I love those little cream-filled tubes! That's for me."

"Okay, you got me. I'll have the same." Sam folded his menu and placed it flat on the little table for two. The sensation of a feminine touch caressing his knee brought a smile to his face.

"Well, I wouldn't say that I've got you yet, Sam, but the night is young."

Sam shook his head. One minute Martha was a little woman in danger and the next she was a charming, if not subtle, seductress. It was as if she changed rapidly from one costume to another and back again. Who was this woman?

The mood at the table changed as rapidly as his view of Martha when Sam spotted two men standing across the room, near the wall under the exit sign. As they talked, the one with his back to the room turned his head. It was Al Turner. The other was a much younger fellow, tall and athletically built. Turner motioned with his thumb, like a hitchhiker, toward Sam and Martha.

The younger man nodded his head after sending a glance in the couple's direction and left the building. Turner spun around and seemed to be heading toward Sam and Martha, then veered off to his left and eased into a chair across from his wife, Elaine, who dutifully waited at their table.

"Martha, don't look behind you, but we have company."

"Huh?" Martha did as ordered and stared into Sam's eyes. Her face became grim, as if a danger alert had just sounded, but she stayed calm. "Let me guess. Whose presence in this place could be most effective at ruining our evening? Don't tell me it's Al Turner."

Sam returned her stare. "Okay, I won't tell you."

"Jesus H. Christ, that's one hell of a coincidence," she said with quiet force.

"Yes, isn't it? Considering what he did today, I'm surprised he'd show his face. If you had just done what he did to Tom West, what would be going through your mind?"

"I'd wonder if Tom went to talk to anybody," said Martha. "Al already figures Tom to be a big mouth, so I'm sure he suspects we might know. Maybe Tom lied when he said he never mentioned our lunch talk."

"Could be," said Sam, his eyes trained in Turner's direction. "Or maybe he just hates us, since he also thinks I turned Cal Powers on to him as a possible suspect. If he knows Tom talked to us today, we're both on his shit list, big time."

"So, what are you going to do, Sam?"

"I'm going to go say hello to the nice couple."

"What are you going to do that for, for Christ sake? Shouldn't we just leave?"

"He already knows we're here, Martha. If we avoid him, that'll just make him more suspicious about us talking to Tom. A minute ago, he was talking to a young guy near the exit, who left after Turner pointed us out. I don't know what that was all about, but if Turner is planning something, he's also setting up another alibi with Elaine. I'll be right back."

"I guess you love Italian food, too," said Sam as he approached Turner's table.

Turner twisted in his chair, acting surprised to see his NSC colleague. "Why, hello, Sam." He fell silent after that, looking to his wife for help in making a decent social greeting.

"Hello," said Mrs. Turner. "I'm Elaine. I don't think we've met before, but I remember you from the basketball game."

Turner rolled his eyes at his wife's clumsy remark. "We come here from time to time. Great food, don't you think? Is that Martha Sanborn you're with?" Al looked across the room toward Martha, pretending he'd just noticed her.

Sam followed his gaze back at his date. Turner's acting left much to be desired. "Yes, we had a dinner date tonight and we enjoy this place, so here we are." Martha waved to them with a forced smile.

"Well, Sam," said Elaine, "why don't you just bring your nice date over here and join us?"

Turner shot a harsh glare at his wife. "We don't want to interrupt the couple's date, Elaine, so I don't think they want to join us. I'd certainly understand."

Sam paused before speaking. If Turner set something up with that other fellow he spoke with earlier, stalling for time might mess up any plans they made. This might be an awkward moment, but it might be one worth stretching out. "You wouldn't be interrupting us at all. In fact, we've finished dinner and were about to order dessert. Why don't we have it at your table? Thanks for the invite. I'll go get Martha." Sam waved to her, signaling to grab her things and move over, before intercepting his waitress to inform her about their move.

Martha slung her coat over her shoulder, clutching her small purse, the bulk of its contents forcing her hand to take a tight grip. When she joined the party, Sam made a polite introduction to Elaine, and Al forced a hello to Martha. They sat in at the table and made their orders as soon as the waitress arrived. Al added a double Scotch to his order.

"Guess what, Martha? Elaine was at the basketball game. Say, wasn't that a lot of fun? Martha had so much fun playing that she could barely keep her pants up." Now Sam was on the receiving end of a glare, this one from Martha.

Elaine let out a giggle. "Oh, my goodness, Martha, was that you? I think you got tangled up with Al, didn't you, and almost lost your pants in the process. Oh, that was funny. Goodness, I hope I'm not embarrassing you." She tapped Martha's forearm.

Al tried to match the light-hearted tone. "Yes, that was a fun game, Sam." He took a swallow from his drink. "We ought to have a rematch someday." He tapped his fingers on the table.

"From what Bob Hill tells me, we'll be doing that during the intramural season," said Sam. "But as you saw, basketball isn't my game. Well, in fact, running isn't for me anytime, what with my bad leg, you know."

"My goodness, Sam, what's wrong with your leg?" asked Elaine.

"I broke it when I was a boy and it never healed properly. It's not bad, but I never became an Olympic sprinter."

Turner fidgeted in his chair, often looking away from his company. When he did, Sam connected with Martha's eyes. His look showed his pleasure in annoying Al. This action repeated itself often while they consumed their dessert and made awkward small talk. Turner ran out of things to say, letting Elaine carry the burden of conversation. After thirty minutes, Sam and Martha thanked the Turners, paid their bill and made a polite exit.

"I hope you enjoyed yourself, Sammy," said Martha as they strolled arm-in-arm to his car.

"It was much more fun than I expected, but I wasn't looking for fun. I was thinking about that suspicious guy Al was talking to. It was as if Turner was pointing us out to him, for what reason I don't know. If we took more time in leaving and that guy was waiting for us in the parking lot, our delay might have put him off enough for him to forget about it. It's getting too cold to sit out here, and I don't hear any car running its engine for heat."

"You may be right, Sam, but sitting next to Turner all that time gave me a chill. Let's go back to my place and get warm." Martha was back on track.

Sam made the gentlemanly effort to open the passenger door for his date and help her ease into her seat, before getting behind the wheel and cranking the engine to his mid-sized sedan. He eased his vehicle out of the lot.

"Shouldn't you let it warm up for a minute before driving? My dad always taught me to do that to get the oil up into the cylinders," said Martha.

"Naw. A mechanic once told me the best thing to do is to start her up and get going, at an easy pace, of course. There's no rush. I know where I'm going and what's at the end of the trip."

"I wouldn't mind the pace, if you didn't have bucket seats in this car," she replied.

Sam grinned at his date and continued slowly along Route 202 toward Henniker, not noticing the large, black pickup truck swinging onto the road behind them until its headlights glared in his rearview mirror. Sam winced at the brightness.

"Are you okay, Sam?"

"Well, somebody behind us seems to think he needs to shine his high beams all the time. And I guess he likes to tailgate, because that's what he's doing now. I don't care for this road much. It must have been an old horse and buggy path years ago. I don't think they put much effort into paving it for automobiles. Some of these twists and turns aren't banked very well, and some not at all. Someone going too fast could get tossed right off the road."

Both vehicles did as Sam suggested, slowing down to get safely through the turns. When they approached a long straightaway with the Contoocook River on his left, Sam held his modest speed, hoping the other vehicle would back off. No luck.

In an instant, the other car's lights flashed in Sam's right side mirror and its engine roared. It sped up alongside Sam and Martha.

"Jesus, what's he doing?" cried Martha. "He's right beside us. Doesn't he know there's no pavement there?"

"I think that idiot is trying to pass us on the right, using the shoulder. That's crazy. He's going to kill somebody if he . . ."

The impact of the big truck slamming into Sam's car gave a loud thumping sound and drew a scream from Martha. The action caught Sam off-guard, but he held onto the steering wheel with both hands, his grip almost viselike. He struggled for control, but lost it as his car swerved to the left, crossing the center line and veering off the road, heading for the cold river waters. Sam hit the brakes in desperation and felt his sedan go into a helpless spin when it hit the soft ground of the river bank. Mud and grass flew up around them.

Sam held his breath, knowing the river's edge loomed only feet away, even though he couldn't see it in the dark. Street lights were spaced far apart on the old road. The force of the three-hundred and sixty degree spin threw the car's occupants around, but also slowed the vehicle's progress toward the river. They lurched one way and then the other before feeling everything stop.

Sam and Martha sat stunned but unhurt, relieved as if they had just survived an airplane crash landing. "Are you okay, Martha?"

"Yes, I think I'm okay. What the hell was that?"

"Can you open your door?" said Sam. There's a pole up against mine. I think it kept us from going into the drink, but I can't get out on this side."

Martha tried her door. It squeaked like a pig, but her effort succeeded. Sam grabbed a flashlight out of the glove compartment before they crawled out of the vehicle, which rested against the large pole. The two sloshed through shallow mud and made their way to the roadside. Once there, Martha looked back at the car and began to laugh.

"You sure can find humor in the strangest places, lady."

"Give me that flashlight." Martha pointed the light at the car, which now sat about fifteen feet away. "Well, I'll be damned. Look, Sam. That pole is for the river tramway. It's sunk good and deep into the ground to support the weight of passengers. The thing must be on the other side of the river, but you can see the pulley and line at the top. Shit, we'd have gone for a nighttime swim if it wasn't for that pole. I always hated that old tram. I think it's an eyesore. Now, I love it!"

Sam took the flashlight and brushed the crash scene with its beam. The car wheels were mired in the muddy grass. He crept closer to the vehicle, but the wet earth forced him back.

"What do you think, Sam, any chance of driving it out?"

"Not a chance. The mud's too deep. All four wheels are sunk halfway into it. Even if I could get it out, there isn't much room to maneuver without slipping into the river. Too dangerous. Looks like we're pedestrians."

Martha peered at her wet feet. "This kind of puts a damper on my plans for our evening together. Good thing I'm wearing flats tonight. Sid's Gulf station is about a mile from here heading back to Henniker. Let's hope he's still open. He often works late in his garage even after shutting down the gas pumps, so we've got a good chance of finding him. Hope his tow truck is tuned up."

The couple sloshed back to the roadside and began their trek along the narrow road shoulder, facing traffic. Sam held the flashlight, aiming its beam at the ground in front of them. Martha clung to Sam.

"That was no accident, Sammy boy. That guy tried to shove us into the river. He waited until the straightaway to make his move. He knew exactly what he was doing. I wish I got a better look at him and his big, bad truck."

"Maybe. There's no way to identify him for certain," said Sam. He patted Martha's arm with his left hand, gripping the flashlight in his right, like a relay runner's baton. "But it had to be that guy Turner was talking to, it had to be. As soon as we get to Sid's Gulf, I'll call the police. Chief Powers is going to find this episode quite interesting. He's already leaning heavily toward Turner as Seth's murderer. I'm afraid we're going to have to violate Tom's confidential talk. Cal's got to know what happened to Tom."

"Yes, I guess so," said Martha, her voice low and repentant. "Hey, if Turner set up this little adventure for us, Tom might already be in danger."

"I was thinking the same thing. That's why we have to break our promise to him." Sam's eyes went upward for a moment as he recalled that his mother said something to him long ago, back in the camp. She said sometimes you have to do bad things to protect good people. He didn't understand it back then. It was much later when he realized that she was talking about herself, that everything she did at the camp was to protect him. She had to keep the doctor happy or her son would be gassed, even if it meant informing on other prisoners and making nighttime visits to the doctor's bedroom. She had to do it.

Chapter Thirty-Five

SATURDAY EVENING, NOVEMBER 2.

The cold fall air, along with wet feet, began to chill Sam to the bone, but Martha kept plodding along without showing fatigue or pain. Sam shot a look her way and broke into a quiet grin, admiring her grit. She had a lot more to her than met the eye.

As they guessed, the station had already closed, but Sid was working in the shop. A couple of hard raps on the door got Sid's attention, but Sam's call for help got a negative reply. "We're closed for the night. Sorry."

Martha, standing with hands on hips, shouted through the door like a drill sergeant awakening troops in the barracks. "Listen to me, Sidney Jasper Sutton. I'm wet, tired and getting a wee bit pissed off, to put it mildly. We just missed taking a swim in the river after getting run off the road, and I'm in no mood for being put off by you. Now, open this door before we burn it down."

Within seconds, the bay door creaked like it hadn't been oiled in a dozen years and began to rise. Martha smiled at Sam. "It just takes a little charm."

Before the door was completely open, the diminutive but trim, fifty year-old Mr. Sutton emerged, wearing a dark blue jumpsuit covered with grease stains from years of use. He showed a welcoming smile across his face. He knew Martha.

"Why Martha, honey," said Sid, wiping his dirty hands with an even dirtier towel. "I knew it was you the minute I heard your sweet voice. Great to see you. It's been, well, you know, a long time since . . . Say, let's keep our voices down, so not to bother my wife. What was that about being run off the road? Whereabouts? How's your car?"

"Well, greetings and salutations to you, Sid," said Martha. "Nice to see you again, too." She turned her head toward Sam, her face twisted in a *once upon a time* look. "Can we step inside? We'll tell you all about it. How's your tow truck running? Got any fresh, hot coffee?"

"Sure, got coffee all right. It's in the office. Just go ahead through that door over there. It's hot, but I don't know that you'd call it fresh."

"It'll do, Sidney, thanks," said Martha without looking back at her host. "By the way, this is Sam Miller."

Sid reached a reasonably clean hand at Sam, who looked at it, took it, and gave it a quick shake. "Nice to meet you, Sid."

Once inside the office, they poured some coffee into paper cups from a stack near the pot and told Sid of their recent road trouble. He responded with expected shock and a curse for all young drivers, "College kids and locals both, it doesn't matter."

Sam twisted his head in all directions before finding his target. A black phone that looked like something out of a Bogart detective movie sat on a corner of the desk in Fred's office. "I need to call the police, Sid," said Sam, pointing to the phone. He made his way to it without waiting for an answer.

"Sure, absolutely."

Sam got through to the police, told his story and nodded his head as he repeated, "Ahuh, ahuh," taking instructions from the desk officer. "You need to get in touch with Chief Powers about this," said Sam. "This may involve somebody connected to the Seth Walpole murder investigation." Sam hung up the old phone and returned to where Martha and Sid stood. The mechanic's eyes roamed over Martha, and he worked the hand towel, trying to cleanse his hopelessly soiled paws.

"The police are on their way and they're calling Chief Powers at home. We can't go get the car until they arrive. They need to take some pictures of the scene." It would only take a few minutes for the police to arrive, including the chief, but the night was far from over for Sam.

✶✶✶✶

A police cruiser pulled into the small parking lot in front of Sid's Gulf station. Two young officers got out and approached the office. In a few seconds, a woman approached from the house that stood well off the road, away from the Gulf station. Sid backed away from Martha as she entered the small building. Sam heard her ask what was happening and watched Sid try to steer her to a far corner where he seemed to be attempting an explanation.

"That would be the missus," explained Martha.

Sam opened the office door to allow the officers in. One was a tall, thin young man with light blond hair. The other was much shorter, with dark hair. Their uniforms looked brand spanking new, gray trousers neatly pressed, dark shirts with shiny badges on the chest. Both wore aviator glasses, which they removed once inside the building.

"Hello, Ms. Sanborn," said the tall one, giving a polite nod to Martha. "Mr. Miller?" He reached a hand to Sam. The introductions were brief, since Sam was the only unknown among these Hennikerites. The officers wanted a rundown of the events, while they awaited Chief Powers. Sam grudgingly complied, knowing he'd have to go over it in greater detail for the Chief. Fortunately for Sam, Cal arrived before he had to go too deeply into the explanation.

Chief Powers didn't bother with pleasantries. "Sam, Martha, please get in my car. We'll go take a look at things and then I'll bring you to the station where you can make your statement. The officers will take pictures and escort Sid's tow truck. They'll look for paint scratches and take samples before Sid puts it up on the lift."

"But Cal . . . Chief, I've already got a car on the lift and won't be . . ."

"Take that one down, Sid. It'll have to wait. This is top priority." The Chief's tone was full of authority, and his words were clear.

Sam and Martha left the office without speaking and moved outside to Cal's police car. Sam opened the back door for Martha and closed it after she slid in. He took the front passenger seat and waited for Cal to take his place behind the wheel. Once inside, Cal started the engine and turned on his rooftop police lights. In a minute they were moving in a short caravan, two police cars and a tow truck, all with flashing lights.

Soon they were looking at Sam's car. Cal stopped just before the accident scene and waved the other vehicles past him. The police cars each put spotlights on Sam's car, while

Sid turned his vehicle around, positioning it for hooking up the tow chain. Once all were pulled off the road, they exited their vehicles for a closer look.

"Pretty close call, Sam," said Cal. "Looks like that pole is the only thing that kept you out of the river. It could've been a lot more serious."

"It is a lot more serious, Cal. There's a lot more to this than meets the eye."

"Yeah, my officer said you think it has something to do with Dr. Walpole's murder. Let's go to the station and talk about it, then I'll take you two home."

When they arrived at the police station, Sam and Martha settled into chairs across from Cal's desk, while the Chief eased into his own chair and faced the couple, his hands folded on the desk. "Okay, let me have all of it."

Sam went into detail about the entire day, from the visit from Tom West to the appearance of Al Turner at Govoni's, and him and Martha being run off the road. Cal's face remained calm, but his eyes showed Sam something that he liked, as if the Chief had made a major decision.

"Let's go talk to Tom West," said Cal. "If he'll press charges, I'm going to arrest Al Turner. Maybe it'll give us enough time to track down the truck that hit you, Sam. I'll talk to people at Govoni's to see if anybody can tell us anything useful. If Turner assaulted West because he blew Turner's alibi, and then had somebody run you off the road along the river, that should convince the District Attorney to issue a warrant for Turner in Seth Walpole's murder. Everything is stacking up against him."

"Can we take Martha home first, Chief?" said Sam. "She's had a long day."

Chief Powers nodded, but Martha spoke for herself. "No, I'm not going home yet, Sam. I'm in this with you, remember? I'm the one who talked to Tom and I was sitting in your car when that mystery man tried to send us swimming. No, I'm not leaving. I'm sticking with you guys."

The men looked at each other, each hoping the other would give good reasons why Martha should go home. None came. She stayed.

They were at the West house in short time and all three went to the front entrance. Bonnie answered Cal's knock. Sam heard a crack in her voice when she greeted the police chief and his companions. "Good evening, Chief Powers. Is . . . there . . . something wrong?"

That was an interesting question, since her husband looked like a train wreck. What story had Tom told to her?

A voice came from behind her. "It's all right, Bonnie. I know why they're here. Let them in."

The fear in Bonnie's eyes reminded Sam of the feeling people at the camp had at the mere sight of an armed man in uniform. But Bonnie's fear couldn't come close to that of the camp prisoners.

They all sat in the living room, with Tom and Bonnie on the sofa. Martha sat next to Bonnie, while Cal and Sam eased into chairs near them. Tom reluctantly made it official to Chief Powers that he had been assaulted by Al Turner. He still didn't want to press charges, but when he heard about Sam and Martha's ordeal, he began to come around to the idea.

"If you arrest him, how long will Turner be in jail before posting bail? I'm afraid he'll come after me again." Tom took Bonnie's hand as he spoke.

"He'll cool his heels in the county jail until Monday morning when he'll be arraigned in the circuit court," said Cal. "Cash bail could be between ten and twenty grand, which I assume Turner can make, but he'll be put under a restraining order to stay away from you. I don't think he's dumb enough to violate that order."

Tom gave a worried look at his wife before turning back to Cal. "But if he has a partner, the one who ran Sam and Martha off the road," said Tom, "we might still be in danger."

"We're going to find him, too. I promise you that. If it will help, I can have a police car swing by your house every hour tonight." Cal's voice rang with authority, making the Wests feel safer.

"Yes," said Tom. "That would be very helpful."

"You're doing the right thing," said Sam. "Martha and I are in this with you, and we want Al Turner behind bars. Is there anything else you need to tell us?"

Tom looked at Bonnie and shook his head. "No, there's nothing else. What do I do next?"

"You need to come to the station house and file a formal complaint," said Cal. "Follow my car. This won't take long. I'll drop Sam and Martha off first before going to the station. You know, Sam's right, Tom. You're doing the right thing. Thanks."

✦✦✦✦

Martha poured a glass of wine when they got back to her place. Sam opted for something stronger.

"I didn't think this night was ever going to end," said Martha. Sam kicked off his shoes and took up a place at an end of the sofa. Martha snuggled in next to him, also stripping off her shoes. They didn't turn on the TV or radio, preferring to enjoy peace and quiet instead. They sipped their drinks without speaking for what seemed an eternity.

"Sam, do you think he killed Seth Walpole?"

Sam held his right arm around Martha's shoulder, his left hand clutching his drink. Her words brought back the dilemma he faced. He had been certain that Arthur Vasile was the killer, but now, everything pointed to Al Turner. And what about Dr. Wirth? Why kill him?

"I don't know, Martha. It's getting complicated."

"Well, I'm ready for something simple, Sam. I just want to get some sleep. Hope you don't mind."

"I'm in total agreement, Martha. I'm too drained for . . . anything else."

They made their way upstairs to Martha's bedroom where they undressed without talking and slipped under the covers. Sam stared at the ceiling for a moment before turning to kiss Martha's bare shoulder. He smiled, realizing she was fast asleep.

Chapter Thirty-Six

SUNDAY MORNING, NOVEMBER 3.

Light already peeked through the curtains in the bed-room when Sam opened his eyes. He felt fully refreshed after the best night's sleep he'd had in weeks. He grabbed his watch off the night table and was amazed that it was after nine o'clock. He slept through the night, something he didn't achieve often. No middle of the night bathroom call disturbed his sleep, but now the bladder pressure was strong.

Sam sat up and swung his naked body around, placing his feet on the floor. He stretched his arms over his head, as if reaching for the sky, and stood up. Walking toward the door, he glanced back to see Martha lying on her stomach, still sleeping soundly. Sam had thrown the covers back when he left the bed and Martha was only covered up to the back of her knees. The sight of her naked beauty might have aroused him if his bladder hadn't made the first call.

After taking the pause that refreshes, Sam ran the shower water until it was suitably warm. The bathroom was large and sported a roomy shower stall, separate from the tub. He stepped inside, found a bottle of soft shower soap and began to lather up. The gentle squeak of the shower door surprised him.

Before he could turn around, he felt Martha's arms encircle him from behind and her body pressed against him. "Good morning, my sweet Sam." She held onto him for an extended time. Her hands were still.

Sam was about to turn to face her, but when Martha's hands began a gentle caress just below his waist, he decided not to break the extremely pleasant contact. Her fingers slid lower, and the lather lubricated his penis, enhancing his arousal. He wanted to speak, to suggest she wait until

they were back in bed, but he was muted by his own or-
gasm.

Having enjoyed a second form of relief within a few
minutes, Sam spun to face his partner. His arms circled
her waist and her hands lay open against his chest. He was
about to kiss her, but a tap from her hands held him back.

"I wanted to take care of your needs, Sam, but I'm not
up to intercourse right now. I just want to feel you close
to me. After what happened last night, well, we almost got
killed, Sam, together. I realized being with you is the best
place for me. Don't panic. I'm not proposing or anything like
that. I just want to keep this feeling for a while, for as long
as it will last."

Sam smiled down at Martha and kissed her forehead.
She buried her head against his chest for a moment and
then looked up at him. "Wash me, Sam. Lather me up and
wash me. I want to feel your gentle hands taking care of
me."

Sam did as requested, spreading the soapy lather over
every inch of her body. He enjoyed touching her smooth
skin, but not in a sexual way. His hands moved in total
compliance with her words, caring for every soft, feminine
inch of her. For the moment, she was a new Martha, still
beautiful and sexy, but also scared and vulnerable and
needy. It was how the women and girls in the camp must
have felt.

Sam returned to his own place after breakfast, prom-
ising to check back with her by noon. He changed into
fresh clothes: tan Levi jeans and a blue Chambray shirt. He
wanted to call Chief Powers, to know for certain that Turner
was in jail, but thought the better of it. *Give the chief some
room.* He decided to scan the Boston Sunday Globe, which
he picked up on his way home. Boston had plenty of its own
problems, as was evident by the front page.

The telephone on his kitchen wall broke the quiet.

Sam moved to the phone and slid his fingers around
the receiver, lifting it from the cradle. "Hello."

"Hi, Sam, it's Carol. How are you?"

Suddenly he realized he hadn't thought about her for
who knows how long. How could that have happened? It reminded him of the enormity of recent events. That he could

have put this woman out of his mind for any length of time seemed impossible. But he had.

"Oh, hi, Carol. I'm fine. How about you?"

"Sam, Arthur wanted me to call you to invite you over this afternoon to watch the Patriot's game and have a little party. We'll get a few others, too. Arthur is working in his study on his project, but is almost done. Why don't you come over about one? You can bring Martha."

She said it without hesitation. *You can bring Martha.* That's how she saw Sam, as a friend who was coupled with Martha. He understood.

"Yeah, that sounds great," said Sam. "I'll give Martha a call. I'm sure she'll love it. You know what a social animal she is."

"Oh, *that* kind of animal." Carol's giggle surprised Sam, and she must have sensed his hesitation. "I'm sorry, Sam. I didn't mean anything. I really like Martha, but you know her reputation. I'm really sorry. I didn't mean to sound unkind."

Mean it or not, it was an unkind remark. He never would have expected that from Carol. Martha knew almost everybody in this town and they knew her. That is, they thought they did. Sam had learned that there was a lot more to Martha Sanborn than met the eye. She had to endure an awful lot from her *friends.*

"Party and football, sounds great. I'm surprised Arthur likes football. I thought he'd prefer soccer."

"Yes, he loves football. He says it's like a war, you know, where one army tries to physically beat back the other and occupy their territory. They're playing Buffalo. He really likes O.J. Simpson."

"Yeah," said Sam, "he's a great running back and all that, but there's something about that guy that rubs me the wrong way. I still say he's no Jim Brown."

"Okay, I'll let you argue that with Arthur. I'll count you two in. See ya."

Maybe Vasile wasn't Seth Walpole's killer after all. At the moment, Sam hoped all hell would come down on Al Turner, but Seth's interest in the Holocaust and his connection to Dr. Wirth, a Holocaust survivor, was too coincidental to ignore. If Arthur Vasile was an escaped Nazi war criminal and Seth found out about him, it would certainly be a motive for murder. He had to learn more about this man.

Chapter Thirty-Seven

SUNDAY AFTERNOON, NOVEMBER 3.

Martha and Sam arrived at the Vasile house at fifteen minutes before one, enough time to meet the other guests and not miss the opening kickoff. Carol greeted them at the door, giving Sam a big hug and a peck on the cheek. Martha got a polite hug and a cheek-to-cheek, no kiss greeting. "Come on in, gang," said Carol. "Everybody's in the living room. Help yourselves to drinks in the kitchen."

"I'm good for now, thanks," said Sam.

"Me, too," chimed in Martha. "I'll hold off until I get food in my gut."

Carol seemed surprised at the no-drink policy for Martha. "Suit yourselves, kiddies."

Sam eyeballed Carol as she led them in. Martha wasn't the loose lush some people thought. *Why can't they give her a break?*

Ian spotted Sam as he and Martha entered the large room. The big man ambled up to the couple and gave Martha a gentle hug, while cradling a beer stein in one hand. "Hi, folks. Great to see you. What's new?"

Sam and Martha exchanged glances before Sam spoke. "I'll bring you up to date soon enough, Ian. How's the beer? I love the stein."

"Vasile's got a nice collection of these. He's got a few frosting in the fridge, along with some great German beer. You ought to try one." Ian leaned in close to Sam and whispered, "At least the guy's good for beer."

"Now," said Sam, "don't you guys start up today. This is supposed to be a party."

"And so it is. Frankly, I was surprised to get this invitation, but here I am. I feel a little funny about it, but, what the hell. I guess it'll be fun. I don't know."

"Where is Arthur, still in his study?"

"Nope. He's in the kitchen fussing with food." Ian turned away for a moment, looking toward his wife, seated on the sofa. Martha had taken the spot next to her. "Hey, come say hi to Judy."

They strolled across the room, and Sam greeted Judy Barnstead. After allowing the hello, Ian tapped Sam's arm and spoke in a low voice out of the side of his mouth. "So, what is the latest news, Sam, you know what I mean? You got anything?"

"Later, big fellow, later." Apparently word about Al Turner hadn't made the rounds yet.

"Okay, have it your way. Come on into the kitchen and I'll get you one of these." Ian held up his stein. Sam nodded and held out his hands, palms up in submission.

In the kitchen, Arthur stood near the stove with another guest, unknown to Sam. "Ah, hello, Sam," said Arthur. "I'm so glad you could make it. I told Carol to call you this morning. We weren't sure if you were . . . around."

Arthur held a large cast iron skillet with both hands, about to place it on the stove. It was full of chopped onions, mushrooms and tomatoes. Sam stepped toward him and extended a hand, expecting Arthur to balance the skillet in his left hand while completing the handshake. But Arthur couldn't let go of the heavy pan with his right hand.

"Excuse me, Sam, but this pan is heavy, so, please . . ." He turned away, placed the skillet on the stove and returned to Sam to resume the hand shake.

Sam stared at Arthur's left hand, recalling what Eli had told him about Dr. Rauf's injury. "Hey, what's the matter, Arthur? A big fellow like you should be able to hold that skillet with one hand. I didn't think a handshake would be such a challenge." He saw a flash of anger in Vasile's eyes, combined with a bit of embarrassment.

"Perhaps you should try handling that skillet with one hand, Mr. Miller. Ah, you are still young. I am getting old, I guess." Vasile tried to move the conversation away from the incident with the pan, but Sam pressed on.

"I guess you won't earn a nickname like Lefty. You are strictly a right-handed man."

"Well, Sam, like I said, we weren't sure if you were around."

"Yes, I'm here in the flesh."

"So I see. So I see. Sam, have you met Jim Kirkson?"

Sam stood wide-eyed before extending a hand. So this was the wealthy alumnus who was going to build Seth Walpole's pet project and help put the college on the map. "Very nice to meet you, Mr. Kirkson."

"Oh, please, it's Jim." He was tall and lean, probably in his early fifties. His brown hair was thick and spotted with gray. He wore straight-legged jeans and a red wool shirt, sleeves rolled up to the elbows. Tan suede boots completed the outfit. It was not what Sam would have expected from this self-made millionaire. Reality could kill a predetermined image.

"What brings you to Henniker this Sunday morning? Or am I asking an obvious question?"

"I have a meeting scheduled with Al Turner tomorrow morning, but Arthur called me a few days ago and invited me over here. We met a couple of years ago at a college function."

Sam's mouth went dry. "Have you . . . called Al?" Sam wondered when the news about Turner's arrest would creep out.

"No, not yet. I'll just wait until our meeting."

Sam thought that was odd and his face apparently showed it. Conversation stopped for an awkward moment.

"Let me comment, Sam," said Arthur. A smile crept across his face. "I think it's safe to say nobody in this room is a big fan of Al Turner, and that includes Jim."

Sam felt the tension in the room ease, and he looked back at Kirkson. *They're all in for a surprise.*

"I don't mean to be rude, Sam, but, frankly, he's not my cup of tea. Losing Seth was a terrible thing in every way, but I never cared for what I've seen of Turner at our meetings. He seems competent enough, but, well, I guess you all know him better than I do. So, I'm in no hurry to see him. I can wait for the meeting."

Sam glanced around the room. "Say, Arthur, Ian tells me you've got some great beer and more of those frosted steins ready to go. I think I'll try one, after all."

Ian's voice boomed. "I'll get it for you. Let Arthur deal with his kitchen chores." He proceeded to extract a stein from the freezer and a beer bottle from the fridge. After popping open the bottle, he flipped the lid to the stein with his left hand and seized the beer in his right. "There's a real art to pouring these babies into a cold stein, Sammy. You've got to take it real slow, or you just might foam up the thing. Behold."

Sam watched Ian perform his artistry with slow precision. "I could grow old waiting for this."

"It'll be worth the wait. Trust me."

Ian emptied the bottle into the stein and brought it to his friend, holding the lid opened. "There you go, Sammy, all set with about a half inch of head. Enjoy."

Sam took the stein and sampled the cold beverage. "Just as you said. It was worth the wait. Thanks."

Arthur forced a smile when Sam held up his stein in his host's direction. "Why don't you gentlemen go into the living room? The game should be about to start."

"Good idea," said Sam, who waved his right arm in the direction of the door, motioning Ian and Jim to go first. He began stepping in the same direction and looked back at Arthur when he reached the exit. His quick glance caught Arthur staring back at him, a stern look that quickly changed to a smile. Sam waved goodbye, holding his stein up high with his left hand. "Look, Ma, one hand," he uttered as he left the room.

The party made for a pleasant Sunday afternoon, even though the Patriots lost. Sam focused on Carol most of the time and didn't pay much attention to football. By four o'clock, people showed signs of sluggishness and were ready to leave.

Martha, who nursed one drink all afternoon, looked at Sam, like a child yearning for attention. "Can you take me home now, Sam? I've had it."

"Of course," he said. In a moment they were making their way around the room, saying goodbyes.

As they left the house and walked past the other cars, Martha noticed a large, black truck. Her curiosity got to her and she headed for it, examining the driver's side with Sam following. She eyeballed the vehicle and then looked straight at Sam.

The front left fender and door were scratched and dented, not totally crushed in, but freshly wounded.

"Sam, do you know whose truck this is?"

"Yes, it's Arthur's. I forgot he has a pick up." They stared silently at one another. "Stay here, Martha. I'm going to check with him about this."

Sam caught up with Arthur as he and Carol were standing at their door, saying good bye to the Barnsteads. "Say, Arthur, your truck looks a little messed up on the left front. What happened?"

The stern look returned to Arthur's face, as if his patience with Sam was running out. "Oh, that. I loaned my truck to a young friend the other day. He said he had parked in a lot in Hillsboro while he went into a store. When he came out, he saw the damage. Somebody must have sideswiped the truck and didn't bother to stop. Probably some half-drunk kids. It's not too bad, though. I'll have to get it fixed soon."

Sam stared at Vasile, digesting every word of his explanation and evaluating it carefully. *Could be, could be.*

"Well, that's a shame, Arthur. It's a nice truck." Sam felt the heat of Arthur's glare, as if he also was being evaluated.

When he turned back to Martha, she held her arms across her chest. She waited for him to reach her. "I heard what Vasile said. Do you buy it?"

"I don't know. I guess so."

"This is creepy. Could Arthur's truck be the one that hit us? Why? We're sure it was someone doing Al Turner's bidding. It had to be. But it's just too coincidental that Arthur's truck has that damage to it. I mean, the one that hit us would show signs of the collision just like the scratches and dents on Arthur's, wouldn't it? Let's get out of here."

Sam put his arm around Martha's shoulder and walked her to her car. She was trembling.

194

Chapter Thirty-Eight

SUNDAY, LATE AFTERNOON, NOVEMBER 3.

Sam dropped Martha off at her place and said he had to take care of something. She looked like a hurt puppy when he spoke, so he assured her he'd return and spend the night with her. Besides, this way he'd be able to pick up some clothes for Monday.

It was getting dark early, with the end of Daylight Saving Time that weekend. Sam had nearly forgotten about it.

Back at his apartment, he realized he'd better be prepared to stay with Martha until his car was ready, so he packed for several days. Martha could use the company. She was badly shaken by the recent ordeal and needed Sam to be close. He was a willing caregiver.

Sam considered the state of affairs in the small town of Henniker. The president of the college had been murdered less than a month ago and now the Acting President had been arrested for felony assault. People wouldn't know what to think. What could be next?

He decided he needed to bring Eli up to speed. He might already know about the murder of Dr. Wirth, but might not know about the Walpole and Wirth connection. He found the piece of paper in his wallet containing the special phone number Eli gave him, a number he could call anytime.

After four rings, Eli answered Sam's call. The greetings were short and Sam got right to telling him what had happened in Henniker and Manchester. Eli's voice was calm, and he seemed very controlled.

"Sam, what Grossman said to you about the German scientists and engineers was correct. In 1943, the Germans realized they were hurting themselves by having numerous scientists and engineers fighting in the infantry. A Nazi officer, Werner Osenberg, compiled a list of them to be cleared for scientific and research duty instead of combat. After the war, that list was used by the United States to identify those whose knowledge and expertise would be beneficial to our government, but most harmful if the Soviets got them. If copies of that list still exist in the hands of ex-Nazis, it could be used to find many of them and to organize them for purposes I care not think about."

Sam swallowed hard. "You mean, for trying to rebuild the Nazi Party?"

"Or worse, Sam. They could be in positions to do great damage to American scientific projects, especially in the Department of Defense."

"And we brought them over here intentionally," said Sam. "Wow. That's like sleeping with rattlesnakes in your bed."

"Exactly. Stay in contact with Mr. Grossman. Perhaps he has more information that can help identify Arthur Vasile. We're getting very close on this, Sam, but we've got to have more evidence before we can take action."

"Yes," said Sam. "Will do."

"Good," said Eli. Oh, by the way, I've sent off a package for you. I don't want to talk about it right now. You should be getting it tomorrow. Remember, Sam, finding the murderer is not your mission. You must help us identify Vasile, at all costs. I understand he might be involved, but what's of greater importance is that we find out for sure if he is really Augustos Rauf."

"I got it, Eli. I'll keep digging."

"Good. And be very careful. He could be capable of anything." Eli didn't wait for exchanging goodbyes. He simply hung up.

Chapter Thirty-Nine

MONDAY MORNING, NOVEMBER 4.

Martha was more like her old self when Monday morning rolled around. She hadn't been interested in love making on Sunday night, but Monday was a different story. Her sexual energy returned in full force and she aggressively went about stimulating Sam in a variety of ways. He rose to the occasion and they satisfied each other vigorously. No Monday morning blahs for them.

They showered together and toweled each other dry. Martha stood with her back to Sam as he patted her down, from the shoulders to her feet and back up again. Then he shifted the towel to her front, clutching her breasts through the damp cloth.

"Sam, I'm sorry if I made a fool of myself the last couple of nights. Don't worry, I'm not trying to tie you down or anything. Tie you up now and then, maybe." They smiled at each other after her little joke. "Like it or not, Al sees us as both being against him. It's funny, you know. Once the whole town thought you and Carol were getting it on, and I had no problem with that. Now they see us being very together. What a turn, huh?"

Sam continued rubbing her front with the towel, slowly and gently, returning to caregiver mode rather than lover. "You didn't make a fool of yourself, not one bit." He hugged her tightly and could feel her heart beating rapidly under his hand. It was like holding a tiny bird in one's palm. They remained silent for a moment before Sam completed the pleasant task of drying her.

"You know, Martha, aside from the drama, this was a pretty good weekend. I mean . . . I enjoyed being with you, really. Now, I'm the one about to sound silly. I guess it's time to get dressed."

"Just one minute there, big boy. It's my turn to do some feeling up." Martha pulled the towel out of Sam's hands and spun around to face him. She wiped his face and then positioned the towel on his chest, rubbing down his torso, all the way. She continued down both legs and drew the towel back up, clutching his crotch. "Hey, is that blood I feel pulsing through your . . . veins?"

Sam felt like an embarrassed schoolboy, caught with a bulge in his pants, only this time it was under a towel. "Hey, hey, that's enough for now. Come on. We've got to get to work."

"Okay, Sam. I was just having a little fun, you know, tit for tat." They smiled at each other and slipped into their clothing.

When they arrived at the library, Sam and Martha expected to get looks as they entered together, but the clerks at the desk went about their business, as if all was as usual. The couple didn't even exchange goodbye looks as they went their separate ways to their work spaces.

The morning passed easily, with Fred and Gene going about their work. Fred helped a student DJ make a pre-recorded program for the radio station, and Gene typed up some film rental orders for faculty members.

Sam caught up on his paperwork and realized he had nothing pressing to do. That's when he recalled Eli sent him a package, due today. His heart rate increased. It reminded him of the feeling when he'd tried a diet pill many years ago. He hated that experience.

A trip to the basement gave Sam a chance to mull about the equipment storage room, checking for anything out of order or needing attention. Negative. He walked across the lobby and entered the radio station, moving quietly into the sitting area. A large Plexiglas window allowed him to look in where Fred was engineering a program. They exchanged waves and Sam retraced his steps out of the studio.

He passed the elevator and opted for the back stairway up to the first floor of the library. The usual number of students scattered about the library, most genuinely studying and some just killing time between classes. A tap on the shoulder got his attention.

"Oh, hi, Bob. Good morning."

"Come into my office for a minute." His boss turned and scurried into his office. When Sam entered, he saw Martha had also been summoned.

"Close the door, will you," said Bob. Sam did as requested and saw his boss gesture to the chairs in front of his desk. He and Martha eased into the seats while Bob sat in his own padded piece of office furniture.

"I'm afraid we've got another strange turn of events around here," said Bob. "I got a call this morning from Carl Mortimer at Security. Chief Powers called him first thing to tell him Al Turner was arrested on Saturday for aggravated assault on a man named Tom West. He's been in the county jail and is being arraigned in the Circuit Court in Henniker this morning. The story made the Concord Monitor and the Union Leader today, so everybody is going to know about it without a big announcement."

Martha and Sam exchanged a quick glance.

Bob folded his hands on his desk, looking like a judge about to hand down a sentence. "Look, I know you two probably have no love lost for the guy, but I wondered if either of you know anything about it?"

Martha was about to speak, but Sam held up his palm toward her. "Yes, Bob, we do. But Chief Powers asked us not to talk about it because it's considered an ongoing investigation. We are closely involved in this thing, so we can't speak up." Sam sat back in his chair, and Martha seemed pleased Sam cut her off and shut down Bob's questioning.

Bob looked stunned and began to tap his hands on his desk. "Oh, I see. Well, if Chief Powers doesn't want you to discuss the case, I certainly understand. It's just, well, you know, after that incident at the basketball game . . . he kind of roughed you both up." Bob shot a little smile at Martha. "Mortimer will call the Chairman of the Board of Trustees to convene a conference call to decide what to do. My guess is they'll ask for Turner's resignation from the college and someone from the Board may take over as Acting President." He paused for a few seconds, expecting a response from his colleagues. None came.

"Okay," said Bob, "if anybody asks you, tell them what I just said about the Board of Trustees. I'll keep quiet about your involvement. I guess you'd better get back to work."

Martha and Sam did as told and were almost out of the room when Bob spoke again. "You know, guys, we sure are lucky to live in a small college town in New Hampshire where nothing big ever happens."

It started slowly at first, but the buzz began shortly after the meeting with Bob. First, Gene and Fred were asking Sam about it. He figured that the staff downstairs was getting into it also. Students were talking about it after a radio station announcer did a rip and read of the local news from the Associated Press machine. He could imagine the turmoil at the administration building.

By eleven o'clock, Sam decided to venture down to the library circulation desk to check for the morning mail. Sure enough, a small pile of boxes and letters were piled up on a table behind the desk, all for Sam's department. Two of the packages were large film boxes with Gene's name on them. A smaller one read, "Attention: Sam Miller."

Back in his office area, Sam placed the two large boxes on Gene's desk and took the rest of the mail to his own. He left the small film box on a desk corner, deciding to wait for his young colleagues to go to lunch, when he could open the package in private. It would be a long hour.

When the time came and Sam had the privacy he wanted, he took hold of the small box and cut the packing tape that kept it closed tightly. There was no film in the package, but a thick film rental catalog instead. It had several unbound papers protruding from between the pages. He slid them out and eased the catalog away.

Between the loose papers covering them were several old, black and white photographs of different sizes, and a hand written note. It said the enclosed photos were a few of the many pictures his agents acquired over years of searching for evidence from Auschwitz. The note was signed, *Your friend, Eli.*

Sam's mouth fell open when he gazed at the first picture. It was an exterior shot of a scene he remembered all too well. Numerous people stood near a wall, what little clothing they wore was torn and dirty-looking, and there were German soldiers, armed with rifles, standing behind them, smiling. This was Auschwitz.

Sam squinted a bit, as if trying to zoom his eyes in on the photograph like a camera lens. He hoped he could

200

recognize some of the faces, but to no avail. They were different faces, but all with the same expression of despair and hopelessness. He knew he was looking at ghosts. These grown men, some of them quite old at the time, must now be dead. They might not have lived much longer after the picture was taken.

He flipped through two more photographs of similar scenes, but stopped flipping when he reached one of an interior shot. A chill ran through him. It showed three people, two men and a woman, standing in a room with what appeared to be an operating table and lights overhead. In front of the people was a small table with surgical instruments. Sam's eyes went right to the woman on the far right. It was Sadie, his mother.

He looked and looked at what he remembered to be her beautiful, warm face. But it was drawn tight and her eyes seemed to be on the brink of tears. The man to her right, in the middle of the picture, held his left arm around her shoulders, squeezing her toward him. He was tall and wore a white lab coat over his clothing, a large smile across his face. It was Mengele, the doctor; the man in charge of the hospital and responsible for the work Sam later learned were experiments on human subjects.

Sam panned across the photo to the man on the left. He was tall and broad at the shoulders, dressed like the other doctor. Sam instantly recognized him, as well, as the other man's assistant, the one who threatened to cut off Sadie's hand if Schmuel dropped his lunch.

Sam's gaze returned to the woman and his eyes began to fill with quiet tears. It was thirty years since Sam had seen his mother's face. He had no pictures of her until now and it tore at him inside that this photo also contained two evil monsters. He reached inside his middle desk drawer and drew out a pair of scissors, intent on cutting her free from those horrible men. But something held him back.

He returned the scissors to the drawer and stared hard at the picture, focusing on the man to the far left. He studied the man's facial features, comparing them mentally to those of Arthur Vasile. He had a full, youthful head of light brown hair, combed straight back. The eyebrows were of average thickness, but the left one seemed to point up noticeably towards the middle of his forehead, while the right one was more parallel to the ground.

Arthur Vasile's hair was thin and gray, to be expected of a man who had aged since this photo was taken. Now that Sam thought of it, yes, Vasile combed his sparse hair straight back. He looked closely at the picture again and saw something that sent cold down his spine. The assistant had what looked to be a bandage wrapped around his left hand. This was Vasile, for certain, only his real name was Augustos Rauf.

Sam felt a sickening ache in his gut. His faced flushed and he felt the warmth of the blood in his veins. He wanted to kill this man, Rauf or Vasile –or whoever he was. He was a monster, and he was married to Carol.

Carol. He had to tell her, to bring her into this for her own good. He couldn't bear the thought of her being with that man. Besides, he would also need her help to find more evidence. He slipped the photographs back between the pages of the catalog and picked up the phone. As he dialed her office number, Sam took several deep breaths, hoping to sound calm and collected when he spoke to her. That was a challenge.

"Oh, hi, Sam. Oh my God, have you heard about Al Turner? What's going on around here? It's one bizarre event after another." Carol seemed to be the one in need of calming.

"Yes, Carol, I know about Turner. The Henniker Police are really earning their pay these days."

"It's crazy, Sam. It's just crazy. I hope we've reached the limit on strange events here. I mean, what else could happen?"

Sam swallowed hard and couldn't find the words to continue. "Maybe this is a bad time, Carol. Perhaps I should call back later."

"I'm sorry, Sam. I'll be okay. Really. Don't hang up. Please. The sound of your voice is always reassuring to me. Arthur just laughed about it when he saw the story in the newspaper this morning. And to think Jim Kirkson is . . . was supposed to meet with Al today. Maybe we could meet for lunch. What do you think?"

Sam took a deep breath and let it out easily, like a basketball player about to shoot a free throw. He had to get back to the reason he was calling her. "Yes, Carol, lunch is a good idea."

"Okay, Sam," said Carol, returning to a calm tone. "Look, I have to run to the bank in Hillsboro. Why don't I do that and meet you at Govoni's in about twenty minutes?"

"That's fine, Carol. I'd be happy to get out of Henniker today anyway. I'll see you soon."

Sam eased the telephone back onto its cradle and sighed, holding the phone down with both hands for a minute, as if he were afraid it would bounce back up at him with more bad news. For a moment, he sat with both hands resting palms down on the catalog, as if he was drawing a measure of goodness from the pictures inside.

In a moment, he gathered up the catalog and headed for Hillsboro. Martha would have to miss her car for a while.

When he arrived at Govoni's, Sam wound through the tables and found one at the far rear of the room and took the seat facing the main door. There weren't many people in that section of the restaurant, so it would provide a level of privacy for their conversation.

Carol appeared a few minutes later and spotted Sam, who was waving to her from his table. His mouth went dry as she got closer. He was about to shake up her life in a way she couldn't possibly imagine. *Can I really do this?*

Carol spoke rapidly as she pulled a chair out and took her seat. There was no embrace. "This is just crazy, crazy, I tell you. What happened with Al? Has he gone completely nuts? I mean, how can a grown man, hell, the Acting President of a college, go around getting into fights? Okay, a fight, but still. The man is in jail. This could cost him his job. Hell, it *will* cost him his job, I'm sure. What on earth is wrong with that guy?"

Sam folded his hands on the table, his fingers interlaced over the catalog. "Carol, do you want a drink or something?" He flagged down a waitress and Carol ordered a glass of Pinot Grigio. Sam stuck with water. He needed all the control he could muster for what he was about to tell her.

"Carol, I'm not here to discuss Al Turner. There's something more important." He gulped more water to fight off the dry mouth and stared down at the catalog in front of him.

Carol furrowed her brow as she sipped her wine. "What? Sam, the college may be falling apart at the seams and you say you have something more important to talk about? I don't get it. Don't tell me you're dying of cancer, for crying out loud." She forced a weak laugh.

Sam sat silently for a moment before lifting his eyes toward Carol. He searched for words. "Here, I want you to see these." He drew the collection of pictures out of the catalog and leafed through them, shuffling and sorting them into a special order. One by one, he slid them to Carol.

"Oh my God, Sam. These look like scenes from a concentration camp." She noticed the film catalog. "Do these go with a film or something? Is there something special about them?"

He sipped more water. He showed her all of the pictures except one, which he held in his fingers by the edges. "They're pictures from Auschwitz."

Carol glanced at the photographs, shaking her head. "It must have been horrible there. Is that one of the camps they talked about during the last Olympics in Germany? Those damned terrorists. They don't ever want peace. They just want to kill people. Those poor athletes."

Sam sipped again. He looked up and stared into Carol's eyes with a look that made her lock onto his face. "This is Auschwitz, where I was a prisoner as a young boy, along with my mother."

Carol stared back at Sam, then reached for her wine, drank some and examined the pictures. "You were a prisoner? You were in the Holocaust? Arthur told me you were originally from Europe, but he didn't say anything about a camp. Where did you get these pictures? Did you know any of these people? Oh, Sam."

Sam's water glass was running low. "I want you to look carefully at this one." He slowly slid the last picture, the one of his mother and the two men, over the table. "That woman was my mother, Sadie. She didn't survive."

"Oh, dear Sam, I'm so sorry." Carol examined the picture closely, admiring the woman. "She must have been very pretty, you know..." Carol meant to compliment Sam's mother, but the awkwardness of the moment stifled her.

"Yes, she was. I wish I had a nice picture of her."

They sat speechless for a moment before Carol started to push the picture back to Sam. He held out his hand to stop her. "Look at it some more, please," he said.

Carol obeyed and finally asked, "Who are the two men? They look like doctors."

"Yes, Carol, they are. The one in the middle is Josef Mengele."

Carol gasped. "Oh my, he was that horrible Nazi. They're still looking for him, aren't they?"

"Yes, they are. Now, look at the other man."

Carol studied the other doctor. "Is there something special about him, too, other than he must have been a Nazi doctor at Auschwitz?"

Sam drank down more water. "His name is Augustos Rauf, Dr. Mengele's assistant."

Carol studied the man's face. "Are they looking for him, too?"

"Yes, Carol, they are. But they've found him and will arrest him soon. He lives here in this country, in New Hampshire, in fact. He goes by another name, Arthur Vasile."

Carol's face transformed. Her eyes opened wide, her face turned pale and her jaw dropped open. Both hands gripped the edge of the table as if she were trying to regain her balance from a dizzying place.

"What? Are you crazy? You're telling me Arthur is an escaped Nazi? Don't be ridiculous." Sam gestured with his hands, pleading for Carol to keep her voice down and she complied. "Sam, don't be silly," she whispered across the table. "You surely don't think I'm going to believe this story. I mean, you hit me with this completely out of the blue, for Christ's sake." Carol grasped her water glass and poured some into her mouth, swallowing hard.

The relationship that they had built over several months, one that Sam wished with all his heart could be more than friendship, was about to crumble to dust if he couldn't succeed in winning her over. He told Carol the man she loved and had been married to for years was a monster, a Nazi who committed crimes against humanity. What's more, he now risked blowing his cover. Once Vasile found out, Sam's life would surely be in danger, and maybe Carol's, too.

"Notice that the man in the picture has a bandage around his left hand. He cut it badly and can barely use it. Arthur has that problem. Carol, I know it's hard to believe, but you must trust me. I wouldn't have met you here if I wasn't certain."

Carol's hands were trembling, due to extreme anger, or fear, or both. She licked her lips, her tongue repeating the action three times before speaking.

"Trust you? My God, you tell me this terrible thing about the man I live with and love dearly and you want me to choose between him and you? Trust you, you say, over my husband. This is absurd, absolutely absurd."

"Carol, please listen to me." He reached across the table for Carol's hands, but she drew them away. "I have a friend in Washington who called me weeks ago. He was at Auschwitz with me in 1944. We got out together and went our separate ways over the years. He works with a group who pursue escaped Nazi war criminals. He's the one who told me Rauf might be at New Sussex College. I agreed to help him search."

Carol's hand was drawn into a fist, lying on the table. "So all this time you were a false friend? Someone out to get my husband on some nonsensical notion that he was a Nazi. And you expect me to trust you?"

"Carol, we became friends long before I got that call. Believe me, this has been very hard, especially after Seth was murdered. I had no reason to think Arthur had done that because there is somebody else very much involved in that case. But you did tell me Arthur and Seth never got along very well. Then there was the murder of Dr. Wirth in Manchester. Carol, he was a Holocaust survivor, as well, and he was in frequent contact with Seth. Seth even wanted Ian Barnstead to develop a course on the Holocaust. Seth and Dr. Wirth were digging into the Holocaust and might have been a threat to Rauf."

Carol slammed her fist on the table. "So you're telling me Arthur killed both of those men?"

"No, no, that's not what I'm trying to say. I think somebody else killed Seth and Chief Powers has a suspect. I mean it's just too much of a coincidence that there is an escaped Nazi in the local area and there are two college presidents digging into the Holocaust—heck, one of them a survivor, and they *both* wind up dead."

Carol drank more wine. She looked all around, as if for an escape. "You're throwing an awful lot at me, Sam. It sounds like you're talking about a movie or something."

Sam leaned forward. "Only it's all very real. And there's more. Saturday night, Martha and I were driving back from Hillsboro and someone in a big pickup truck tried to run us off the road. They slammed into the passenger side and forced me off the road toward the river. We spun off the road and onto the grass. The only thing that stopped us was the tramway pole. Otherwise, we'd have been sunk. Someone tried to kill us."

Carol looked at Sam, speechless. She began to rub her thumbs across her fingertips, her head turning slowly from side to side.

"As we were leaving your house yesterday, Martha and I noticed the damage to Arthur's truck, dents and scratches on the driver's side. The truck that hit us would have such damage. I know, Arthur said that he loaned the truck to a young friend who claimed the truck was sideswiped while it was in a parking lot. That may be so, but perhaps I should tell Chief Powers about it and have the police check Arthur's vehicle for paint residue to see if there is any and whether or not it matches my car's paint. Is he driving the truck today?"

"My God, Sam, you're serious. You think Arthur is lying. You think his friend drove you off the road with Arthur's truck."

"No, Carol, I find that hard to believe, too. I mentioned another suspect. That man was here at Govoni's Saturday night when Martha and I were here for dinner. The man had been talking to somebody else at the door. He and Tur . . . the other guy, looked our way before the fellow left and the suspect took a seat with a woman, I assume his wife. I was certain that my suspect's young friend was the guy who caught up with us and hit us, until yesterday. When I saw Arthur's truck, well, I didn't know what to think. How many coincidences are there going to be? Of course, a check for paint residue could exonerate Arthur on this."

Carol wet her lips. "Even if there is matching paint residue, Sam, it doesn't mean Arthur had anything to do with it. Maybe his friend was also the friend of that suspect of yours."

"Yes, that's true. So why not have the police check it out? If there is a match, Arthur can tell the police who the young man is. If there is no paint, then Arthur is totally exonerated. Where is the truck today?"

Carol brought her hands up to her mouth, her elbows on the table. Sam thought he could see the wheels of thought spinning in her head. "He dropped it off this morning at Sid's Gulf station. I followed him and drove him to work."

Sam's face showed a slight grin, but he remained silent. *Imagine, both vehicles are side by side at Sid's.* He finished his water and looked at Carol. She had calmed down and appeared to be trying to digest all the information he'd laid on her in these few minutes. Sam watched as she reached for the photograph, picked it up and studied it again. A seed of doubt had been planted.

"Yes, your mother was pretty. I can see that."

"Please, Carol, don't tell Arthur about this conversation. I think it would be best for everyone if you just kept quiet about it."

She nodded. "Okay. I'll be quiet, but I'm still not buying this escaped Nazi stuff."

Sam paused, furrowing his brow and searching his thoughts for a final word that might help. "You know, Dr. Mengele was fascinated with twins. His research before the war centered on the whole phenomenon of multiple births. Then, he went mad, doing unspeakable things to twins at the camp." He ended his comment right there and stared into Carol's eyes. They were growing moist. She knew full well what he was driving at.

"I think I'm going to go back to work, Sam. I'm not very hungry after all." Carol began to rise from her chair, then suddenly sat back down. She took a pen from her purse and scribbled on a table napkin. Sam watched her, puzzled and somewhat amused. *Good thing they used paper napkins at Govoni's.* When she finished, she slid the paper to Sam, who read the scribble, Colonia Dignidad.

"Do you know what that is?" she asked. Sam shook his head.

"I never heard of it, either," said Carol. "Arthur got some mail with that on the return address. He got very upset because I saw it and he accused me of prying into his work. Please, find out what that is and let me know, quietly. I hope it's just a fruit vendor."

He watched her get up and turn away without further words. In a few seconds, she was gone. Sam had also lost his appetite, so he paid for the wine and strolled out to Martha's car, clutching the film catalog. He hoped Chief Powers was in his office.

Chapter Forty

MONDAY, LATE MORNING, NOVEMBER 4.

The short drive to Henniker seemed longer by the time Sam reached the police station, where he met with Chief Powers. He explained about Arthur Vasile's truck and the coincidence that both cars currently sat at Sid's shop, waiting to be fixed.

"Let me get this straight, Sam. You don't think Arthur Vasile was driving the truck, but you think it might have been the truck that hit you, correct?"

"Yes. I'd like you to have an officer check it for paint residue. There might be some that matches the paint on my car, which is right next to it in Sid's garage."

"Okay, we can do that. But I hope you understand a match is not conclusive evidence. It would only mean that the truck hit another vehicle with paint similar to your car's, but it won't prove that it was your car, just one with similar paint. And the driver told Vasile he was away from the truck when it got sideswiped?"

"I know, I know, but it's a start, and it's a hell of a co-incidence, don't you think?"

"Sam, there are a hell of a lot of black pickup trucks around here, but you're right. To have a truck with driver side damage and paint residue similar to that from your car, yes—that would be a hell of a coincidence. I'll send an officer over there today. I'd go myself, but I have a meeting today with the Board of Selectmen. I'll let you know what we find about the paint."

"Thanks, Chief. I appreciate your help, as always."

The next stop for Sam on his journey was his own apartment. He needed to contact Eli.

"We may have something, Eli," said Sam after the number he called was answered in six rings.

"That would be good." Eli's voice was calm, as usual.

"Do you know anything about a place in Chile called Colonia Dignidad?"

Eli's tone changed. "Sam, how did you hear about that place? Yes, we know of it."

He told Eli about the Vasiles' argument over his mail.

"Sam, that place is a stronghold for Nazi ideas and methods. We have agents who infiltrated it, and know it's used for spreading Nazi doctrine. German officers who made it to South America are hired as consultants to spread their poisonous ideas about social control. They even teach torture techniques, as well as abduction and execution methods. It's a breeding ground for Neo-Nazism. Sam, this is it. If Vasile is corresponding with Colonia Dignidad, then we have the proof we have been looking for. He is Augustos Rauf."

"It's incredible, but that monster has been right near me all the time I've been working here." Sam's breathing grew labored and quick. "To finally be sure he's Rauf is unbelievable, but true. What do we do next, Eli?"

"First, get that letter. That would be solid physical evidence. Second, don't try to approach him. I'll be on a plane today and meet you tonight. Tell me where to find you."

Sam gave Eli the information he needed to find the apartment and said goodbye. How would Eli take Vasile . . . Rauf? If it got violent, he had to be certain Carol would be safe, but how? It would be a very long afternoon, and somehow Sam had to remain cool, like nothing happened, like he wasn't on the same campus as the man who wanted to kill him as a ten year old boy. He had to call Carol.

She agreed to meet him at the steel bridge over the river on Ramsdell Road, just outside of town. It was late enough in the fall so that freshmen no longer had a fascination with the spot, and they would have privacy—something very vital, considering the topic for discussion.

When Sam arrived in Martha's vehicle, Carol's car was parked just north of the bridge where there was enough shoulder to get a car off the road. He pulled in front of her, but paused before getting out. He hated that he was destroying her happy life with Arthur, but he knew that was going to happen eventually. He hated that hurting her was the only way to save her. They exited their cars simultaneously and stepped toward each other, stopping between vehicles.

He wanted to wrap his arms around her, squeeze her tightly to him in a protective gesture, but he thought the better of it. She resisted physical contact at Govoni's earlier. It wasn't likely she'd welcome a bear hug from him now.

"What is it, Sam? Did you get an answer from your Washington friend so soon?"

He felt a pain in his gut and watched Carol's face turn pale as he told her about Colonia Dignidad. The light that was always in her eyes went dim, leaving her altogether. She turned in silence and walked the short distance to the bridge, with Sam hustling after her. They stopped and took up positions leaning on the steel rail, gazing down into the flowing water a few feet below. This was a spot frequented by new students each year, a spot where young men would play the romantic with the young women, wooing the new love interests in their lives. It was a spot where relationships had their beginnings. Today, a woman's relationship with her husband would come apart.

She had lost the anger she felt before toward Sam. He stood to her right and watched as her gaze turned upward, as if she were following the flow of the river. The life she'd known with Arthur was floating away.

"I'm sorry, Carol, so sorry. I don't know what else to say."

She continued to gaze down the river as she talked. "What are they going to do, Sam, those Nazi hunter friends of yours? Are they going to steal him away and take him back to Israel to stand trial, like Eichmann?"

"That's their plan, I believe," said Sam.

"But aren't you risking everything by telling me? Are they going to take me, too, to keep me quiet?"

"No, no, they would never do that, I'm sure. But you are in danger. We both are, from Arthur. There's no telling what extremes he'll go to in order to avoid capture."

"So what do we do, just sit around until your Nazi hunters arrive? When will that be?"

Sam took a deep breath. "Eli said he'll be here tonight. He'll meet me at my apartment." Sam's chest heaved as he shifted the conversation. "Carol, we need your help. We have to get that letter Arthur received from Colonia Dignidad. It's the proof Eli needs."

Carol turned toward Sam and he saw the tears falling from her eyes in the late afternoon light. "You're asking me to help find the evidence you need to send my husband to prison, maybe even to the gallows. You're asking me to help kill him." She gripped the bridge rail, as if holding on for dear life.

"Yes, I guess that is what I'm asking," said Sam, watching Carol struggle to hold herself together. "Will you help us?"

Sam watched as she returned her gaze to the river, and the silence seemed to last forever as she contemplated her answer, the only sounds coming from the water.

"There really isn't much choice, is there, Sam?" Her voice was soft and cracking. "Well, your timing is good. Arthur is going away again tonight, to see his colleague in Massachusetts. He should have left by now. So, bring your friend over tonight. We can have a jolly good time breaking into Arthur's study and rifling through his files. I'm sure you'll find what you need. Maybe you'll even find another picture of your mother."

Sam looked down and swallowed hard. The thoughts in his mind raced back to the camp, where his mom did whatever it took to protect her son. His thought was interrupted by Carol's soft voice.

"Oh, I'm sorry, Sam. I didn't mean anything hurtful. Please, forgive me."

Sam reached for her and pulled her to him, his arms gently enfolding her.

Holding Carol in a tender, tight embrace should be thrilling, but it wasn't what Sam wanted. There was no excitement in this moment. Her body trembled as she wept against his chest. Without looking up, Carol uttered simple words. "Call me tonight when your friend arrives and you're ready to come over."

Sam felt her pull away from him, and his arms fell by his sides. "Okay, Carol, we'd better get back to work. Martha's going to think I've stolen her car."

She moved away quickly, before Sam could put a consoling arm around her shoulders. "Not me. I'm going home.

I'll call my boss and say I'm not feeling well. That would be an understatement, but it would be true."

Sam watched her go back to her car and drive away. On previous occasions when he was invited to be with Carol at her house, he felt a rush of emotion and urging. Tonight there would be a different type of excitement.

Chapter Forty-One

MONDAY EVENING, NOVEMBER 4.

The Turners barely spoke on the tense ride home from court. Elaine, always the dutiful wife, went to the bank and withdrew the needed cash to make Al's bail. He didn't cast so much as a glance at her in the car, as if she was his enemy. Or perhaps he was too deep in thought, making new plans.

At home, he tore off the necktie and sport coat she brought for the court appearance, and threw them on a living room chair. Al homed in on a bottle of scotch. Chivas Regal, neat in a highball glass, was his sanctuary. He downed several before stretching out on the sofa and floating into much needed sleep.

As daytime became evening, Al stirred awake while his wife eyed him from a chair. "Al, dear, come into the kitchen and have some food. I've made sandwiches. Please, you need to eat something."

It had been a long morning in court, and Al couldn't dismiss the emptiness in his belly, so he silently complied with his wife's urging. Scotch in one hand, the bottle in the other, he sauntered into the kitchen and eased into a chair at the table. Elaine sat at a comfortable distance across from him.

"Everything's going to be okay, dear, you'll see. You just had a misunderstanding with Tom and it got a little . . . well, you got excited and he must have said something to make you angry. I'm sure he'll forget about it soon . . . ."

"Oh, stop that foolish blather, woman," he interrupted. "It wasn't a misunderstanding, for Christ's sake. He opened his big, fat mouth to that Sanborn woman about my meeting with him the night Walpole . . . well, you know what. He should have kept his trap shut." He bit into his sandwich.

"But dear, it was just a meeting about the club. I know that and it didn't have anything to do with Seth. Oh, don't even think about that night. Tom is a good man and I'm sure he'll forgive you for hitting him."

Al poured another scotch and gulped it down. "Jesus Christ, you are a goddamn dumb bitch. Tom's not going to *forgive* me. He's going to *ruin* me." He poured another.

"Al, dear, please don't shout at me and call me that name. I'm your wife and I love you. I'm just trying to help."

Al shot up from his seat, staring down at Elaine, who pushed back in her chair as if there might be an escape hatch to it. She folded her arms, the only shield available, across her chest. Her face paled.

"West knows what happened that night. Now Sanborn knows it, too, and Sam Miller with her. Now it's too late to do anything about it. Don't you get it? I'm finished, ruined. My career is over. I'm going to spend the rest of my life in goddamn prison."

"Al, dear, what are you saying? You just had a little fight with Tom. They won't send you to prison for that. What do you mean the rest of your life?"

Al eased away from the table, glass in hand. Elaine was too frightened to stand and was still in her chair when her husband staggered back into the kitchen, his face flushed with Satanic hatred. Both hands were occupied, a glass of Scotch in his left and a fresh bottle in his right. He poured from the big container to the small one and drank it down. Right hand to left hand to mouth, three times, with a juggler's rhythm.

"That good for nothing Seth Walpole. He knew about the club, don't you see? He practically threatened to expose us, but he knew that would be bad publicity for the college. It didn't matter. He had to go. I couldn't take any chances. It would have worked fine, just fine, if it weren't for that snooping little bastard, Sam Miller. I was going to get him, too, somehow. I don't know how, but I would have."

The truth struck Elaine Turner harder than any physical blows her husband ever delivered. Her husband killed Seth Walpole. She burst into tears and jumped out of her chair, racing in a fearful dash out of the room. She tried to squeeze past Al, escape the only thing on her mind.

She was too slow. Al flung the glass at the wall and reached out with his left arm, circling her waist. With drunken force, he threw her staggering back through the room. Halfway across the kitchen, her tangled feet sent Elaine in a backward tumble that ended with her head crashing against the edge of the granite counter.

Al watched the blurred image of his wife's head striking the counter, followed by her crumpled body landing on the floor, almost in a seated position against the cabinet. Blood streaked the cabinet door and gushed around her collar. He took a swig of scotch straight from the bottle.

"Oh, what the hell, woman, we both have to go anyway." Al pulled pen and paper out of a counter drawer, eased his wobbly body into a kitchen chair and scratched out the tale of his hatred for Seth Walpole and how he killed him in the man's neatly decorated office. When finished, he signed his name, underlining it. Before dropping the pen, he added, *fuck Sam Miller and his bitch.*

Al shook off the wooziness in his head and stumbled into the basement. He made his way to his unlocked gun cabinet and withdrew a .38 caliber handgun. Reaching up to the shelf holding ammunition, Al fiddled for a single bullet, which he loaded into his revolver, spinning the cylinder with a chuckle.

He struggled up the stairs and staggered his way back into the kitchen. He gathered the scotch bottle closer and slid into a chair at the table. "Time for a game, little woman," he said to his dead wife. "Spin the fucking thing until you're dead." He spun the cylinder again, placed the barrel in his mouth and pulled the trigger. Click. Turner spit out the barrel in a hardy laugh, taking a swig of scotch as a reward. He repeated his deadly game. Click. Another laugh. Another swig. Repeat. Click. Laugh. Swig. Repeat.

This time there was no click and no laugh, just the loud boom of a gun, sounding the end of Al Turner's sorry story.

Chapter Forty-Two

MONDAY EVENING, NOVEMBER 4.

Martha sat in the passenger seat of her own car as Sam drove her home from work. She wanted to caress him, to light a fire in him, but she could tell this wasn't the time. His face showed a faraway look that worried her.

"What is it, Sam? I can see the wheels turning in your head, like you're planning the Normandy invasion. Maybe I shouldn't ask, but after all we've been through lately, I think I have a right to know."

Yes, she does have that right, but I can't tell her yet. He explained it was probably best if she didn't know what was about to happen.

"Look, if you've got some plan to take down Al Turner, then I should be there to help. Hey, I'm not some damsel in distress. Like it or not, we're both in this thing. Besides, I'm not real thrilled that Turner is probably out on bail and might be looking for us. He's a nut case, Sam."

Sam kept driving and soon pulled up to Martha's place. "You've got a gun, don't you? I suspected that's what was in your purse before. Keep it handy if it will help you feel better, but you can't be with me tonight and I can't tell you what's going on. I'm sorry, but you must trust me."

Martha looked at Sam before opening her door. "How'd you know about the gun? Did you snoop though my drawers?" No answer. "Yeah, well, okay, you bet I'll keep it close." Martha took a breath and puffed it out. "Deniability. That's the word, I believe. If I don't know what it is, I'm in the clear. Okay, I get it, but be mighty careful with that crackpot." She slid out of the car and ran up to her front door, disappearing into the apartment.

Once inside his own apartment, Sam grabbed the film catalog he brought home from the office. Sitting at the kitchen table, he selected the picture with Sadie and the two men. Her sad eyes spoke volumes about her pain, the inner conflict she must have felt from doing Mengele's bidding, serving him in despicable ways and doing it all for Schmuel. His guilt dissipated over the years, but his love and admiration for her grew. Her strength had been remarkable.

After munching on cheddar cheese and crackers from his kitchen, Sam took the pictures into the living room where he continued to examine them while resting in an easy chair. His eyes grew heavy and the time sped by while Sam succumbed to sleep.

His limbs stiffened when the doorbell startled him awake, his eyes jolting open. Shaking his head, Sam tried to emerge from his grogginess. Success came and he felt alert and thrilled when he opened the door. A tall, thin, dark-haired man stood quietly in the doorway, a smile breaking across his handsome face as he uttered, "Schmuel, I presume."

Tears filled Sam's eyes as he recognized his boyhood friend and fellow campmate. They clutched each other in an embrace, a silent hug in which time flashed back for both men.

"Eli, my dear old friend, come in, come in." His friend carried a black tote bag, strapped over a shoulder. He wore grey slacks, a white shirt and a dark blue sport coat. His black shoes were soft and silent as he moved.

"Are you hungry, Eli? I'm afraid I don't have much food in the house, some cheese and crackers were my dinner." Sam gave a gentle laugh about the state of his food stores.

"I'm fine, Schmuel . . . er, Sam. I grabbed a sandwich at the airport. I'd like to get going. We'll have another time for getting reacquainted, but we must get to our business. I want to get two things tonight, that letter and Rauf. There are two other men in my car. We are prepared to do whatever we must. Can you draw a sketch of the floor plan at his house?"

"Yes, but he's not in town tonight. Carol, his wife, met with me this afternoon and she told me he went to Massachusetts, as he has often done lately, to work with a colleague as consultants on a special project. He won't be back until tomorrow."

"What is her state of mind? This must be a terrible shock to her, and perhaps she isn't going to be helpful."

Sam feared Carol's suspicion that she might have to be kept quiet was correct. A chill raced down his spine. "She was devastated, of course, but when I told her about Colonia Dignidad she knew it was all true. Now she knows she married a Nazi monster, even though she loved this man he pretended to be, Arthur Vasile, for many years. She is terribly hurt, but she'll help us. I should call to let her know we're coming. Their house is just a short drive from here, a couple of minutes."

"Good. Make the call. It's good that he is away. That will give us time to make our plans. We need to be able to surprise him and take him quietly, if we can."

Holy shit. It is a real life Mission: Impossible. Sam's palms grew clammy as he moved to the kitchen phone and called Carol.

They moved briskly outside and Sam spied the two men in Eli's car. His friend walked up to it and motioned for one to roll down his window. After giving instructions, Eli returned to Sam and took his place in Martha's car, as Sam's passenger. "They'll follow us and park a short distance from the house. We don't want the neighbors noticing strange cars in Rauf's driveway."

Rauf. It was still hard for Sam to believe that Arthur Vasile was, indeed, Augustos Rauf, a butcher of human flesh. It was like the Jekyll and Hyde story.

Chapter Forty-Three

MONDAY EVENING, NOVEMBER 4.

Carol's house had the usual exterior illumination, floodlights on the garage and a lantern outside the front door. Sam turned left, pulling Martha's car up to the garage, while the two associates of Eli stayed on the right side of the road, stopping two houses past the Vasile house. The associates stayed in their vehicle, shutting down the engine and lights.

Carol greeted Sam and Eli at the door. As they stepped inside, Sam made a brief introduction. Carol extended a cold hand to Eli and gave him an even colder look.

"I assume you want to search Author's study first, Sam. It's locked but I don't think that will keep you people out," said Carol.

You people. Sam motioned for Eli to follow him, and Carol trailed behind. Sam made the necessary effort and easily worked the lock open. Turning toward Eli, he noticed his friend wore tight fitting, dark gloves, adding to the atmosphere of intrigue. Sam found the light switch as they entered the room.

Eli made the assertive move of taking up a position in the desk chair. "Carol, what can you tell me about your husband's big project, the one that took him away tonight?"

"Well, he works as a consultant for a chemical company in Massachusetts. Norwood, I believe. He's very excited about it. Why, he even told me some recent developments. That's something he doesn't usually do."

"Like what?"

"For one thing, it's going to be located in northern New Hampshire. That pleased him a great deal. He says it will be easier for him to travel to it that way."

Eli looked directly at Carol. "What is this thing that has him so excited?"

"A training center, he said, for this chemical company. It will have offices, classrooms and modern equipment,
whatever that means for a chemical company. Oh, and he
said it will have overnight facilities, meaning a dormitory. I
guess he still plans to take some overnight trips."

Eli turned his gaze to Sam. "We need to find any and all
correspondence with Colonia Dignidad, not just that recent
letter. If this project is what I think it is, and is secretive, I
fear it may be a local facility resembling Colonia Dignidad,
a center for training young Nazis. Their mission could be
not only to teach Nazi ways, but to plan industrial sabotage
here in the United States via terrorism. We've got to stop it."

Sam's mouth went dry as he tried to speak. "My God,
Eli, almost thirty years after the war and we're still fighting
them, not only in South America, but right here, too."

"And we helped them get a foothold here through Paperclip," said Eli.

"Paperclip, what's that?" asked Carol.

"I'll explain it to you later, Carol. Let's get started.
What's that?" Sam pointed to a door across the room.

"That's a closet. I haven't looked in it since Arthur took
this room as his study."

Sam tried the door and found it locked. In a minute
he had it opened. A naked light bulb hung from the center
of its ceiling, with a pull string switch. Once on, the light
revealed stacks of cardboard boxes, all numbered alpha-
numerically. Sam looked back at Eli, who nodded. He took
it as a command and began opening the boxes, pulling out
file folders. The first file in the top box was labeled "Master
List." The other files each had men's names on the tabs.

Sam was watching as Eli searched the drawers in the
desk and found a small, locked box in one of them. He saw
Eli frown upon not finding a key. "Check the center drawer."
His friend found several keys in a bunch. Sam went back to
his file folders. In a moment he called back to Eli. "Look at
this." Sam took a few steps and handed the master file to
Eli, who examined it. There were many papers, making it a
much thicker file than the others. The paper smelled of old
mimeograph fluid and some of the names were smudged,
but all were legible. There must have been a dozen sheets
and over a thousand names.

"Sam," said Eli. "Do you remember when I told you about a list of scientists and engineers that was compiled by a man named Osenberg? The one later used by Paperclip to help us determine who we'd bring into this country and get them jobs? I believe this is a reproduction of that list. The fact that it is mimeographed tells me there are others. This is very important. Once we take Rauf, I'll arrange to collect these boxes."

Eli found the key to the box, opened it and eyed the old diary lying inside. He carefully lifted it and placed it on the desk in front of him. Sam started to step back into the closet, but waited for a moment, intrigued by Eli's find. There was something about the box and its contents. The fact that it had been under lock and key added to its mystery.

While his friend opened the cover to the diary, Sam drew closer, moving to Eli's right side and peering at the book. At the top of the inside cover, the name of its owner was penned in faded ink, A. Rauf.

Sam stared at it for a moment, taking in the full impact of the moment. There was no longer any doubt. The two men studied it before their eyes met in silent acknowledgement.

Carol had never seen this book, so she edged to Eli's left side to see what the men discovered. Her eyes began to water as she saw the name, erasing any possibility that this was all a big mistake. That her husband was not the war criminal they claimed he was.

Arthur Vasile was, indeed, A. Rauf.

The quiet of the room enshrouded them, holding them perfectly still, until the sound of a car pulling into the driveway shook them awake.

"Carol, could that be Arthur?" asked Sam. "I thought you said he was gone overnight?"

"I don't know. He rented a car, so I don't recognize the sound. I don't know who it is. We'd better get back into the kitchen. Your friend can hide in the basement."

Eli closed the book, dropped it into the box and slid it into the drawer, closing it quickly. Sam folded the mimeographed paper roughly and pushed it into his hip pocket. After shutting off the closet light, he was the last to exit the study, without time to try to fidget the door into a locked position. After switching off the room light, he trailed the others into the kitchen.

Carol pointed Eli toward a closed door. "That leads to the basement. Hide down there." He obeyed, quietly closing the door behind him.

Sam spotted the half-finished bottle of wine on the counter among the other bottles, grabbed it and found two glasses in the cabinet. He quickly poured some wine into each and handed one to Carol as they heard the front door open.

Augustos Rauf, a.k.a. Arthur Vasile, let his voice fill the house. "Hello, Sam," he said, before he was in sight. As he appeared in the kitchen, he halted before getting close to Sam or Carol. He was wearing a long overcoat, holding a briefcase in his right hand.

"It's good to see you again, Sam. You know, I'm glad you're able to keep Carol company when I make these trips. You're a good friend. I see you've already started with wine. Carol, dear, would you pour me a glass?" Arthur strolled back down the hallway. Carol and Sam shot looks back at each other. She whispered, "What'll we do?"

Arthur spoke as he walked. "Let me just hang my coat and drop my case here by the coat rack." There was a sound of something dropping to the floor near Arthur. "Ah, my case fell open and some papers spilled out. I'll be right with you. Just a minute." Arthur's voice faded, as if getting further away. Time seemed to crawl. *He's taking too long.* Sam heard his footsteps as Arthur returned.

Arthur reentered the kitchen, rubbing his hands together. "Now, that wine will taste great," he said as he took the glass from Carol, gave her a hug and kissed her cheek. He sipped the wine, put his glass down on the counter and stepped back from Carol.

"I'm surprised to see you, Arthur. What happened?" said Carol.

Arthur stared at his wife and then Sam. "As it turned out, we finished much earlier than expected and I didn't feel like spending the night there after all, so I came home. I can see you are quite surprised. I didn't mean to ruin your evening of friendship."

Sam stood in silence, watching Arthur's movements. He wondered if Eli had found a way out of the basement.

"Carol said you are making great progress with your project," said Sam. "Are you going to continue to work with the company for the long term?"

"Yes, I believe I will be involved for the *long term,* as you say."

"Carol said it'll be a long drive from here. Will you two be leaving New Sussex College?"

"Why, no. Although I may need to take a leave of absence at some point to help get the facility up and running, I expect to stay on right here. Would you miss us if we were gone?"

Sam glanced at Carol. She was looking down, avoiding eye contact with both men, as if she were trying to retreat into another world.

A creaking sound shot up suddenly from the beneath the kitchen. Sam's face drew taut and Carol looked his way. Arthur showed a wry smile.

"Carol, look at poor Sam here. He looks like he's just seen a ghost. Perhaps we should go into the basement and look for it."

Sam stood frozen in place. *Please, Eli. Get out of there.*

Arthur grabbed his wine glass and took another sip before placing it back on the counter. "You really do look a little spooked, Sam. But don't worry. I am certain the sound we just heard did not come from a ghost. These old houses have many odd sounds, now and then. Most of the time, it's just old wood, usually the floor boards and joists that call to us."

Sam forced a weak laugh. "Yeah, I guess you're right. I don't think I'll ever get used to old house sounds. When I was a boy, I used to live in a place that had lots of them. Hey, why don't we go sit in the living room and get comfortable?"

"If you don't mind, I've been sitting in the car for a long time. I'd prefer to stand a while and stretch my legs. Let's stay here a little longer. Don't you want to know more about the project?"

Sam swallowed hard, struggling to hide his tension. "Sure, it sounds really interesting, but it can wait." Sam looked straight at Arthur, but his eyes betrayed him with an instant shot at the basement door. It wasn't lost on Arthur.

"Well, a minute ago you were filled with curiosity about my project, but now you say it can wait. And I think you are still concerned about that noise from the basement. I guess there is more than one place in this house that has your interest."

Arthur took hold of his wine glass with his left hand while his right slid into his sport coat pocket. "How sloppy of you to leave my study unlocked . . . again. Tell me, did you find everything you were looking for . . . Schmuel?" Arthur gripped a pistol when his hand emerged from the pocket.

Sam glared at the pistol. The only weapons near him were kitchen knives, but they were out of reach.

"Yes, Dr. Rauf, I found everything I needed to find. I found your true identity and know what you are doing. So, you plan to build a Colonia Dignidad right here in New Hampshire? How ambitious."

"So, my loving wife has grown quite talkative. Too bad you'll never see it."

"You're not going to shoot me, are you? How will you get away with that? You'll have some explaining to do." Sam hoped Eli had gotten out and alerted his associates.

"I came home and found you fucking my wife. I went crazy with rage, but shot you in self-defense. You see, you'll have a weapon in your hands, too."

Sam needed time. "You're so deliberate in your plans, Rauf. But tell me, why did you kill Seth Walpole? That was pretty messy. I know he was learning about the Holocaust and may have been a threat to you, but not enough to warrant killing him."

"Ah, that was a bit of luck, you know. I didn't do it, but I think I know who did. You see, I have a young friend in the police department. He's going to help me with this unfortunate event tonight. He told me about Chief Powers and his suspicion of Al Turner. Thanks to Turner's foolishness, I didn't have to kill Walpole. What a dumb fool, that Turner."

Sam looked puzzled. "Am I missing something?"

"Yes, you are. My colleague in Massachusetts set into motion another part of the plan. We have knowledge of certain Jewish figures in this country who survived the war and the camps. Dr. Ike Wirth was one of them. We planned to kill him and eventually as many of these Jews as possible, especially those in positions of authority and influ-

ence, like a college president. There will be others. But the
training center, that is our major accomplishment. Many
young people in this country hate the U.S. government. Mi-
litiamen, survivalists; they call themselves different things.
With the numerous Germans transplanted after the war
becoming our teachers, we'll motivate those people and
convert them into young Nazis, teaching them to do great
deeds."

Sam heard the same kind of hatred and madness he
heard at the camp. "What about Carol? Are you going to kill
her, too? How can you be so brutal?"

"It's not brutality, Schmuel. It's efficiency. My wife
served me well these years, but now she will die with you.
Oh, I won't kill her. You will, with the gun I will plant in
your hand."

Sam had not fully comprehended Arthur's madness, or
the extent to which it could go. He'd been married to Carol
for over ten years and she loved him completely. But apparently it was all a well-calculated charade. He used her to
help him fit in wherever they lived, all without the slightest
concern that he might have to discard her at some time.
That time was now.

Sam saw the anguish in Carol's face. It was as if she
and Sam were synchronized in their thinking. She was seeing her husband as he really was for the first time. Her face
flushed with terror.

Sam's anger grew, but he was without any means to
fight the man with the gun.

"You're feeling helpless now, aren't you Schmuel?" said
Arthur. "You see, you are not truly out of the camp. You're
still a prisoner, a helpless prisoner. Only now, your mother
is no longer here to protect you."

Sam raised his hands, his fingers bent as if grasping a
weapon. Vasile laughed at Sam's helpless motions. Carol,
too, felt helpless, and their collective anger increased. But,
unlike Sam, her desperation led to action. The heavy glass
wine bottle was within her reach.

Carol's shriek echoed through the room as she grasped
the bottle, hurtling it at Rauf. It caught him on the side
of his head with enough force to hurt, but not enough to
knock him down. He staggered for a few seconds and in
an instant Sam was on him. He clenched his right hand

into a fist and swung at Rauf, striking the man's jaw with all his might. Again, Rauf staggered, but did not fall. Sam repeated the blow, and this time Rauf dropped to one knee. He glared at Sam and raised the gun in his hand, aiming it at his attacker.

Hearing the struggle, Eli flung open the basement door. With the Nazi in his sights, he squeezed the trigger of his own weapon three times. In a reflexive motion, Rauf spun and managed to fire one shot, the bullet striking Eli in the chest, knocking him to the floor. Blood spattered the floor and wall behind Rauf as Carol covered her face with her hands, screaming.

Sam rushed to his friend, who lay collapsed on the floor. There was no sign of blood. Slowly, Eli eased himself up onto an elbow. With one hand, he unbuttoned his shirt, revealing his bullet proof vest. "You know, Schmuel, these things are great, but it still hurts when a bullet knocks you down and you bang your head."

Sam smiled, relieved. Carol was another story, however.

In a matter of hours her world had turned upside down. She stood in a corner of the kitchen, as if trying to get as far away from the chaos as possible, sobbing and holding her arms across her chest. Sam went and wrapped his arms around her, hoping to bring her comfort, but her sobs continued as if he wasn't there.

Eli examined Rauf for a pulse, but he had none. The evil doctor, assistant to Josef Mengele, was dead.

The little New Hampshire town had experienced another violent death, but this one marked the end of a long road in a young man's journey. Sam would never look back on his time at the camp in the same way again. He would never try to put it out of his mind, or keep it buried in the past. He truly was a Holocaust survivor. Soon he would help his friend Ian create a history course about the experience. It was the next step.

Epilogue

SATURDAY NIGHT, DECEMBER 14.

"You're still thinking about her, aren't you, Sammy boy?" Martha's voice was soft as she cuddled up to Sam on her sofa, the fireplace crackling across the room. His face had a faraway look.

"No, no . . . well, yes, I guess I am."

"It's okay, Sam. I understand. You've been through an awful lot. I guess we all have. Poor Cal Powers. I'll bet he's never had so much paperwork in his life." The remark brought Sam back from his thoughts of Carol and he smiled at Martha as she snuggled against him.

"Carol has a rough road ahead," said Sam. "Everything changed for her. Once the smoke clears, I think she's going to move far away. I can't blame her."

"Cal's world sure got a jolt," said Martha. "It was bad enough he had Seth's murder to deal with, but he never knew he had a Nazi hunt going on at the same time. And one little neo-Nazi right in his own station! That kid left town in hurry. Do you think Cal will ever get over the fact that you left him in the dark about the whole thing?"

"Yeah, I think so. Cal's a good guy at heart. He didn't like what we were going to do with Rauf, you know, kidnapping him and taking him out of the country, but it didn't happen, so . . ."

"But what about that guy in Massachusetts? You know, Arthur's buddy? It didn't take long to nail him."

"True enough," said Sam. "Rauf's last speech sealed it for that guy. The police were right on him for his role in the Ike Wirth murder. He's cooked, and that whole enterprise to build a Nazi training center is up in smoke now. I'm sure glad there are men like Eli who will never give up in their search for the war criminals. Just imagine what could've happened if Rauf and his pals had succeeded."

Martha inched closer to Sam. "I'm mighty glad there was a man like Sam Miller watching my back."

Sam pulled Martha closer, hugging her and kissing her cheek. "I think I'll keep an eye on you for a long time, Martha Sanborn." Her body warmed him in a very pleasant way. He could get accustomed to this.

"Sam, something bothers me about this, more than just Vasile, or Rauf, whoever he is. That list you and Eli talked about. You said there are maybe over a thousand Nazi engineers, doctors, technicians, scientists, all brought here after the war. That's less than thirty years ago, so most of them may still be alive, and in the United States! Even though you stopped Raufie, there might be somebody else with the same ideas. That's enough to keep a body awake at night."

Sam hugged Martha more tightly. "Yes it is, Martha. Yes, it is."

About the Author

Although he describes himself as a "card carrying New Englander," Steve lived for twenty-six years in Maryland while pursuing a career spanning four federal agencies. His background has enabled him to serve as a project manager at the National Security Agency, the Environmental Protection Agency, the National Fire Academy and the Centers for Medicare and Medicaid Services, where he worked with teams of experts in various fields to develop state-of-the-art training for both classrooms and distance learning technologies.

A "Baby Boomer," Steve took up fiction writing as he moved into his career final frontier. Married since 1975, a father of three and a grandfather, Steve and his wife Louise own a home on Cape Cod that will serve as his private writer's colony for the years ahead.

His first novel, Connections, was published in 2012 by Gypsy Shadow Publishing, an ebook publisher from Texas. It is the first in a series featuring Detective Jack Contino, battling crime in New England in the 1970's. The other two in the series are Aberration and Calculation. In his fourth mystery, Steve departs from the Det. Jack Contino crime stories and features Sam Miller teaming up in a strange way with Martha Sanborn to solve a murder while hunting for an ex-Nazi in rural New Hampshire.

Steve holds a Master's degree in Educational Technology from Boston University and a B.A. in Business Administration from New England College and spent over thirty years in the Education/Training field, including posts in higher education and the federal government. In 1999 he won a finalist Telly award, for writing, producing and co-hosting a training video on the Emergency Education Network (EENET), a cable network that serves firefighters and law enforcement emergency responders.

Steve has served the Board of Directors for the Cape Cod Writers' Center (CCWC) and holds an administrative position with the Cape Cod Senior Softball League, as well as swinging a quick bat.

WEBSITE: www.stevenmarini.com
TWITTER: https://twitter.com/StevenPMarini
FACEBOOK: https://www.facebook.com/StevenPMarini
BLOG: http://babyboomerspm.blogspot.com/